surface rights

surface rights

a novel

Melissa Hardy

DUNDURN
TORONTO

Editor: Shannon Whibbs
Design: Courtney Horner
Printer: Webcom

Library and Archives Canada Cataloguing in Publication

Hardy, Melissa
　　Surface rights / by Melissa Hardy.

Also issued in electronic format.
ISBN 978-1-4597-0715-3

　　I. Title.

PS8565.A63243S87 2013　　C813'.54　　C2013-900815-2

1　2　3　4　5　　17　16　15　14　13

| Conseil des Arts du Canada　Canada Council for the Arts | Canada | ONTARIO ARTS COUNCIL CONSEIL DES ARTS DE L'ONTARIO |

We acknowledge the support of the **Canada Council for the Arts** and the **Ontario Arts Council** for our publishing program. We also acknowledge the financial support of the **Government of Canada** through the **Canada Book Fund** and **Livres Canada Books**, and the **Government of Ontario** through the **Ontario Book Publishing Tax Credit** and the **Ontario Media Development Corporation**.

Care has been taken to trace the ownership of copyright material used in this book. The author and the publisher welcome any information enabling them to rectify any references or credits in subsequent editions.

J. Kirk Howard, President

The publisher is not responsible for websites or their content unless they are owned by the publisher.

Printed and bound in Canada.

Visit us at
Dundurn.com | @dundurnpress
Facebook.com/dundurnpress | Pinterest.com/Dundurnpress

Dundurn	Gazelle Book Services Limited	Dundurn
3 Church Street, Suite 500	White Cross Mills	2250 Military Road
Toronto, Ontario, Canada	High Town, Lancaster, England	Tonawanda, NY
M5E 1M2	LA1 4XS	U.S.A. 14150

For my own sister,
Pamela Rooks

The author would like to thank the Ontario Arts Council for its ongoing support over the years.

Prologue

When a massive coronary took out Verna's father in the Keele Street TTC station, she was down in Cocoa Beach prepping the condo for sale. The Rothmans next door took the dog for the interim — while Verna was dealing with her grief, of course, and then the funeral and the settling of her father's small estate. She had sort of hoped they would offer to take Jude off her hands permanently, but Sue Rothman hadn't realized how much work he was. "I'm hardly ever home ..." she explained, handing Verna the leash. "It wouldn't be fair to the poor dog. And here's his toy and his dishes and his Iams ... you'll need more of that. You have no idea how much he eats."

As she took the half-empty bag of dog food, Verna thought, *What on earth am I going to do with a dog?*

Tuesday, May 17, 2005

Verna Macoun Woodcock drove north. It was ten o'clock on a Tuesday morning — a workday, or what would have been a workday had she not retired from the Ministry of Agriculture the previous Friday. After twenty-eight long years in a cubicle overlooking Bay Street, Verna could no longer be described as "a worker ant." That was what her twin sister Fern had insisted on calling people who, unlike herself, got up every morning and punched in at some soul-eroding job. Not that Fern's liberated lifestyle and free spirit had done her much good — dead four years come October. Verna sniffed and shifted in the seat and peered through the windshield at the 400 unrolling before her through sleet the consistency of a slushy.

"Hey, Jude!" she asked the black Lab perched on the Volvo's back seat — Jude, her father's dog, hers now. "Starting to look familiar?" Jude must have made this particular journey with her father a dozen or more times. Whenever they hit a curve in the road, he banked like a pro. She pointed the Volvo toward Barrie and hunkered down for weather.

It was the Tuesday before the long Victoria Day weekend — May Two-Four. According to Canadians this celebration of a dead queen's birthday marks the beginning of summer. More often than not, the weather fails to support this contention; indeed, sleet, hail, and frost are more typical of the long weekend than sun and warm breezes. Nevertheless, this perception — that Victoria Day serves as some kind of magic portal through which summer's blessings flow — provides an occasion for binge-drinking while scantily clothed, for the reckless commitment to the earth of surely doomed annuals, and for opening cottages. The latter activity, when multiplied by a factor of thousands, routinely results in bumper-to-bumper traffic stretching along the 400 from Toronto to Huntsville, and, now that the Muskokas have become so expensive, points north. That was why Verna was travelling on the Tuesday — to beat the traffic — and what she had woken up this morning, a middle-aged woman in her little-girl bed in her dead father's house, and headed north to do — to open the family cottage. But that's where the whole cottage thing ended. As soon as it was prepped for sale, she planned to engage the services of a real-estate agent in nearby Greater Gammage — "Carmen the Cottage Lady" — to list the property for sale. Verna had found her on the Internet.

"Hey, Jude!" she sang slyly.

The dog opened his mouth and panted lightly.

"Don't be afraid!"

The dog yelped.

"Take a sad song …"

Bark!

"And make it better!"

Ruff! Ruff!

It was a routine that her father had worked out with the dog, their *schtick*. Donald Macoun would sing a line and Jude would bark and everyone would clap and laugh.

"There. Feel better?"

Certainly the interchange seemed to have raised the Lab's spirits. He fluffed up to the extent a short-haired dog can, sat up straighter, and, opening his mouth, beamed at her. At least he looked like he was beaming. Not for the first time Verna thought, *What am I going to do with a dog?*

In addition to prepping the cottage for sale, Verna had set herself another task for this sojourn into her past — scattering the ashes, or, as the woman from the crematorium solemnly insisted on calling them, the *cremains*, of father, sister, husband. Accordingly, ranged beside her on the front seat of the Volvo were three identical white cardboard boxes the size of a phone book. To each of these a typed label had been affixed: Donald Macoun; Fern Macoun; Robert Woodcock.

Her father had wanted his ashes scattered in the glen up at the cottage. Purported to be an old Ojibway burial ground, it was also the place where generations of Macouns had laid cats and dogs and several parakeets to rest and where Fern had buried the placentas of her various children — what she called "Offerings to Gaia." The ashes of her grandfather, George Dewey Macoun, were scattered there and those of her aunt Margie and Joan Macoun, Fern and Verna's mother. Joan had died as a result of "complications following the birth of twin girls." That is to say, she had bled to death on Verna and Fern's birthday, putting a considerable damper on that event the girls' entire lives — their father stricken, the girls tip-toeing about, afraid to make a noise, a pall cast over birthday cake and presents.

Fern had never specified where she wished to be laid to rest, so, for the past four years, the carton containing her cremains had sat tucked away on a shelf in the hall closet of the Indian Crescent home. It was Verna who had taken matters into her own hands and decided to make of Fern's ashes her own "offering to Gaia."

As for Bob, he had requested that his ashes be scattered from a prop plane over the Space Coast. *Too bad*, Verna thought, feeling steely. *Maybe if you'd been nicer. Maybe if you'd been true.*

They careened past the exit to Highway 9 that led to Schomberg, Arthur, and Orangeville to the west and Newmarket to the east. The exit to 89 came and went — Alliston, Rosemont, Violet Hill. Then the exit to Wasaga Beach. Barrie unfolded to their right in new subdivisions emanating from boulevards lined with fast-food outlets. Verna ignored the ramp and got on Highway 11.

Her father would have been eighty-four had he lived another month. Verna had been down in Florida when he died. She had just gotten around to putting the condo her husband had insisted on buying in Cocoa Beach on the market. It was Bob who had liked Florida, not Verna. Too hot, too far away, and altogether too much weather.

"So, here we are, Jude," Verna told the dog, "all that's left of the Macouns. A menopausal woman and a ravenous dog. The end of the line. Well, not really, I suppose." After all, there were Fern's kids: Parsley, Sage, Rosemary *or* Thyme. That was how Donald and Verna referred to Fern's lot. In fact, it was Paisley, Romy, and Tai, pronounced *tie* — ridiculous hippie names. As near as Verna could reckon, Paisley would be closing in on thirty by now, while Tai (a boy) must be in his late twenties. As for the baby, Romy, she would be in her late teens or early twenties.

They slid past the exit to Atherly on the way to Gravenhurst.

Fern had been all over the place in her child-bearing years — the Kootenays, Arizona, Brazil for a time. Verna and her father hadn't seen her for years at a time, never mind the children. All Verna could remember of those few, brief visits with her sister and nieces and nephew was spilt apple juice, a constant flow of mucous and hot, salty tears, and cacophony — something pitched squarely between bedlam and mayhem and punctured by the occasional high-pitched, eardrum-splitting scream.

"It was enough to put you off children altogether," Verna told Jude. "And they smelled worse than you."

Over the years, one by one, the fathers of Fern's various children had parachuted in to whisk their offspring away to one of the earth's four corners. Fern, they said, was an unfit mother. The children were not safe with her. And, indeed, as far as Verna could tell, Fern hadn't seemed to mind over-much. Time passed, efforts to reconnect failed, everyone lost touch. Neither Verna nor her father had heard from any of them in years.

So her father's house in the High Park area of Toronto — not a bad red brick Victorian semi-detached on Indian Road Crescent — became Verna's. The cottage up north became Verna's. The 2004 Volvo, not even a year old with scarcely a kilometre on it became Verna's. Jude became Verna's. Everything became Verna's.

She glanced back at the Lab. "You miss him, don't you? Dad?"

Jude looked confused.

"Of course, you do." Turning back to the road, she squared her shoulders and peered through the veil of sleet at the road ahead. "You miss him more than I do. He was your everything, whereas for me, he had become a burden.

I'm a cold, unfeeling person, Jude. Really I am. He was a wonderful father and a lovely, gentle man, but to me he had become a burden. How selfish is that? What a terrible daughter." Yet in another way, she reflected, both Donald and Fern seemed more real to her now than while they had been alive. It was as though their loss were an amputation that had not healed so much as scarred over; so that, every time she went to stretch, there was this tightness, this sense of restriction to remind her where they had once been connected to her. Bob, not so much.

Bracebridge came and went. Then Huntsville and Sundridge and South River. She stopped for gas in Callandar and to walk Jude, who took a huge dump in a parking lot behind a stack of shaggy firewood and then proceeded to gleefully consume someone's discarded hotdog. They stopped again in North Bay to refill Verna's thermos of coffee and to pick up a bag of ice and two big bottles of Russian Prince at the LCBO before continuing on 11 toward Temagami and Cobalt.

In the District of Temiskaming, northwest of Kenogami Lake, Highway 11 crosses the Arctic Watershed. There is a rest area there, with porta-potties and a sign and a plaque. Whenever they had made the long drive north as children, her father would always stop at the rest area, and, because the high school history teacher that he was could never resist a good plaque, he would make them wait, dancing from foot to foot and holding their crotches, until he had read the words aloud. Only then would he release the two little girls from their agony, calling after them, "From here on out, as long as we are north of this place, your pee will drain north, not south!"

For old times' sake Verna pulled over at the rest area, got out of the Volvo, put Jude on his leash and walked him over to the plaque.

The height of land known as the Arctic
Watershed crosses Highway 11 at this point.
North of here, water drains into Hudson
Bay; rivers, lakes and streams to the south
flow into the Great Lakes. As the northern
wilderness came under development, the
erratic line of the watershed defined territo-
rial boundaries. It marked the southern limit
of Rupert's Land, the vast territory granted
to the Hudson's Bay Company in 1670.
Two centuries later, it formed the northern
boundary of lands ceded to the Crown by
the First Nation Ojibwa in the Robinson-Su-
perior Treaties of 1850.

"Signed," she concluded, "'Ontario Heritage Foundation, Ministry of Culture, Tourism and Recreation.'" She
looked down at Jude, who returned her gaze expectantly
and Verna suddenly realized that, long after she and Fern
had ceased to accompany their father to the cottage, he had
probably continued to stop at the Arctic Watershed rest area
every time he went north. Indeed, he had probably made a
point of reading the plaque aloud to the dog of the day —
whichever of that succession of canines at whose side he had
walked through life and of which Jude was only the latest
and last. "Okay, go on," she told him.

Jude wagged his tail, then dragged her over to a pile of
rocks. After circumnavigating it several times, nose twitching, he hiked up his leg.

The cottage had come down from her paternal grandfather,
George Dewey Macoun, an eminent geologist and cartographer who had died when the twins were seven. Verna

remembered a tall, stooped man with liver-spotted skin, who smelled of Black Cavandish pipe tobacco and was always patting about his person for his pouch. A quiet, abstracted man, he was genial, but vague.

It was George who had bought up all the parcels of the land around the lake in the early twenties; by 1925, he had built the cottage, the boathouse, and the dock. An old photo of him hung in the hallway of the house on Indian Crescent. It had been taken in Golden City, northern Ontario, around the time of his marriage to Verna's grandmother — Miss Frieda Ekhert of Kingston — and preserved the grainy image of a lanky and somewhat awkward-looking young man, long-faced, hollow-cheeked, and sporting the paramilitary uniform favoured by surveyors of the time: khaki, a kerchief, and Stetson hat. He would have looked almost like a white hunter on safari had it not been for the black-and-white cow chewing her cud beside him. Betty was the Holstein's name and she had belonged to Mrs. Flowers, the woman who ran the boarding house where George stayed when he was up north. Betty played a pivotal role in the Macoun family mythology — it was upon the bovine that George pinned the blame for his long absences from home.

"She kept eating your grandfather's journals," Donald explained to Fern and Verna. "The notes he took for the Bureau of Mines. And then he would have to stay up north longer, because he had to start over again."

"Why did he let her eat his journals?" the girls wanted to know.

"I think he did it on purpose," their father replied. At that he had fallen conspicuously silent, as if to imply that there might be more to that story than anyone knew. What had been up with that, Verna wondered. Had her grandfather had a secret? Did that explain why he had always seemed faintly perturbed to her — as though he was expecting someone who had yet to arrive, someone whose appearance, when it finally happened, would cause him to beam and say in his scratchy voice, "Why, there you are! I'd almost given up on you!" Verna shook her head. Whatever that secret had been — *if* there had even been one — it would have died with Donald. *That's how it is with family secrets,* she thought. *We haul them along with us everywhere we go like some tiresome, but vital pieces of luggage that we are afraid others might steal or open; we guard them with our very lives. Then one day we die and they are buried with us. What had seemed to us so shocking turns out to be of no concern to anyone else. How could we have known that shame has an expiry date?*

Temagami. Then Latchford. Cobalt to New Liskeard. Then Englehart to Kenogami Lake. Bourkes and Ramore and Beverley, where they would finally leave Highway 11 on the ten-mile jog of county road that began in Beverley and just as abruptly ended in Greater Gammage. Verna glanced at the Volvo's clock. They would be there by five — five! That special time, that portal to ease: the cocktail hour. According to Verna's private rule book, drinking before five was verboten. It was a good rule, essential if she wished to remain functional. Were she ever to start drinking before five, she was quite certain that all hell would break loose or freeze over or do whatever it was that hell did. Nearly five. Nearly there. Thank God.

Verna had just pulled off 11 into Beverley when it occurred to her that she wasn't entirely sure where the cottage actually was relative to Greater Gammage. Was it north … or south? Or maybe west? Or northwest? She could bring to mind her father's old Mercury Comet bumping down a pitted gravel road to get from the cottage to Greater Gammage, but which road was it?

Exasperated with herself, she thumped the steering wheel hard with the heel of her hand. Damn it! What had she been thinking? That the magnetic pull exerted by Lake Marguerite on Macouns was so strong that it defied time and space? That the lake's coordinates were somehow hard-wired into her brain and tangled up in her DNA? How on earth could she have thought that she could climb into a car, drive north, and seven hours later find herself at a cottage she hadn't seen in thirty-eight years?

There was nothing else for it. "I can't remember how to get to the cottage," she told the dog. "We'll have to stop in Greater Gammage and ask."

Ten minutes out of Beverley, she rounded a bend, and, sure enough, there was Greater Gammage, clinging to the riverbank like a stubborn stain. Greater Gammage could hardly be said to look like a town so much as the weathered, rusted-out remains of a head-on collision that had taken place long ago at a crossroad. Born in hopes and dreams, a convergence of strangers who had come together for no other reason than to get rich off the gold and silver discovered in the region, who stayed because they were too poor to leave, Greater Gammage lived out its days in disappointment. Verna remembered how that particular, local brand of disappointment had smelled — of mould and wood smoke. She braked to take the old timber trestle bridge across the Black River. As a child she had had nightmares about that bridge; it had never seemed entirely reliable. Now it creaked ominously, like an old tree swing in the wind.

Coming up was the Maple Leaf Bar and Grill (or bar, at any rate; the word *Grill* had a big black *X* through it) — Verna remembered this from her childhood — and the Pump and Munch, some sort of hybrid born of a gas station and a convenience store — this was new. There was something else new, as well. "Look!" she told Jude, pointing to a sign that read BLACK RIVER REALTY, CARMEN BEAUSÉJOUR, BROKER. "That must be Carmen the Cottage Lady. Realtors usually know where things are. In any case, I might as well check her out if I'm thinking about giving her the listing."

Parking in Greater Gammage had never been a problem. Verna pulled into the space in front of the real-estate office next to a glossy Buick LaSabre the colour of an eggplant. "Guard the car!" she instructed Jude and, turning, crossed the sidewalk to peer for a moment at smudged feature sheets taped to the inside of the store-front's window. These depicted various alleged cottages listed by Carmen the Cottage Lady — from Norembega to the north, Holtyre to the east, and Barber's Bay to the west. They appeared dodgy for the most part — hastily thrown together from salvage, then dug out each spring to be repaired and added onto as families expanded. Often a property had two or more buildings on it. In addition to the main house, there would be a vintage Airstream that some uncle from down south had parked on the prop-erty decades before and then laid paving stones in front for a patio or a ramshackle one-room sleeping cabin for the noisy overflow of teenagers. There were a few proper cottages, as well; wooden, stained a dark and intracta-ble brown, with sloping wraparound decks or A-frames, pitched like tents on the marshy edges of still lakes. By comparison with these, George Macoun's cottage would appear grand. There was no doubt in Verna's mind that the woman would kill for this listing.

She opened the door a crack and peeked in. Except for a battered file cabinet in one corner and the metal desk beside it, Black River Realty was furnished entirely with dilapidated lawn furniture — a collection of stacked green resin chairs and three aluminum chaise lounges in one of which a mountainous woman sprawled precariously. One hand rested, spread-fingered, on her bosom; from the other dangled a lit cigarette. Red flip-flops swung from the toes of her swollen, purplish feet. Was she asleep? Her eyes were closed and her red hair was set in jumbo foam rollers. But what about the cigarette?

Verna slid into the room, closing the door behind her. "Uh ... excuse me?"

The woman's eyes popped open, widened with alarm, then, assessing the situation, she blinked. "Oh, hello, dear," she said. "Just resting. Not that it's hectic. Just that I'm the size of a barn. The slightest effort wears me out. Have to conserve energy. I didn't ask to be this big, but you got to play with the hand you're dealt ..." Turning to the glass-topped table beside her, she ground out her cigarette in an ashtray overflowing with butts. "Say, dear, can you help me up?" She planted a foot on either side of the lounge and extended two hands to Verna. She looked like an enormous child asking to be picked up.

"Please, don't bother. I just ..."

"Got to get up sometime!" the woman insisted. "Otherwise the blood pools. Don't want the blood to pool. No, not that. Terrible thing. Aneurysms. And I can tell you, the last thing I need is an aneurysm. Would just about finish me off. Come on, dear. Give us a yank. By the looks of you, you've got one good yank in you."

Verna took the woman's hands and braced herself.

"On the count of three," the woman instructed. "One ... two ... three!"

Verna pulled. The woman strained. It was touch-and-go for a few seconds, but then there the woman was, on her feet, yanking into place around her bulk the faded gingham housecoat — in the struggle it had gotten twisted around and hiked dangerously high up above her elephantine knees. "Thanks," she said. "If you hadn't come along, God knows what would have happened to me!" Then, at the look of Verna's face, "Just kidding! My name's Carmen, by the way." She glanced over her shoulder in the direction of a greasy dog-eared poster taped to the wall. IF YOUR DREAM IS TO LIVE AT THE BEACH, it advised, CALL CARMEN THE COTTAGE LADY! There, wearing a gauzy turquoise cover-up and seated behind a dainty rattan desk set up on a sandy beach was a younger, slimmer Carmen — the type of swarthy redhead found only among French Canadians. A smile lit up a handsome face; she held a fountain pen in one hand; by the looks of it she was on the verge of signing a lucrative deal. "Oh, that's me, all right!" she said ruefully. "Or half of me, at any rate. Several hundred years ago. Who would have thought ... but no. Enough about me. Water under the bridge. So ..." She rubbed her palms together with affected relish. "What can I do you for? Want to buy a cottage? Of course, I sell anything and everything. Doesn't have to be a cottage. Mobile homes. Quonset huts. Geodesic domes — their popularity was brief. I've got a laundromat listed and a nice little corner store. Great business opportunity there! No former grow houses, though. Nope. Never again. Got burned on that one. So, what is it you're looking for? God, I need a cigarette. Do you want a cigarette?"

"I don't smoke."

"Of course, you don't. So many southerners don't these days. They make such a point of it. You're wondering how I know you're a southerner. Your accent. You mind?" Without waiting for Verna's answer, she retrieved a package of Du Mauriers and a blue Zippo lighter from the table and lighted up. "They say nicotine'll kill you, but I'd put my money on the extra hundred and fifty pounds. You know what they say."

"No," said Verna, bewildered, because, after all, *they* have been known to say a whole lot of things.

"Nobody gets out of here alive!" Carmen informed her and hooted. The hoot modulated into a honk, which culminated in a terrifying bout of coughing, chest-thumping, and stomping.

"Are you all right?" Verna asked. "Can I get you something? Some water, maybe?"

"No, no!" the realtor demurred. "Not to worry. I'm fit as a fiddle, bright as a new penny, good to go. Just a little bronchial spasm is what that was."

"I saw your ad on the Internet," Verna said uneasily. She was beginning to think that she might have to look further afield for a realtor — to Beverley, perhaps even Timmins. Carmen could hardly be described as "professional," even when you took the fact that she lived in Greater Gammage into account. Was she even capable of representing clients? "You might know my family — the Macouns. We have a cottage on Lake Marguerite."

At this Carmen beamed broadly. "Lord thundering Jesus!" she exclaimed. "Why, I'd never ... It's Verna, then? Why didn't you say so?"

Verna blinked at her. "Excuse me?"

Carmen pounded her on the back. "I didn't recognize you! What's it been? Thirty years? Forty?"

Verna stared blankly.

"Oh, don't tell me you don't remember! We knew each other when we were kids."

"I'm sorry ..."

"Oh, sure you do! A skinny, red-headed kid with freckles?"

"Nope. Sorry."

Carmen gave up. "Ah! Don't matter! You were a teen-ager and there's nothin' more ornery and ungrateful than a teenager. How'd you think I got this big? Think I did it on my own? Four teenagers did this to me. Worried me into a state of obesity. Thank God they're all gone. Pack of wild Indians. Now I can live out my days in peace."

"Yeah, well," Verna agreed. During the last few summers she had spent at the lake — her fourteenth and fifteenth — her moods had seemed to swing between two extremes: either soggy despair or molten fury at poor Donald for forc-ing her to leave behind her friends and all the excitement that was Toronto in the summer. Obviously neither state had proved conducive to her remembering that there were locals at all, much less individual locals who grew up and out to become Carmen the Cottage Lady. In fact, the only image of others that she could dredge from her memory of that period was of a shadowy cluster of urchins, looking more like extras from *Les Miz* than viable representatives of her own peer group.

"You got kids?" Carmen asked, then answered herself. "No, that's right. Fern said you never had any."

She had touched on a nerve. Verna had wanted kids. Bob had not. Then, after a while, she hadn't wanted them, either, or, to be more precise, she hadn't wanted Bob's. "So you knew Fern?" she asked.

"I sure did. Now, she was something else! Remember how she used to draw the boys?" She chuckled.

"Like flies." Verna was rueful.

Carmen laughed. "A pheromone machine, that's what Fern was. 'Course we were all a little boy-crazy in those days. Well, I certainly was. Now ..." She shrugged. "Now I wouldn't give two red nickels for the whole lot of them. Men! Why, if some man were to walk into my life right now, do you know what I'd do?"

"What?" asked Verna.

"I'd escort him to the door and I'd say, 'Don't you come back now! I mean it! Scoot! Get the hell out of here!' Oh, but say!" Remembering, she turned solicitous. "We were all real sorry to hear that Donald passed. He was one of the good ones."

"Yeah, well," said Verna glumly. "Thanks."

"How old was he?"

"Eighty-three. Almost eighty-four."

"Well, you see!"

"Actually I'm thinking of putting the cottage on the market," Verna said. "Would you be interested in listing it?"

"Are you sure you want to do that?"

"Well, yeah." Verna was surprised. "That's what I'm thinking."

"Then I'd think twice if I were you. A cottage like that — better to keep it in the family."

"Hold on," Verna said. "Let me get this straight. You're a real-estate agent and you're telling me *not* to sell?"

"I'm telling you what I *think*," Carmen clarified. "And I think you don't want to be making a decision you might regret someday. That's a real nice cottage. You got your own lake. Your own *lake*. Not many people in this wide world got their own lake. There might come a time that lake'd come in handy."

Verna was annoyed. Why should she have to explain herself to Carmen? If she wanted to sell, she wanted to sell. It was hardly Carmen's business. "It's too far from Toronto," she said curtly. "I haven't been up here in over thirty years. I hate blackflies and mosquitoes and no-see-ums and horseflies, and deerflies. As for 'the family,' I'm it. All she wrote. End of story."

"What about Fern's kids?" Carmen countered. "She had a passle of 'em, if memory serves."

Touché. "Yeah, well, we have no idea where they went," Verna said. "Disappeared off the face of the earth. M.I.A. Haven't heard from them or their fathers in years." She winced, remembering how, a couple of weeks before his coronary, her father had asked, "If Parsley or ... any of the others surface, you'll help them out, won't you?" He couldn't remember their names, either. He asked this not once or twice but five or six times in the course of a single morning. And every time he had asked, she had replied with mounting irritation, "Of course, Dad. Of course I'd help them out. What do you take me for?" How anxious and agitated he had been toward the end; it was almost as if he could hear his inner clock winding down, losing its crank. It hurt her heart now to think how cross she had been with him, how often she had given way to irritation in what turned out to be the last few weeks of his life.

"If there's one thing I've learned," Carmen told her, "it's that the cat comes back." She patted Verna's arm with a plump, cocktail-ring-encrusted hand — pink zircons and smoky topaz. "Hey?" she cajoled. "Come on! What's the big hurry? Wait a little. Think it over. Take your time. Donald's barely in the ground."

"Actually he's in the car," Verna said, suddenly miserable. "His ... ashes, at any rate. Fern's, too. I've come to scatter them. That's why I'm here. One reason."

"Well, then," said Carmen.

Verna rallied herself. *Enough already. Get on with it. It's nearly five.* The Cocktail Hour. "Actually why I stopped by is ... this is embarrassing, but could you tell me how to get to the cottage from here? For the life of me ..."

"*Tabernac!* And why didn't you say so? The lake's always been devilish hard to find, especially if you don't know where you're looking. *Eh eh!*" She jabbed Verna in the ribs. "Don't worry. I'll take you there."

"No, Carmen!" Verna protested, panicking. It was going to be hard enough seeing the cottage for the first time in so long and after all that had happened. The last thing she wanted was an audience. "It's really not necessary. I'm sure …"

"Oh, sure, but it's no trouble at all," Carmen assured her.

"But I've got the dog in the car …" Verna was desperate. "There's no …"

"Oh, I'm not intending to go in your car," Carmen said breezily. "Wouldn't fit. No, I'll lead you to it in the Carmen-mobile. It's got a pop steering wheel and extra long seat belts."

"But … you're not dressed!" Verna grasped at straws.

Carmen reached up, grabbed hold of the jumbo rollers in her hair and pulled them out. Hair the colour of fire tumbled in shining waves to her shoulders. "Now I am!"

Verna followed the unwieldy Buick as it toiled past the handful of listing, boarded-up storefronts that constituted the remainder of Greater Gammage and down the ragged spur of road that hugged the river. Another kilometre and the road veered off into deep forest. Two more and the Buick slowed to make a wide right turn onto a narrow gravel road. *Of course*, she chided herself. The service road. How could she have forgotten the kilometre-long winding laneway that tethered her grandfather's cottage to rough civilization? The entrance to this road was so hidden amid the tamaracks, birches, and cedar that, unless you knew what you were looking for, you almost always missed it. As children, she and Fern simply accepted the fact that the road was problematic — magic was clearly involved. It was a secret passage, a magic porthole, maybe even a wormhole.

As a teenager, she had blamed it for her isolation, for the fact that she could not be found with ease by whomever she hoped was seeking her ... although, now that she thought about it, it had clearly not proved an insurmountable obstacle to boys sniffing out Fern over all those summers. Nevertheless, Verna had forever been after her father to erect at the laneway's entrance one of those cozy little signs by means of which cottagers lay claim to their bit of bush and waterfront — "A Snail's Pace," "Sunny Beach Hideaway," or, less coyly, "The Wickerson Family."

"Why can't we?" she had pleaded. "Other families do."

But Donald would ask, "Who would like a Doctor Pepper?" Pretending that he hadn't heard, or, "I'm going to have to make a trip into town for bread. What do you want? Wonder or Hollywood?" Donald, she realized, had had no wish to be found and now neither did she.

The Volvo bumped and lurched after the lumbering LeSabre — the road was badly washboarded.

Carmen rolled down her window. "It's been years since your dad had this road re-graded," she called back to Verna. "You might want to do that. Otherwise your suspension will be all shot to hell."

A few minutes more and the road creaked open to a view of the lake on Verna's right. The size of a football stadium, Lake Marguerite had started life as the footprint of a glacier preserved in the granite of the Canadian Shield. Now, with dusk fast approaching, the oval mirror that it held to the sky reflected a sun setting in a cascade of sparkling shards.

At the sight, or, perhaps, the smell of water, Jude struggled to attention, made a muffled noise, and shook his tags. His ears pricked up and his nose quivered. He made his way across the backseat to the window to stare raptly at the lake as though its shining waters, rippled like corduroy, were the portal to paradise. He was a water dog, after all, bred to swim. Bred to retrieve soft, dead things from the water and lay them at his master's feet, all for a little praise and love. No, it wasn't the dog's reaction to the lake that caught Verna by surprise. It was hers.

Dad, she realized. *He's gone.*

Her throat constricted. Sharp tears pricked like needles at the corner of her eyes. It was as though the realization had tackled her head on. Knocked the wind out of her. She hunched over to absorb the blow and, as she did, popped the clutch, causing the Volvo to lurch to a halt. *He's dead*, she told herself. *I've lost him. Lost!* What a strange notion that was! As if the old man had been mislaid. As if she and he had become separated in a store or an airport. What was it they say — those whose job it is to break bad news? What the OPP officer said — the one who called to tell her that he and his partner had found Fern dead in the cottage. What the policewoman said — the one dispatched to tell her of Bob's fatal accident. What the paramedic said — the one who responded to the 911 call at the Keele Street Station. The standard line, what they all say: "I'm sorry for your loss." Sister, husband, father. It was as though they had been kidnapped from a shopping mall while she was busy doing something else. While she was not paying attention.

"What's up?"

Verna looked up to see Carmen leaning out of the Buick's rolled down window, peering back at her.

"Nothing," Verna managed.

"Is there a problem?"

"No. Give me a moment."

The LeSabre's door swung open. Carmen's foot appeared, then portions of the rest of her.

Oh, dear God! Don't get out! "I'm fine," Verna called desperately, hoping to forestall her.

But it was too late. Carmen appeared at the window of the Volvo. "Tell me you're not having a heart attack."

"I'm not having a heart attack."

"You think you're not, but do you know for sure?"

"I think I'd know if I were having a heart attack!"

"Not necessarily. I had a client once had a heart attack on the way to a showing. One minute he was tailgating me like you wouldn't believe, the next he was over the embankment and into the river. Forty-eight years old. Angry son of a bitch. I can't say anyone was sorry to see him go."

"Well, I'm not having a heart attack. Just a stitch in my side." Verna succeeded in straightening up, but not without difficulty. "There. See. It's better."

"Sometimes heart attacks present as gas," Carmen insisted.

Verna turned the key in the ignition. "Well, this was a stitch. Lactic acid. I'm fine. Really. Let's go."

Carmen shrugged. "If you say so." She lumbered back to her car.

Another half-kilometre and the cottage rose into view on a foundation of mortared fieldstone a metre high. It was a log house, made of northern white pine harvested from the surrounding forest and roofed with cinnamon-coloured, hand-split cedar shakes. The cottage was not the first human habitation to have commandeered the lake's northern end. That distinction had belonged to a roughly hewn log cabin — just whose had been unclear. George Macoun had shrugged when asked. "Probably some French trapper who wandered off one day," he had replied, sucking on his pipe. The cabin had burned down some time before George had bought up the land around the lake. He had the cottage built over top of its smoke stain and rubble remains. It was, after all, the best place for a house, the lake's sweet spot.

A screened-in porch, fully half the cottage's frontage in length, peered out towards the lake through hooded, mesh eyes. The trim was white — the porch, the windows, the lintels. The doors and shutters had been painted a dark green. The shutters on those windows facing the water were always closed against the wind, which boiled up from the cauldron of the lake with some fury during storms, while the remainder of the windows, those that looked out over the more quiescent forest, remained unshuttered throughout the winter. In front of the cottage extended a lawn of sorts, ending in a semi-circular cobble beach. Beyond the cottage lay the two-slip boathouse and next to that a dock set on cribs — logs spiked together into crude boxes into which large rocks had been dumped. These gave the foundation weight and stability and made it less susceptible to manipulation by ice over winter. At the very end of the dock was a weather-beaten Muskoka chair turned toward the south; her father would sit out there in the evening, using battered binoculars to watch loons feed on ciscoes or moose munch salty water lilies.

Enough space had been cleared on the near side of the cottage to park up to four vehicles. Verna pulled up next to the LeSabre, got out, and opened the back door for Jude, who promptly bolted.

"No! Shit! Wait! Jude! *Jude!*" she screamed. But it was too late. The Lab flung himself into the lake with abandon and paddled joyfully about, gulping water.

Carmen remained in her car with the window rolled down. She laughed uproariously — "Ha! Ha!" — and smacked the outside of the car door with her hand.

"Damn it all!" Verna cried. "Shit! Now I have to spend the night with a wet dog!"

"There are worse things to spend the night with than a wet dog," Carmen pointed out, then, "Well, I'm out of here."

Verna remembered her manners. "Thanks, Carmen. For showing me the way and all. About the other ... I'll be in touch."

"Hey! *No problema*," Carmen assured her. "But remember what I said, Verna. Give it some time. Never make a hasty decision, particularly when it comes to real estate. That's my philosophy and I've been in this business for thirty years." With that she threw her car into reverse and executed a wide turn.

"Thanks again!" Verna watched as the Buick trundled down the laneway and out of sight. She continued to stare at the gap in the forest into which the car had disappeared, postponing that moment when she would have to turn around and climb the stairs to the porch, and, all by herself now, only her, negotiate this mausoleum of memories, this repository of her past. *There's no help for it*, Verna, she told herself. *No one is going to rescue you. No one is going to do it for you. Because there is no one. Just you. And you've got to go in. Otherwise, what was the point of coming all this way?* She closed her eyes and first summoned, then organized her meagre ration of resolve. She turned around and, steeling herself, climbed the four stone steps that led from the parking area to the patch of lawn, then up the couple of steps leading to the door of the screened-in porch, her heart thudding dully and her throat constricted. She took as deep a breath as she could manage, then opened the door and stepped inside.

The porch was as she remembered, though more confined, darker, and damper. It gave off an acrid smell that reminded her of hummus. The furnishings were the same sagging wicker furniture that had always been there — the Bar Harbor Triple Cross set and the two Heywood rockers, the colour of wet wood. Clay pots in which the spines of long-dead ferns languished. On her way to the front door she accidentally kicked over an old Eight O'Clock coffee tin filled with cigarette butts and rusty, standing water — that must have dated to Fern's tenure of the cottage, she thought, stepping around the mess. Between bouts of colon-cleansing and various gradations of vegetarianism, Fern had chain-smoked, as if working herself up to the next ordeal of healthy living. She had been very particular when it came to brands, Verna remembered — she made a point of smoking only Virginia Slims, Ultra Lights — "You've come a long way, baby!" Its marketing evidently spoke to her, assuring her that she was making progress, that things were going well. Verna had never smoked. She despised smokers as weak. She drank instead. *"Ne quid nimis,"* their father had always enjoined. "'All things in moderation'," but neither Fern nor Verna had ever proven capable of much restraint.

Verna fished in her pocket for the ring of keys she had taken that morning from the rack beside the door to the breezeway of the Indian Crescent house. With unsteady hands, she tried first one, then another, but it was the third key that slid easily into the keyhole. "Three's the charm!" That's what Donald would have said. He had had a saying for everything. It had been both endearing and irritating. *Damn him*, she thought, as tears once again picked at her eyes.

Verna turned the key and pushed open the door. Wood swollen with damp, it stuck a little. She peered in. The sun had yet to sink, but its slanting rays could not penetrate shutters drawn tight against the rigors of the past winter. It was dark and smelled musty, close, but alive somehow, as though the house were not a concoction of stick and stone and mud, but some large, hibernating creature curled in on itself. This was not the first time such a notion had occurred to her. As a child entering the closed-up house for the first time after the long winter, she remembered understanding somehow that it was a kind of inchoate being — asleep, but on the verge of waking. The idea had been terrifying, but also compelling. To think such things had been irresistible to Verna; indeed, she could not *not* think them. "Verna is a fanciful child," her grandmother had said once — the twins had just turned six when Frieda, lightly dusted with confectioner's sugar, slipped first into a diabetic coma and then out some existential back door to what was referred to in the Macoun family as, "The Other Side." Although Verna could barely assemble enough fragments of memory to compose an image of the old woman in her mind, she could remember this observation on her part, which Frieda had made in the same way she might have said, "Verna is a tiresome child," or, "she has always been so difficult." (On the subject of Fern, Frieda had this to say: "Fern is such a sunny child," which led Verna to conclude that she herself was not so sunny and that this was not a good thing.)

Verna fumbled for the light switch, relieved to see the light come on. She had thought far enough ahead to get the electricity turned back on before making the trip. Orange candle-shaped bulbs screwed into bracket fixtures wobbled on, bathing the wide hall that bisected the house with nervous, yellow light. She glanced to her right — to the living room, pine-panelled, with a big window that looked out over the lake when it was not shuttered up. A card table and chairs had been pulled up underneath the window, but the focal point of the room was an imposing river-stone fireplace that extended all the way from the pegged oak floor to the wood-lined ceiling. Huddled before its soot-stained hearth were a lumpy sofa and two armchairs slip-covered in dark green corduroy, the ribbed fabric worn shiny in spots by the assorted rumps of three generations of Macouns. She crossed to the sofa and fingered the corner of a black, loden green-and-navy-blue afghan — just one of the many fruits of Frieda's lifelong love affair with the crochet hook. Both the cottage and the Indian Crescent house were littered with afghans, tea cozies, wash cloths, bizarre holiday decorations, and pot holders worked in quad rosettes and six-pointed stars and granny stitch in Red Heart acrylic yarn purchased at Woolworth's and favoured for its washability; its texture — something like that of cotton candy — had always set Verna's teeth on edge. Opposite the window was the door to what they had always called "the study," first George's, then Donald's, and directly over that door's lintel, a woe-begone-looking, moth-eaten moose head. Someone at the Bureau of Mines had shot the moose while on a hunting trip in the Soo and had its head mounted. When his wife, a robust vegetarian, refused to have it in her house, he gave it to George. The moose's antlers measured an impressive sixty inches across. George had figured the moose's age to have been between ten and twelve years old when he took the bullet. She and Fern had named it Bullwinkle, of course, after the cartoon character.

At the sight of Bullwinkle, a light went on in Verna's head. Dad's Scotch, she remembered. Macallan Highland single malt. His favourite; George's too, father and son. Verna checked her wristwatch — nearly six o'clock. The cocktail hour had been underway for close to an hour. What was she waiting for? As it was, she was going to have to play catch-up. She crossed to the study, switched on the light, and quickly scanned the small room: floor-to-ceiling shelves crammed with moldering books and old magazines — decades of dog-eared copies of *National*

Geographic and *Life* and *Maclean's* and boxes of maps folded and stacked; the big oak desk piled high with papers; and, there, right in its accustomed position on the credenza, the Bohemian lead crystal decanter, coated with dust and flanked by two wide-bowled, tulip-lipped Scotch glasses. From within its fortress of crystal the single malt winked a golden eye at her. "Howdy!" it said in a voice that only Verna could hear.

She crossed to the credenza and let her fingers fall lightly onto the decanter's stopper. How Donald had sung the praises of his father's Scotch. Its sweetness and its complex flavour, how it had matured in carefully selected, hand-crafted oak casks, but casks with a difference, casks that had held rich, rare sherries for at least three years before being shipped from Spain to Macallan's Speyside distillery in Scotland. "It's the interaction between spirit and wood that does it," Donald had told the twins, swirling his glass and sniffing the whisky, adding a few drops of water, then sniffing it again. He had made a ceremony out of everything.

Tears leaked from Verna's eyes. *Ridiculous*, she chided herself. *It's just bloody Scotch. Bloody, expensive Scotch.* She dabbed at her eyes with a wad of tissues, took a glass, and gave it a perfunctory wipe on the tail of her Black Watch flannel shirt. She poured herself two fingers of the whisky and wandered back through the living room and into the shadowy hall, where she paused to lean against the varnished wainscotting and hold the glass to the wobbly light — the Scotch glimmered a rich mahogany. She took a sip and rolled it around in her mouth like a marble, coating it. Then another.

Now this, she thought, eyeing it, *is a proper drink*. A man's drink. Verna was proud that she drank like a man and not like a girl, which was to say, not like Fern. Fern had drunk (and never hesitated to mix) blush Zinfandels and strawberry wine and Jell-O shooters and B-52s and mini Baileys and Peach Schnapps and pails of Welch's grape juice mixed with vodka. Sweet drinks that made her giddy, then hurl. She had been one of those girls who became one of those women who could be counted on to throw up and/or faint at the slightest provocation — an excitable woman with unstable equilibrium. Verna shook her head. *What a child*, she thought. Never taking the probable consequences of her actions into account. Always surprised by completely predictable disasters.

She peered into the glass. No more Scotch. How did that happen? *Never mind*, she consoled herself. *Plenty where that came from. Well, not plenty, but some.*

She checked her wristwatch. It was six o'clock.

Verna returned to the study and poured herself another two fingers. *Maybe I should add some water*, she thought. *That's what Dad always did. Something about releasing the flavors, the aromas …*

She headed for the kitchen. The board-and-batten walls painted a butter cream, the floor of buckled linoleum a counterpane of white and brick red squares, the bead-board cabinets with water-glass cabinet door inserts, and the big, roughly finished pine trestle table, a new refrigerator since she had last been at the cottage and maybe a new stove … otherwise pretty much as she remembered. Right down to the fire-engine-red wall-mounted rotary telephone by the back door. Verna crossed over to the old farmhouse sink and turned the tap. The faucet coughed dryly and emitted a slender drool of rusty water. *Damn*, she realized. *The water's shut off. Of course, it's shut off. Dad always shut it off at the end of the season.* She would have to turn it back on. But how? And where was the valve, anyway? And how would she recognize it if she saw it? Some time before, her father had given her sketchy instructions on how to open the cottage in the event of his demise — instructions that might possibly have included the shutting off and turning on of water, that she did not now recall. That and a scrap of paper on which he had written the name and phone number of the Ojibway handyman from the nearby reserve — Lionel Madahbee. She was to contract with him to affect any needed repairs. "You keep an eye on Lionel," her father had warned her. "He's melancholy."

Melancholy? What had he meant by that?

Turning on the water is a job for Lionel, she decided.

Woof! Woof!

Verna jumped, slopping Scotch onto her jeans.

Woof!

"Jude!" Verna gasped. "Jesus, Mary, and Joseph! What a start you gave me! Where are you?"

Woof!

The sound came from out back.

Verna set the remains of her drink on the counter, crossed to the door to the back porch, and unlocked it. Jude hurled himself through the aperture, planted all four paws on the floor, and shook, beginning with his head and ears and vibrating all the way down to the tip of his black tail. Muddy water splattered everywhere.

"Jude!" Verna backed up in an unsuccessful attempt to stay dry.

Jude barked joyously and bounded off toward the hall. He galloped up the stairs, still barking.

"Yuck!" Turning, Verna opened one drawer, then another, looking for a tea towel to mop up the water and mud. Upstairs she could hear Jude running up and down the hallway. What in hell is he doing? Then she realized what he was doing. He was looking for Donald.

Shit.

Verna slammed her eyes shut and squeezed back the tears. "Enough with the waterworks!" she scolded herself. Locating a tea towel she wiped first herself, then the floor. Jude continued to tear up and down the upstairs hall, yelping.

"Jude! Hey, Jude! Come down! He's not there, Jude! He's in the car!" Then, when there was no response, "Jude! Suppertime! Kibble! Chow! Come on, now. You know you love it!"

The sound of claws clicking down the stairs. Jude stood in the door to the kitchen, his black fur shining with lake water. He looked disappointed, but hopeful.

"Let's go out to the car and bring your food in," she told him. "And Sister's vodka."

Did I really just refer to myself as the dog's sister? She thought. *Because that's what Donald had always done.* "Tell Sister it's time for school." "Tell Sister she has to wear socks."

She went onto the back porch and past the woodpile to the Volvo. Opening the trunk, she retrieved Jude's dishes and the bag of Iams. It was then that she noticed the two big bottles of water tucked into the trunk's right-hand back corner, part of what looked to be a sort of emergency road kit that Donald had assembled — a couple of rolled-up Hudson's Bay blankets, assorted bungee cords, a ball of string, a sheathed buck knife, jumper cables, flares, and a big red Canadian Tire flashlight. She shook her head. *Semper paratus,* she thought, removing the bottles of water from the car and setting them on the ground. *Still, it means I don't have to wait until Lionel comes to have water. This should do us until morning, maybe longer.*

She grabbed the bag of dog food and one of the containers of water and carried them into the house. She came back for Jude's dishes, which she set on the floor in the kitchen. She poured water from the container into one and kibble from the bag into the other.

"Oh, boy," she said. "Dog food *again!*" That's what Donald had always said when he fed his various dogs. "Jude!" she objected. "You're drooling on my foot!"

Jude tore into his food while Verna returned to the car and brought back the evening's necessities — her overnight bag, the other container of water, the bag of ice, a bottle of Russian Prince, and one of diet tonic water.

She removed two empty ice trays from the freezer — the old-fashioned tin kind with the lever — setting them on the counter, then thrust the bag of ice into the freezer along with the bottle of vodka. "Remind me to make ice in the morning," she told Jude, who was noisily lapping up water from his bowl. She put the bottle of diet tonic in the refrigerator, went to the study, and retrieved the decanter, which was still more or less full. More or less. She poured herself another drink and splashed some water from the bottle into it.

Between sips and trailed by Jude, she made trips to the car. First to get her suitcase, next the grocery bag of food, and the other bottle of Russian Prince. Then a book of crossword puzzles and the previous Saturday's *Globe and Mail*, followed by the dog's leash, a bag of rawhide strips and another of pigs' ears. Finally the three cardboard boxes that had ridden shotgun on the passenger seat of the Volvo — the remains. No. The *cre*-mains. The boxes containing her father and sister's ashes she brought into the kitchen and set on the counter. Bob's she placed on the back porch next to the woodpile.

"Remember Bob?" she asked Jude. "Fussy, old, self-satisfied, full-of-himself Bob? Oh, you know — the reason I could never have a dog, the one who didn't like dogs. You, for example. The one who didn't like you."

Jude's face sagged.

"Oh, don't look so worried," Verna reassured him. "He didn't like me, either. Toward the end. No, before that. Of course, I didn't like him much, either. Actually, if you want to know the truth, I hated him. Maybe it'll rain on you," she told Bob's ashes. "Maybe a raccoon will come to scatter your ashes. Maybe a bear will come along and paw your box to smithereens. Maybe a fox will see you and try to drag you to its hole. Good luck with that, you two-timing bastard!"

Rummaging about in the bag of groceries she retrieved a microwaveable President's Choice chicken curry and peeled back its lid — dinner. She set it on the counter next to Fern and Donald's ashes.

It was then that she noticed her drink was gone. "That won't do!" she informed Jude and poured herself another, bigger this time. "I never did like Scotch," she said. "It always seemed so complicated, so rule-bound. Slow down, take your time, savour it. As if to do otherwise would be to blaspheme. As if it were some sort of religion with, you know, followers. No. Not a religion. A cult. That's what it is. A cult."

Well, there was nobody around to tell her what to do and, besides, the Macallan was hers now. She had inherited it and nobody, but nobody, was going to tell her how to drink it. If she wanted to guzzle it, she was going to guzzle it. And that, as they say, was that!

This time the drink she poured herself was even bigger than the last. It all amounts to the same thing in the end, after all. Four little drinks. One big one.

"Come on, Jude," she rallied the dog. "Let's get this stuff upstairs."

The Lab took the lead. Verna followed, carrying the suitcase in one hand, her drink in the other, and the carry-on bag slung over her shoulder. When they reached the top, "Whew!" she said. "I seem to be a little tipsy. I'd better slow down. Jude, will you remind me to slow down? Will you?"

But Jude was dancing on his claws in front of the door to Donald's room. The door was shut. So was the door to her old room. So were all the doors — the door to Fern's room; the door to what had always been referred to as the "guest room" (despite the fact that there were never any guests); even the door to the bathroom at the end of the hall. That was not surprising. Some families shut doors; others leave them open. The Macouns liked their doors shut; they liked their privacy, their secrets. Still, it was a little creepy — all these closed doors with nobody on the other side.

"Kind of like arriving at the Mickey Mouse Clubhouse long after all the Mousketeers have grown up and gotten fat or MS or become alcoholics or died of a drug over-dose. No one left to say, 'Here's your ears!'" Verna told Jude, who just yelped at her as if to say, "What? Who? Let's get on with it; I want to see Alpha Dog!" "Okay. Fair enough," she said. "Mickey Mouse Club. Before your time. But Alpha Dog's not in there, Jude. I'm sorry, but he's just not."

She set the suitcase and the carry-on bag on the floor, and, summoning up her courage, turned the knob on Don-ald's bedroom door and shoved it gingerly. It creaked open to reveal a slice of white-washed tongue-and-groove walls and ceiling and a rocker drawn up close to the dormer that looked out over the lake. Eager to get into the room, Jude squeezed between her legs and the door, causing it to open the rest of the way. He let out a happy bark, then fell silent when he discerned that his master was nowhere to be seen.

Verna came alongside the dog. She laid her hand on his head. "Sorry," she said.

Jude sat down. Then he lay down. He looked abject. But, then, dogs always look sad when their mouths were closed. Those big eyes. Who was to say whether Jude was happy or not? Still, Verna knew he was sad. Hell, she was sad!

She sat down next to him on the floor. "You're stuck with me from now on," she told him. Then she looked around the shadowy room. There was the bedroom set from the Eckert house in Kingston, her grandmother's house — the oak bed with the high headboard and the matching chest of drawers topped by the splotchy bevelled mirror and the steamer trunk in the corner. But there were other things, objects that she recognized as being her father's, his artifacts: the battered sheepskin slippers beside the bed, a half-full bag of generic eucalyptus-flavoured cough drops, an old pair of reading glasses from Shoppers, a photograph of her mother on their wedding day, looking a lot like Fern had at that age.

"Here," she said, reaching out and pulling one of the slippers out from under the bed. "You can have this to remember him by. I bet it smells like his feet. It smells like somebody's feet." Jude sniffed the slipper, then looked up at her. "It's Okay," she urged him. "You can have it. It's yours." Jude lifted his chin and then lowered it, so that it was resting on the slipper.

Verna gathered her knees to her chest and rocked back and forth on her sitz bones. She looked up at the shuttered dormer. "I should get Lionel to open up the shutters," she told Jude. "That's what'll sell the place. Lake views."

She drank thoughtfully. Which is to say, her head was full of thoughts while she drank, all jostling for space, half-formed and circling some sort of inner drain. After a few confused moments, she stirred. "Well," she advised the dog. "One door down. Next!"

Her legs felt a little shaky, so she crawled over to the bed and used it to drag herself up. She collected the glass from the floor with a swoop and wobbled unsteadily to the hall, trailed by the black Lab with the slipper in his mouth. "I'm here!" she told Fern's door, then leaned back against the banister to gather her strength. For this was not simply the bedroom in which Fern had slept when they were children. This was the bedroom in which the OPP officer and his partner had found her four years earlier — the room in which she had died. Had died alone.

"It wasn't the cancer that killed her. Did you know that?" Verna asked Jude. She shook her head solemnly. "Nope. It was something called 'sepsis.' I had never heard of it, so I looked it up." She laughed. "Of course, I did." Super Grammarian — that's what they had called her at the ministry — behind her back, of course, but then Bob had told her. Of course he had. Couldn't resist, even though he knew it would hurt her feelings. Maybe *because* he knew it would. Because she was such a stickler for detail, so uptight and rule-bound, because it was important to her that everything — spelling, grammar, diction — be just right. "Come on, Verna!" he had cajoled her. "Lighten up! It means that you have super powers. The ability to parse. To conjugate. You and you alone can save infinitives from being split! It's funny, Verna. Can't you take a joke?"

To which she had replied somewhat stiffly, "Apparently not."

"What was I talking about, Jude? Oh, right," she continued, "sepsis. You'll be interested to know that the word derives from the Greek word for *putrefaction*. Yes. That's right. My twin sister putrefied to death. Alone. By herself. How do you like them apples?" Verna's throat ached. Her eyes burned. "Jesus!" she muttered. "How did that happen?" She peered at the closed door to her sister's room; it looked back at her — accusing, reproachful. Her stomach did a little jig. Not a good sign. "I can't go in there, Jude. Not yet. Tomorrow. I got to get something in my stomach. Otherwise I'm going to pull a Fern."

She headed downstairs carefully, followed by Jude, and crossed into the kitchen. She looked at the aluminum tin of curry. Suddenly curry did not seem to be a good idea.

"No more Scotch *pour vous, madame*," she said sternly, pouring herself a vodka and tonic instead. She slipped on her jacket and tottered out to the screened-in porch and set the drink down on the lacy little Queen Anne table that, together with the Heywood rockers, made up a set. She made a second trip, this time for the bottles of tonic and vodka. These she set on the floor behind the table, so that she wouldn't accidentally knock them over. "For that," she informed Jude, "would be a tragedy of the first magnitude!" *What*, she wondered, "*is the first magnitude*"? She was certain she used to know what that meant. She would have to look that up. Of course she would. "Because that's what I do!" she said aloud. "Because I'm Super Grammarian." She plopped down in one of the rockers and gazed foggily out at the lake. Jude appeared in the doorway, carrying the slipper in his mouth.

"Is that your WOOBIE?" Verna slurred. She hated it when she slurred. Good thing it was just the dog. "Ah, is that your WOOBIE?" For that's what her father used to call the discarded stuffed animals that the succession of soft-mouthed retrievers who had informed his life felt compelled to carry about with them. WOOBIE. An acronym for Wonderful Object Occasionally Bitten in Earnest. Because, in some cases, after a brief period of infatuation, the dog of the moment ended up shaking the WOOBIE to death, then pulling out its eyes and nose and eating a good deal of its polyfil stuffing. (This invariably returned to haunt whoever was scooping up after them.)

Donald used to buy stuffed animals at the Goodwill for a quarter apiece. He had felt bad about it. Embarrassed. "I don't tell the cashier they're for the dog," he had confessed. "It doesn't seem right when that's all that some parents can afford for their kids." A real bleeding heart, her father, dyed-in-the wool NDP.

"Come on!" Verna encouraged Jude. "Come here!" Jude approached. She patted his head. "Good dog! Keep me company, why don't you? Heck! What else do you have to do? I'm it! The main attraction."

Jude grinned, a huge pink triangle of tongue lolling out of one side of his mouth, before oozing onto the floor the way retrievers do, suddenly boneless, flat like a bearskin rug.

It was coming on to a quarter past eight. The sun was setting, but, in the absence of any large settlement in the vicinity, there was no brown light to soften the descending edge of darkness. Mist began to rise up from the lake in wisps, like ghosts from a graveyard.

"Beautiful," she murmured. "Beautiful." She rocked and drank. Jude fell asleep and snored. She nudged him with her toe. "Stop snoring!" Eventually, after shadows had wrapped the house round in a dusky embrace and light had drained from the sky, the stars popped out. That's when she remembered what the phrase, "of the first magnitude" meant. It meant the brightest stars in the sky, beginning with Sirius, the Dog Star.

"See!" Verna pointed out drunkenly. "Sirius, in the constellation Canis Major. That means 'Big Dog.' Are you a big dog, Jude? Sure you are! Golly, but that's bright!"

At some point she fell asleep, only to startle awake, half-frozen.

"What?" she muttered.

She staggered into the house, Jude at her heels. She shaded her eyes and peered at the stairs, which seemed exceptionally steep to her. Unreasonably so.

Nope, she decided and wobbled off into the living room, where she lowered herself onto the lumpy couch, assumed a fetal position, covered herself, more or less, with Frieda's scratchy afghan and slept. Jude curled up with the slipper on the rag rug before the hearth.

She woke only once, when a sound like a loon makes poked into her sleep, prodding her into a kind of temporary lucidity. *Loons mate forever*, she remembered, before the thought slipped away from her and she sank back into a churning ragout of dreams.

Wednesday, May 18, 2005

She woke into a cacophony of loud banging and hysterical barking.

"What?" she managed, rearing up a couple of inches, then, "*Oh!* Ouch!" Her head felt like a mangled screw top, half off. "Jeez!"

"Anybody home? *Yoo-hoo, eh?*" Someone on the porch, at the front door. "Anybody home? Hey! Got eyes, don't I? Can see the car. Give it up, eh? I know you're in there! Oh, *yoo-hoo!*" A monotone exhortation, like the clanging of an infernal bell.

"Just a minute!" Verna clawed her way out of her grandmother's afghan (no easy task), set her feet on the floor, and, taking her thunderous head in her hands to steady it, rose with extreme caution. *One for* homo erectus, she thought, before noticing that she was in her stocking feet and wearing the same jeans and flannel shirt as the day before, only now they were rumpled and stuck to her in places. "Oh, God!

Did I sleep down here?" she muttered. Then, when the pounding resumed, "I'm coming! Hold your horses!" She wobbled into the hall, and, with some difficulty, dragged Jude away from the door, interposed herself between him and it, and pushed it open.

On the other side of the screen door stood a Native woman wearing a red-and-black plaid flannel shirt, jeans with the bottoms neatly rolled up, and white running shoes. Her straight black hair was pulled back into a loose pony-tail and she wore silver dream-catcher earrings. She was no more than five feet tall, four inches shorter than Verna, and perfectly spherical. Not so much fat as round. Her face was also round and she wore John Lennon granny glasses.

"Yes?" Verna managed, struggling to hold Jude back.

"Woke you, eh?"

"I'm afraid ..."

"You don't look so good," the woman observed. "Bad night, eh? Looks like you've been drinking. Smells like it, too. Whew!" She pinched her nostrils in the universal ges-ture of "P.U." Verna fell back a foot, lest she offend further, and gaped at the woman. She was at a total loss for words; her brain seemed to be stuck in neutral. The woman was not so inhibited. She pointed to Jude and said. "He's happy to see me. Wants to say hello. Wants to pee."

"Oh, yes," Verna agreed in a rush. "Right. Of course."

The woman took a step backwards and Verna let go of Jude's collar. He exploded through the door and plunged his head between the woman's legs in frenzied greeting. Verna stepped forward to grab his collar and pull him back, but the woman told her, "Don't worry." She paddled the dog's wagging behind with both hands. "Just docking, eh? Dogs, they do that, don't they, Jude? They dock. Yeah. I'm glad to see you, too." She pushed him away, and, crossing the porch, opened the door to the outside. Jude galloped through and began to zig-zag across the lawn, anointing this rock, that tree until he reached the water's edge. He waded in, barking joyously.

"Excuse me," Verna sagged against the door frame in a forlorn attempt to remain upright, "but you are ..."

"Winonah."

"And you knew my father?"

"All my life. I'd sit down if I were you. You look like you're going to hurl. Don't want to clean up hurl."

Verna opened the door, tottered forward a couple of steps, and then carefully lowered herself onto one of the Heywood rockers. She closed her eyes in order to re-establish equilibrium.

"Like a smoke?"

Verna grimaced. She shook her head.

"Cause I can get 'em for you real cheap, eh. From the reserve."

"Don't smoke," Verna murmured. *Did everyone from around here smoke?* She wondered. *Oh, right. They did.* "Remind me again why you're here?"

Winonah extracted a cigarette from an unmarked pack in the breast pocket of her plaid shirt. "Carmen Beauséjour give me a call," she replied. "Said you'd need help opening up the house. Seeing as how you never done it."

"Thanks, but Dad gave me a name. The guy he always used."

"Who?"

"Lionel Somebody."

"Lionel Madahbee?"

"Something like that. Yeah. I've got his number. Somewhere."

"*Uh huh.*" Winonah nodded. She lit the cigarette and took a long drag on it. She exhaled. "Good luck with that."

Verna blinked at her. "What do you mean?"

Winonah cocked her head to one side, smoked, blew smoke rings. "Dead," she said.

"Dead? I'm sorry. You're talking about Lionel?"

Winonah nodded.

"So you know him? *Knew* him, I mean?"

"Yeah," Winonah replied. "Somewhat. My brother."

"Lionel was your brother?"

"My twin brother."

"Oh!" Verna was flummoxed. "Did he kill himself?" she asked. "I'm sorry. That was insensitive of me. It's none of my business. It's just that Dad said he was ... melancholy."

Winonah stared at her. "Yeah. And?"

"I just thought ..." Verna fumbled. "I mean, if he was depressed ..."

"Melancholy is not depressed." Winonah's tone was firm. "What Lionel was — he was numb."

"Numb?"

The woman nodded. "That's right. He suffered from intermittent numbness. That's different from depressed."

She seemed so convinced of this that Verna hadn't the heart to pursue it. "Was this recent?" she asked. "Because just a couple of months ago, Dad —"

"April," Winonah cut her off. "Spring Pow Wow down there in Michigan."

"Was it an accident then?"

Winonah shook her head. "He died in competition," she said, sitting down in the other Heywood rocker.

"I'm sorry." Verna was confused now. She had pictured Lionel as looking like a bear — big and shaggy and lumbering. "Was he an athlete of some sort?"

Winonah shrugged. "I suppose. If you call eating a sports event."

"What do you mean?" Verna asked. "Like a pie-eating contest or a how-many-jalapenos-can-you-choke-down or hamburgers or ramen noodles or hot dogs?"

Winonah looked offended. "Hardly," she said, putting out her cigarette and tossing it into the rusty coffee can. "Not much skill involved in that. Just … capacity."

"What then?"

"Chubby Bunny Contest."

Verna stared at her. "Excuse me, but … what?"

Winonah looked at her with a mixture of pity and contempt. "You've never heard of the Chubby Bunny contest?"

Verna shook her head.

"Well," observed Winonah, "you don't get out much, do you?"

Verna considered this. "I guess not."

"What happens is you stuff one marshmallow into your mouth at a time, then you say 'chubby bunny' until you can't say it anymore," Winonah explained. "If you gag, choke, or spit out the marshmallow, you lose."

"So what happened to Lionel?"

"One of the marshmallows got lodged in his throat," Winonah said. "They couldn't get it out in time."

Verna was horrified. "How awful!"

"Pretty stupid, if you ask me," Winonah replied grimly. "Chubby Bunny Contests have killed a lot of our people over the years. It's a silent killer. Ojibway didn't have marshmallows before the white man came. Turns out they are just another way to kill our people — like blankets infected with smallpox. Some Traditional Pow Wow. I'm leading a movement to do away with Chubby Bunny Contests at Pow Wows. I have a petition with eighty signatures on it so far. So, have you primed the pump yet?"

Verna blinked at her, then shook her head. "Uh, no," she said. "Excuse me, but are you talking about the water? Because I don't know where the shut-off valve is. You don't happen to, do you?"

Winonah was stoic. "Lionel and me were twins," she replied. "We had this psychic bond, eh? Everything Lionel knew, I know. And you can't just turn on the water. Got to prime the pump first."

Had Dad said anything about priming any pump? Verna couldn't remember. Still, she was certain that she had heard the phrase before, "to prime a pump." Used metaphorically in all likelihood. "I had a twin," Verna recalled. "But I don't think we had any psychic bond." *Or any bond at all*, she thought. How sad was that? She wanted to weep, but didn't have the energy. Instead she collapsed in on herself, heavy and wistful.

"I knew Fern," said Winonah flatly. "It was you we didn't know."

Priming the pump turned out to be an almost Herculean task, which Winonah accomplished with what could only be described as plodding implacability. It entailed hauling water in buckets (eighteen, all told; Verna counted) from the lake and pouring it into holes in the top of the pump until the intake pipe connecting the cottage to the spring out back was full. She then checked the pipes for loose connections, and, finding none, released the shut off valve. The valve, as it happened, was on the back porch next to the woodpile.

"Hey!" Winonah appeared at the door to the porch carrying a partially filled trash bag in one hand and the now damp cardboard box of Bob's cremains in the other. "I found this carton by the woodpile, eh? Is it yours?"

"Not recently," Verna replied.

"Robert Arthur Woodcock." Winonah read the label.

"And? So?"

"So what do you want me to do with it?"

Verna considered this for a moment before saying, "Throw it out."

Winonah dropped the box into the bag, pulled the drawstring, and tied it. "There's water now. Maybe you want to get us some coffee."

"Good idea!" Verna wondered if she actually could get up from the rocker. From her shoulders down it felt like she was made of slabs of concrete; from the neck up it just hurt.

"I'm not making it," Winonah warned her.

"Okay! All right already!" Verna wondered if handy persons were supposed to bully their employers. And had she actually hired her? She didn't remember that part. No, to the best of her recollection, Winonah had just started working and Verna, for her part, had failed to stop her. Not a contract in the strictest sense of the word, but now that she had proven herself useful at a time when the same could not be said of herself, she was loath to dismiss her. Also, she suspected that it was ill advised to cross the round little woman. Who knew what she was capable of? "But you've got to help me up," she extended her hands in Winonah's direction. Winonah set the garbage bag down, crossed to Verna, took her by her wrists and, without any preamble, yanked, catapulting Verna to her feet. "Ouch!" Verna complained.

Winonah appeared unrepentant. She picked up the garbage bag and headed into the house.

Verna limped after her. "Say, what are you going to do with that bag?"

"There's a Dumpster on the way to town. I'll drop it off."

They arrived in the kitchen.

"There are filters in the drawer next to the fridge," Winonah informed her.

"How do you know that?"

"I told you. I know everything that Lionel knew."

"And he knew where the filters were?"

"Of course. What's this?" She peered into the now unfrozen President's Choice chicken curry.

"Oh." Verna remembered. "It was supposed to be dinner. I didn't get around to it."

"It's been sitting out all night?"

Verna nodded.

Winonah loosened the drawstring on the garbage bag, picked up the container, and, tipping it, slopped its contents into the bag. Verna could just make out one corner of Bob's cardboard box as the sticky rice and congealed sauce slid over it.

"He always hated Indian," she murmured.

"What?" Winonah bristled.

"Nothing," Verna said quickly. "Nothing at all. So where's the coffee?"

"Beats me!" said Winonah.

"So Lionel knew where the filters were, but not the coffee?"

"That's right," Winonah replied. "Lionel drank tea."

While Verna foraged for coffee, Winonah checked the drain valve at the bottom of the water tank to make sure it was closed, went upstairs, opened the hot water tap in the claw-foot tub and let it run until water started to squeak out of it. She returned downstairs, opened the cold water shut-off to the tank, and turned the tank on. Then she checked both the tank and the drain valve for leaks.

While Verna, shaking, loaded the coffeemaker with Eight O'Clock Coffee from the can she had found tucked away in one of the cabinets, Winonah checked plumbing traps to make sure they were connected. "You're missing a drain plug in the downstairs bathroom sink," she told her. "I'll pick one up when I'm in town."

While Donald's Mr. Coffee Machine, vintage 1972, sputtered into geriatric action, burping hot brown liquid into a stained decanter, Winonah prowled around the foundation of the cottage, scouting for heaving or cracks, before taking a walk out to the dock to see if it was twisting or creaking and checking for corroded or missing supports and popped nails.

While Verna crept back to the front porch, precariously juggling two mugs of steaming coffee, Winonah assessed the state of the power lines. "There's been a lot of deadfall," she told Verna as she relieved her of her mug. Verna sank back into the Heywood rocker, grateful to have succeeded in making and transporting coffee without undue mishap. Then she took a sip of coffee and burned her tongue. "Damn!" she exclaimed. "God, I hate that!"

"Hate what?" Winonah asked.

"I burnt my tongue! I'm always burning my tongue."

Winonah shrugged. "That's because you're in too much of a hurry, eh? You got to slow down. You know what Lionel used to say?"

Verna, infuriated, stuck her tongue out and fanned it.

"'Don't hurry. Be happy.' That's what."

Rolf!

Jude, who had spent the better part of the morning paddling in the lake or chasing ducks, stood aquiver at the door to the porch, his tail in violent motion.

Rolf!

Winonah let him in.

The Lab charged over to Verna, planted all four feet, and shook joyously, drenching her.

"Jude!" Verna cried. "Yuck! Jude! Go away! You hear me! Over there! You smell like a swamp!"

"Those power lines," Winonah said. "They're okay, but there's some fraying at the pole. You'll want to call Hydro about that." She peered at Verna. "On second thought, I'll call Hydro." She blew on her coffee, took a sip, and grimaced. "This is no Timmy's."

Verna lay back in the rocker and closed her eyes.

"What's for lunch?" Winonah asked.

After a meal cobbled together from Verna's meagre groceries and a can of Campbell's Chunky Clam Chowder that had over-wintered in the pantry, Winonah wiped her mouth with a paper towel, stood, and stated her intention. "Shutters."

Verna countered with, "Nap," and proceeded to drag herself upstairs, dogged by the redolent Jude.

She had intended to sleep in her old room. It was, after all, her room. However, when she pulled down the faded comforter on the old spool bed — the same blue-and-white-checked gingham counterpane edged with ragged eyelet that she remembered — she saw that there were no sheets. There were, however, mouse droppings.

"Damn!" She had forgotten about the mice.

Verna sat down on the bed's edge and glanced forlornly around her. The wobbly rocker with the caned back, the bookcase, seriously askew, the bedside table with the pink porcelain lamp, its tipsy yellowed shade festooned with dingy pompoms — all as she remembered, only shabbier, smaller. She felt sad, glum, the sole survivor, the last of the Mohicans. To be the last man standing — where was the fun in that? For one thing, who was there to notice? Idly, disconsolately she pulled out the top drawer of the bedside table — it stuck a little — and peered inside.

Treasures and junk. Detritus from a previous life. Stray jacks, a pair of pink plastic sunglasses, stale candy cigarettes, and a worn set of playing cards. A Duncan yo-yo from the mid-sixties, white on blue. Unlike Fern, she had never mastered the yo-yo. Or the hula hoop. Or anything else requir ing a modicum of coordination and the ability to commit. She had been full of trepidation, a spaz — that's what kids had called her. She shut the drawer.

The room smelled musty, as though it had been sealed up for a long, long time. *Well, who knows?* she thought. Maybe it had been. Maybe once she was gone, it had fallen into disuse and had remained, decade after decade, shut in upon itself. For all she knew, she might have been the last person to sleep in this bed. The Macouns were not the sort of family that invited guests to their cottage, after all. It was too far north for that to be convenient and, besides, they were ... well, not that sort. Not very friendly. Too tucked in around the edges. Too chary of their secrets.

She looked up to see Jude standing in the door with her father's slipper in his mouth. He looked animated.

"What?" she asked the dog.

Jude dropped the slipper and yelped.

"Yes? And?"

Jude yelped again, retrieved the slipper, backed up, and trotted down the hall.

"I'm not sleeping in Fern's room, if that's what you're thinking!" she called after the dog. "No way I'm opening that Pandora's box!" She stood and walked into the hall. Jude was standing expectantly in front of Donald's door. "Oh, I get it,' she said. "You want me to sleep in Dad's bed." She considered for an instant not shutting the door to her room — in all probability it could do with a good airing. However, leaving the door ajar seemed to her reckless somehow, an invitation to mayhem. So she carefully closed it, making sure that the latch caught and held. "Let's see if he left the sheets on," she said, opening the door to her father's room and following Jude inside. In the half darkness, she made her way over to her father's bed and pulled down the Hudson's Bay blanket stretched across it. Eureka! Sheets. She stood for a moment, looking down at them. *Dad slept on these. There's probably dander ... old skin cells of his on these sheets, his dust.* She sunk into a momentary reverie, then bestirred herself. "Well, it's like they say, Jude: beggars can't be choosers and I don't feel like figuring out where the rest of the sheets are." She crawled into the bed — no point in taking any clothes off, what with the Daddy dander and all — and pulled the covers up around her neck. Jude came up and pushed the now soggy and matted slipper at her face. Reaching up, she took it from him. "What?" she asked. "Yuck!"

He backed up.

"Jude!"

He took a run at the bed.

"No!"

But it was too late. All four muddy paws on the bed.

"Jude! You're still wet!" Verna complained.

Jude happily retrieved the slipper, clambered over her, and began to describe a circle in the bedclothes next to her in preparation for lying down.

"Jude!"

But the dog paid her no heed. He continued to circle until he had flattened the bedclothes to his liking. Then he lay down.

"You stink," she told him.

Unperturbed, Jude closed his eyes. A moment later he was snoring.

"Cut that out! You're worse than Bob!" Grumbling, she adjusted her position to accommodate the dog. Moments later sleep's undertow dragged her toward it and then sucked her below the surface, drowning her in dreams.

Verna's burning eyes creaked open to light ricocheting at a slant off the lake's surface and through the dormer window in a tremulous shaft. Where was she? Oh, yes. The lake. Her father's bedroom — the white-washed walls chalky in the tinny afternoon sun, the steeply sloping ceiling mottled from the reflection off the water, the smell of wet dog — *eau du chien humide*, as her father would have said.

"P.U.!" Verna muttered. Narrowing her eyes to slits in order to put some distance between her burgeoning headache and the razor-sharp light, she took stock: throbbing brain, too big for its bony case; stomach, a cauldron of uneasy acid; the poor sack of aching bones that was her too-tender skin. And to finish it off, she thought, to conclude with a flourish, Canine Swamp Creature, parked right in the middle of the bed with his lumpy back pressed firmly against hers and his legs twitching. The dog had managed to appropriate so much of the bed's surface that she found herself relegated to its very edge, teetering on its brink two-and-a-half dizzying feet above the floor.

Out of an indeterminate somewhere in the room — a location that sounded like the bottom of a well — swam a voice. Reverberant. Bendy. "How are you feeling?" it wobbled.

Verna eyed the distant floor with trepidation. An inch more and off she would roll. Given the height of the bed and her present entirely wretched state, that was bound to hurt. Her ears rang. "Precarious," she ventured. "I feel precarious."

"Woof!" Jude yelped, but softly, a muffled bark. He was dreaming about chasing rabbits. At any rate, that's what Donald would have said. But who knew what dogs dream about?

"Dreaming 'bout rabbits, eh?" Again the voice. But whose? And where was it coming from? The location was hard to pinpoint. It seemed to bubble up from somewhere down below, before breaking through some skin of surface to half-pulsate, half-ooze across the room — *blub, blub, blub*. Oh, yes, of course, she remembered, it must belong to that Native woman, the indefatigable one, the one with some country singer's name.

"Winonah," the voice took on more form, substance. "Actually it's an old Ojibway name."

What? Verna thought. *Just a minute. I didn't say that aloud, did I?*

"Winonah, the daughter of No'okomiss," the voice continued, plumping up, rounding out. "*Winonah* means, 'to nourish' in our tongue."

"I'll take your word for it." Verna hoisted herself onto one elbow, twisted to the right, and tried to shove the dog more toward the centre of the bed. To no avail. "Jude!" she complained. "Good God, dog! How much do you weigh?" For a few moments she forgot all about the voice, locked as she was in a struggle with the comatose Lab for a modicum of the bed's real estate. Then it dawned upon her — the room was no longer dark. This gave her a bit of a jolt — as though someone had *pinged* her with a cattle prod. She stopped wrestling with the dog and crouched down. What the hell had happened to the shutters?

"Oh, I took 'em down about an hour ago. That's the last of them."

Verna fell back onto her elbows. *Of course*, she told herself. After all, Dad would have had a ladder tucked away somewhere and Winonah, through her psychic bond to Lionel, would know exactly where that was — probably in the shed off the back porch. While she was working this out, Jude handily regained, by a simple act of expansion, the small amount of turf that she had managed to win for herself. He inhaled and, as he exhaled, his body swelled in size.

"You win," Verna conceded victory to the Lab. She rolled herself back onto her left side. "Porker!" she grumbled. "Enormous, fat chow hound! If you were a cat, I would have thrown you across the room by now. Hey, Winonah! How did you manage to take down the shutters without waking us up?" Laying a damp palm over her clammy forehead, she closed her eyes. If recollection served, taking down shutters was a noisy process, filled with clatter. And what time was it, anyway?

"Oh, it's getting on to half past three."

Half past three? I must have ...

"And, by the way..." Chuckle. "I'm not Winonah, eh?"

Verna froze. After an instant of convoluted panic during which her thought process skidded screeching into a patch of black ice and spun onto two wheels and out of control, she regained such command of her faculties as to realize that, of course, the voice with whom she had been randomly conversing over the past few minutes belonged not to the handywoman, but to some unknown man. Of course it did; a man who didn't sound anything like a woman. How could she have failed to notice the difference? Although, to be fair, the properties of the voice seemed to have changed from the time she had first heard it to the present moment — before it had seemed to come from everywhere and nowhere at the same time, now it seemed to emanate from one locus; before it had been without character or tonality, now it had depth and roundness.

It was then that she noticed the rocking chair.

When she had come to bed, it had been drawn up close to the dormer window. Of course it had. In life there are objects that are capable of being moved, but that are, for one reason or another, not. Ever. Case in point: the rickety old Muskoka chair at the end of the dock. She could not remember a time when it had not occupied that vantage point or had been turned to face any direction but due south. As with the Muskoka chair, so with the rocker in her father's bedroom. Its place was to the right of the bed and the left of the dormer window, toward which it was turned at a forty-five-degree angle. This was its place, its watch; where it had always been. After all, the whole point of the rocking chair was so that its occupant could sit, looking out over the lake.

Now, however, the natural order of things, at least insofar as they related to the rocking chair and its place in the world, had been utterly violated — it was most decidedly *out* of place. In fact, it had been dragged away from the window and some five or six feet across the floor and placed so that it was turned away from the bed and the lake; instead, it faced the closed door to the hall. What was even more unsettling, however, was that, through its caned back, Verna could just make out the bulky outlines of a man's broad back and the faded red-and-black plaid of a lumberjack jacket — a match to Winonah's. Just make out, because she couldn't *quite* make them out, not *quite*. Still …

She panicked. "Jude! Jude! Wake up!"

The dog stirred, then lifted his head to look over his shoulder, first at her, then at the man in the rocker. He lifted his muzzle and sniffed. His ears perked up. His tail thumped against the bed. His mouth opened. He smiled.

"Hey, Jude!" The possible man in the chair greeted the dog. "Long time no see, eh?" A local, Ojibway, judging from his accent — the words flat and spread, open at the end, not quite finished, the intonation contained between narrow margins. "Come here, boy!"

Ignoring Verna's protests and her flailing attempts to restrain him, the Lab struggled to his feet, jumped off the bed, and ran around the rocker to the stranger, docking between his legs as he had done earlier with Winonah. His entire back end wagged as the stranger bent over and paddled him on the rear, again, in much the same way as Winonah had done that morning.

"Hey, Verna," the man said. "I didn't mean to scare you there."

"Who are you?" she stammered, her heart racing at the same time as her ears filled up with fog.

"Lionel Madahbee."

"Lionel Madahbee? But ... but that's not possible!"

"Why?"

"Because ..." Verna shuddered. "Because he's *dead*."

The stranger shrugged. "Be that as it may."

"Turn around so I can see you!"

"Are you sure? I'm dead, eh? Maybe I look okay. Maybe I don't. Choked to death, eh? Not too pretty."

"But Jude ..."

"Dogs are good at sensing spirits. How you look don't matter; it's how you smell. And I smell pretty good, don't I, boy? Yes, I do."

Jude laid his head on what would have been the stranger's knee and sighed.

Verna wrung her hands. Had it come to this — to seeing things, ghosts, in broad daylight? Was it the drinking? Had it gotten that bad? Or maybe, just maybe, she was crazy. "What are you doing here? If you are here, that is."

"Oh, I'm here all right!"

Verna winced. "I was afraid so."

"Why afraid?"

"Because you're a ghost and only crazy people see ghosts," Verna explained. "I don't want to be crazy."

"So it's all about you?" Lionel asked.

Verna reflected on this for moment. "In this case, I'd have to say yes."

"Well, too bad," said Lionel resolutely. "Because I'm not going anywhere."

Verna was alarmed. "Ever? You're not going *ever*?"

"Well, of course, *ever*," replied Lionel. "What do you think? When I'm through waiting. Then I'll be gone. Then I will take the three-day road to the Sky World."

"And what exactly is it that you're waiting for?"

"To be returned to the earth."

"Uh … This might sound rude, but can't you wait somewhere else?"

"Nope," said Lionel.

"Why not?"

"Too crowded downstairs."

"*What?*"

"Too many spirits. Go back to sleep, Verna. When you wake up, I'll be gone."

"Am I asleep now and dreaming you?" Verna asked.

"Maybe," said Lionel. "Or you could be having a vision. It's hard for me to tell. Are you on a quest?"

"I don't think so," replied Verna. "Maybe. I've been thinking of changing my life around, shaking things up, you know?" Her glance snagged on the spotty mirror above the chest of drawers. Given the position of the rocker — turned at an angle toward the door — she should have been able to see Lionel's reflection in the mirror — but the chair appeared empty. Verna gasped and slid back down into the bed. "How come I can see your back, but not your reflection?" She pulled the covers up to her chin.

"How should I know?" Lionel asked and began rocking. The chair groaned; the floorboards creaked. Verna rolled over to the side of the bed nearest the wall, pulled the covers over her head, and cowered until, little by little, the sound of the rocker squeaking against the floor grew more and more indistinct and she slept.

Verna sagged against the lintel of the door to the kitchen. She felt groggy and weak, but her headache was of an altogether lesser magnitude than previously and her stomach, while sullen, was not so rambunctious. "How long have I been out?" she asked Winonah, who sat at the trestle table with a mug of tea and a can of Eagle Brand condensed milk in front of her.

"How should I know? It's four-forty-five. Soon as I finish my tea, eh, I'm out of here."

Beside her was the large green garbage bag that contained, among other detritus, Bob's cremains, and, at her feet, Jude. The dog was wet — must have gotten into the lake again. Verna didn't remember him leaving the bedroom. Who had opened the door for him? No! She told herself. No! No questions. Nobody opened the door. Maybe Winonah opened the door. Ask her. No, don't. Instead, "You're going?" Verna struck out on her wobbly own across the floor and ratcheted down into the chair opposite Winonah. "Really? I thought Lionel was the tea drinker."

"I've been here since nine," Winonah reminded her. "And I take both."

"Will you be back? I mean, isn't there more to do?"

"The cottage is opened, if that's what you mean. That'll be two hundred. Make it cash and I won't charge you the tax."

Suddenly the last thing Verna wanted was for Winonah to go. Her brush with Lionel, whatever the nature of that brush had been, had rendered the idea of being alone, except for a dog who liked everybody, in the woods in the dark extremely unattractive. "But surely there's more to be done?"

Winonah shrugged. "There's always more to do."

"Like what?"

"Like cleaning out the gutters, like checking the roof and the chimney for birds' nests ..."

"Well, that's all got to be done, hasn't it?"

Winonah eyed her suspiciously. "If you say so. What's up?"

Verna ignored her question. "So you'll come back tomorrow?"

"If you want. *What's up?*"

"Nothing's up. Nothing at all," Verna blathered, then brightened as she had an idea. "In fact, why don't you stay the night? Then you wouldn't have to make that long drive back."

"Ten kilometres?" Winonah asked.

"Still! You could sleep in Fern's old room."

"The room where she died? No way! That room's got bad vibes."

"Bad vibes?" Verna was appalled. "What do you mean 'bad vibes'?"

"Bad vibes," Winonah repeated. "Besides I got to make supper for my no'okomiss before she goes to Bingo."

Verna froze. Her no'okomiss? Hadn't Lionel mentioned something about a *no'okomiss?* "Your *what?*"

"My no'okomiss. My old granny. If I don't feed her, she'll die."

But Verna was desperate. "Can't she feed herself? I mean, if she can go to Bingo, surely she can eat something!"

"Can," replied Winonah. "Won't." She stood.

"But why? Wait a minute," Verna bargained. "How about I pay you fifty dollars to stay the night?"

"How about you pay me the two hundred dollars you owe me now?"

"Yes, of course! Now where did I put my purse?" Verna rose from her chair and looked anxiously around before spotting it on the counter next to the three boxes of cremains ... *Wait a minute*, she thought, *what's Bob doing here? Didn't I put him out by the woodpile where Winonah found him? Didn't she throw him into the garbage bag along with the curry? Am I making that up too?*

Winonah solved the mystery. "Oh, that box, there," she said. "That's Lionel."

Verna blanched. "Who?"

"Lionel. My brother. His cremains."

"His cremains ... are *here*?"

"Either that or he gave me somebody else and told me it was Lionel. I wouldn't put it past him, that white undertaker." Winonah's eyes slanted toward the purse. "Are you getting me the money? Because right about now Granny's asking herself, 'Where's my fishsticks?' I don't like to keep her waiting. She's old. You got to show respect for elders."

"The money, yes!" Verna made a raid on the counter, returning with her purse. As a rule she didn't carry much cash, but, thinking that Greater Gammage might be lacking in ATMs, she had gotten a wad of cash back at the North Bay LCBO. She counted out ten twenties and was on the point of adding another fifty when Winonah's hand closed on the cash.

"I'm going," Winonah told her. She stood.

Verna leapt to her feet. "I have an idea. You could bring Granny here."

"Granny doesn't want to come here," Winonah said flatly. "Granny wants to go to Bingo." She started towards the back door.

Verna followed her. "But after Bingo!"

"After Bingo she wants to go to bed." Winonah opened the door.

"She could go to bed here!" Verna followed her out onto the porch.

"Look, Verna." Winonah was firm. "Granny was sent to a residential school. No-Talking-Indian School — that's what our people called it. Because kids were beaten if they spoke our language. She ran away once. They locked her in the boiler room for two days, down in the basement where it was hot and dark and full of spiders and big rats. They would have locked her in the broom closet, but another runaway, she died, eh? From breathing ammonia and bleach fumes for so long. Going to that school put my granny right off most kinds of white people."

"But …!"

"And even if she did trust white people long enough to close her eyes when she's around 'em, the last thing she wants to do is go to bed in a house full of dead ones. Me neither." She headed toward the rusted-out Chevrolet Impala parked next to the Volvo.

"Winonah!"

"See you in the morning!" She climbed into the car and rolled down the window.

"Winonah, wait!" Verna started down the stairs.

"Mind your socks, there," Winonah warned her, gunning the Impala's engine. "That grass, it's wet, eh?" She ground the car into reverse.

Verna glanced down to see that she was still in her stocking feet. As she did, the Impala lurched forward and began to toddle lopsidedly down the service road in the direction of town.

"Wait! Wait!" Verna wailed. "Winonah! Wait! You forgot Lionel!"

"See you in the morning!" The Impala melted into the forest.

Thursday, May 19, 2005

It was tender sunlight that woke her, that and the bright sounds of the forest briskly reconstituting itself. Tiny white-throated warblers, scissor-tailed flycatchers, gray-crowned rosy finches — neotropicals come north to breed, singing as they feasted on insects. An all-you-can-eat buffet; an orchestra tuning itself. A slight breeze ran its fingers through the boughs of fir and larch and thumbed the ruddy buds of birch. She could hear the lake lapping against the cobble beach below, like water sloshing in a shallow bowl.

What day was it? Of that she wasn't quite sure. Really, she advised herself, when you look at it, what day it was depended on whether yesterday — that being Wednesday to the best of her recollection — had ever actually ended. She didn't remember it ending.

Oh, wait a minute. She did.

She remembered being frightened — or, at the very least, creeped out — when Winonah left. Not that she believed in ghosts; she just didn't want to be alone with the idea of them. She remembered tossing around the idea of throwing the dog and her suitcase into the Volvo and driving back to Beverley so that she could stay the night at the Vi-Mar Motel or the Bel-Air. She remembered having a couple of drinks — V and T's, not Scotch (she had an uncanny feeling, all of a sudden, of being watched, and, therefore, a greater need for circumspection; see, she wasn't an alcoholic; see, she could temper her drinking) — then deciding rather emphatically that she was fifty-four bloody years old, that there were no such things as ghosts, and, in case she were wrong about this, Lionel's had seemed disinclined to harm her. In fact, all he had wanted was to hang out in the rocking chair — hardly sinister. Later she remembered eating room-temperature chili from the can and feeding the dog something slightly less appetizing before letting him out and then in. She remembered locking up. She remembered unlocking the front door and putting the three boxes of cremains out to overnight on the screened-in porch — for some reason, she wasn't entirely sure why; well, yes, she was — before relocking the front door. Finally, she had made herself a big drink, gone upstairs, repositioned the rocking chair in front of the window, checked for any further evidence of Lionel, and, finding none, unpacked her suitcase and arranged the contents of her overnight bag on top of the chest of drawers. And she had done all this riding the fluttery edge of a panic attack like one of those freaky Jesus lizards skittering across the surface of the water. Then she had turned in early. Really early. Old-person early — eight o'clock, maybe. That's right. That's what had happened. That long nap must have confused her, thrown her off. *Naps wreak havoc with one's circadian rhythm*, she told herself. *Naps make you see things, people that are not there. No more naps.*

She sat up, pushed off the sheets, and examined herself. An old navy-blue T-shirt — no bra, she scarcely needed one — and a raggedy pair of "pitters." That's what Fern called underpants with a high waist, because they came, as she would say, up to your armpits. Fern always wore bikini briefs and sometimes, to Verna's horror, thongs — thongs had always reminded Verna of the string tied around roasts by butchers — the way they pressed into flesh. As for the jeans and flannel shirt Verna had worn for the past two days, they lay in an unceremonious heap on the floor, next to a slumbering Jude in his iconic bearskin manifestation. Apparently she had undressed before coming to bed. That, as Martha Stewart would say, was a good thing. A sign that things were returning to normal, when she did not sleep in dirty, two-day-old clothes.

She swung her naked legs over the side of the high bed. Not a pretty sight. Ricotta cheese came to mind. Maybe she could have liposuction when the cottage sold. Have all the loose, wobbly bits sucked out of her. And why not breast implants while she was at it, so that, in her old age, she could go bob, bob, bobbing along? The prospect was grotesque. She dispensed with it.

At least the rocking chair had stayed put, she noted with relief. No ghostly rearrangement of the furniture overnight to contend with. And who knows? Maybe she had dreamed up the entire enchilada — the repositioning of the chair, her conversation with Lionel. Of course she had dreamed it. But maybe not. It was disconcerting — this not knowing.

She slid off the bed and padded over to the window. Mist mantled the lake; it emanated from it in spiralling wisps. Donald had been fond of pointing this out — the way the threads of mist spun up from the water, like cotton candy wound onto a stick. "Ojibway ghosts," he would remark. "On their way to the Happy Hunting Ground."

Except for one, that is. Except for Lionel, whom, now that she focused, she could just make out sitting, with his back turned to her, on the stone wall that separated the lawn from the beach. At least, it looked like Lionel — the same broad back, the same red-and-black plaid lumberjack jacket. She forgot about talking herself out of seeing him the previous day; that seemed counterintuitive given the fact that he was right there. And what was that in his hand? A long stick? Was he whittling? Could ghosts whittle?

Verna unlatched the casement window and leaned out. "Lionel!"

He flinched, but did not turn around.

"Don't go anywhere!" she cried. "I'm coming down." She closed the window and latched it. "Come on, Jude!" She prodded the somnolent dog with her toe. "Wake up! Lionel's downstairs. Let's go see him! Lionel, your buddy Lionel! Come on, you lazy dog, You're supposed to protect me! Are you even listening?"

The Lab half-opened one sleepy eye to peer unseeingly at her before rolling over to his side. He sighed heavily; the one eye closed.

There was no time to waste, she told herself. Snatching her jeans off the floor, she clambered into them — they felt simultaneously stiff and clammy — and, still zipping, headed for the hall. She didn't want Lionel disappearing on her before she had time to ask him … what? What did she want to ask him? She had no idea, but she knew that whatever it was, it was urgent. Taking the stairs two at a time in her stocking feet, she unlocked the front door, hurtled across the porch, and burst through the screen door to collide head-on with Winonah.

The impact sent both women staggering backwards. Winonah's red Canadian Tire Toolbox exploded open, spewing wrenches and bits and clamps onto the grass.

"What the …?"

"Sorry!"

"Are you okay?" A wraith of a girl, age indeterminate, leaning on the hood of Winonah's battered Impala, her arms wrapped tightly around herself as if to keep herself warm. She was faintly yellow in hue and knobby, with pale blue protuberant eyes that stared at Verna — ogled her, actually — and limp, patchy blond hair crammed into a banana clip. "Are you okay?" she repeated. A knob of Adam's apple rode up and down her crane-like neck like an exposed elevator up a shaft.

"Holy Moses! You knocked the wind out of me!" Winonah complained.

Verna remembered Lionel. She wheeled around and looked toward the stone wall on which she had seen him sitting a few moments earlier. Gone. He had disappeared without a trace. *Damn! What? Wait!* "The stick!" she cried.

Gleefully she hopped across the wet expanse of lawn to retrieve the stick Lionel had been whittling. "See!" She held it up for the women to see. It was a metre long with a natural curve at the top. The ghostly Lionel had managed to peel the bark from it and had just begun to carve something into the curved portion when she had routed him — the head of a bird, from the looks of it. Holding the stick in one hand, she hopped back across the lawn. "See!" She showed the stick to Winonah and the girl.

"It's a stick," said Winonah.

"I know it's a stick, but, look. Someone has peeled the bark off it. See? It's a bird. See the beak? And there's its eye."

"It's a stick," Winonah repeated.

"But …" Verna caught herself. *Slow down. They'll think you're crazy.* "Why, yes it is," she agreed, leaning the stick up against the porch. She blinked at the girl. "I'm sorry. I didn't catch your name."

"Romy," the girl replied.

"Romy?" Verna repeated carefully. The two syllables tugged a little at her brain.

"Yes, Romy," the girl said. "Your niece Romy."

Verna stared at her. "My *what*?" she asked.

"Your niece," Winonah informed her. "The youngest one. Fern's baby. I picked her up outside Beverley. She was hitchhiking."

"The bus goes to Beverley," explained Romy. "It doesn't go here. I would have called, but I didn't know the number."

"She knows," Winonah said. "About Fern."

"Oh!"

"About her being dead and all. Some neighbour told her."

Mrs. Rothman. Verna grimaced. "Ah!"

Winonah squatted down to collect the scattered contents of the toolbox. She looked up at Verna. "Are you going to stand there gawping or are you going to help me?"

"Gawping," Verna repeated carefully. In the sudden maelstrom that the word "niece" had unleashed in her, Verna clung for dear life to "gawping." *Interesting*, she thought as she skimmed the fragile skin that had immediately formed over her inner turmoil. *I don't believe I've ever heard the word "gawping" used in a sentence.* Then the skin broke and down she toppled into the swirl of turbulence. "You'll have to excuse me," she murmured and went to sit down in a chair, only, of course, there wasn't one, which meant that her descent was a controlled one for about a foot and a plummet for the remaining twenty or so inches. *"Oof!"* she exclaimed as her coccyx hit the ground with a smack. "Ouch!"

"Are you okay?" asked the girl, all elbows and knees and bony wrists. She bent down, palms on thighs. "Did you hurt yourself?"

"I'm fine." Verna waved vaguely.

The girl gave her a look — she didn't believe her. "If you say so." Hunkering down, she helped Winonah with the tools as Verna surreptitiously scrutinized her, searching for traces of Fern. The eyes, maybe. The bump of nose.... She was wearing a heap of clothing, one layer on top of another, the palest shades of blue and white and gym-suit gray. What the younger women at the Bureau would describe as a layered look, only taken to some absurd extreme. Maybe she didn't have a suitcase. Maybe she carried her wardrobe on her back like a homeless person. Was she a homeless person? No. She looked too clean to be a homeless person. Spotless, actually. *Well, that's a relief,* thought Verna. *My niece is not a homeless person.* Whatever the case, the super abundance of clothing failed to disguise the central fact that the girl was thin, bone-thin. It looked as though her cheeks had been hollowed out with a trowel and her eye sockets with a melon baller. God knows how old she would be, Fern's last baby. Twenty? Twenty-four? Trying to figure it out made Verna's head ache. From a distance the girl looked like a teenage waif; up close she looked like a little old man.

A moment later the handywoman was snapping the tool-box shut and Romy, *Romy, her niece,* was standing. "Need a hand?" she asked, extending one to Verna.

Verna eyed it with trepidation. She had seen more meat on a soup bone. Shaking her head, she struggled to her feet on her own, joints protesting.

Winonah looked at Romy, who looked downcast, then at Verna, who looked stunned. "Well, this is a heartwarming family reunion," she observed. "I'm going to make coffee." She picked up the toolbox and went into the house. "Where's Jude?" they could hear her shouting up the stairs. "Yoo-hoo! Where's *The Dog?*"

Verna peered furtively at Romy. "I'm sorry if I don't sound … It's just that …"

"You're freaked out." Romy sounded aggrieved herself — brittle, her voice strained, eked out. Red-rimmed eyes, the scleras faintly pink. She'd been crying. "How do you think I feel? Some stranger tells me my mother is dead."

Verna considered this; as she did, remorse waylaid her, bowled her over. "I'm sorry you had to find out this way," she said feebly. "It's just that you and the others … Your fathers took you away. One by one. You were there and then you were gone. Vanished. Years and years passed. We never heard from you." If she sounded this lame to herself, what must she sound to Romy?

"Did you ever consider 411?" Romy asked. "We're in Canada, for God's sake. How hard is it to find anybody in Canada? How clueless are you? You could have hired a detective."

"We didn't think of that," Verna admitted, wondering why that hadn't occurred to them. Maybe she hadn't wanted to find Fern's children. *Okay*, she thought, *I can see how that might happen, but what about Dad? Surely he would have wanted to know where his grandchildren were.* "We did think about Googling you," she remembered. "Or I did, at any rate."

"Yeah, right," said Romy. "You have to have done something to be on the Internet. I haven't done anything."

"But your father…. Didn't he do something? Wasn't he an artist of some kind?"

"An escape artist," Romy replied.

"At any rate, I couldn't remember his name. His last name. In fact, now that I think about it, I can't remember his first name."

"Yeah, well," said Romy, looking stricken. "It's Paul. Paul Doucette."

Desperate, Verna took her by her stick arm. "Let's get some coffee," she suggested.

Romy and Verna sat on the screened-in porch, holding mugs of coffee and watching Jude paddle around in the lake. The box containing Fern's cremains sat in Romy's lap. As for Winonah, she was up on the roof, making thumping noises.

"What's she doing again?" Romy asked.

"Checking the chimney for birds' nests," Verna replied.

"Oh," said Romy. She paused. "Did Mom look like you? I mean, you were twins, weren't you?"

Verna winced. She closed her eyes. "We were, but no, we didn't actually look alike. We were fraternal twins. Well, actually, *sororal.*"

"Which means …?"

"Not identical," replied Verna grimly.

"Good," said Romy. She sounded relieved.

Verna bristled. "Thanks a lot!"

"Nothing personal."

Don't be cranky, Verna admonished herself. *After all, you're long past your "best-before" date. The best you can hope for now is "presentable."* She glanced down at herself — the same shirt and jeans, and, more to the point, the same underwear she had arrived in two days earlier. Had she washed her face even once since then? Had she combed her hair? She had to admit that, at the moment, she fell fairly far short of even the presentable mark. *What is up with me? Am I coming undone? I wonder if I smell.* She rallied herself. Clearly Romy wanted to learn more about the mother she had never known. You'd think someone who had lost her own mother at — what was it, two hours old? — could spare a little compassion for someone in similar straits. And hadn't the poor girl just learned of her mother's death? What a shock that must have been! If Romy had been anything like Verna, she had built Fern up in her mind to be some sort of saint and/or goddess. Verna winced, remembering how she had put Joan Macoun on a pedestal, then used her as a stick with which to beat poor, mild, stricken Donald. For a while, at least. During her terrible teenage years. Then not so much. In the end she had let it go, the way she had let everything go — Fern, Bob, herself. Zen-like, really. *So, belly up to the bar. Tell her about Fern. And be nice.*

"If there was 'the pretty twin,' then Fern was it. In case you're wondering," she said, remembering the way boys had sprung up like mushrooms after a rain the moment the Macoun family's white Mercury Comet made its annual appearance at the intersection that was Greater Gammage. And, pretend though Donald valiantly might that they came for both Verna and Fern, everyone understood that they came for Fern alone. Just thinking about it triggered a hot flash in Verna; she was consumed by sudden heat. *Now, Verna,* she reasoned with herself, *if living equates to winning — and surely, in the greater scheme of things, it must — then it's you who have won, not Fern. You.*

"Really?" Romy pounced. "Pretty? How? Describe her to me!"

"She had these big, big eyes and this, like, I guess you could call it, *nimbus* of strawberry-blond hair ... dyed, of course ..." She couldn't resist that. "And then there was her complexion. My father insisted on describing it as peaches and cream, although really, between you and me, it was more splotchy than peaches and cream."

"Was she thin? I imagine her as wispy. Was she wispy?"

Verna considered this. "No, not thin," she remembered. "More ... blowsy. But she did manage to retain some semblance of a figure into middle age, despite having borne all you kids. Which is to say," she clarified, "she had a waist."

Fern's figure was a sore point with Verna, whose body, meagre to begin with, had gone all stringy with age. (Well, what
about Fern wasn't a sore point?) "You look like a boiling
chicken," Bob had once observed. Unkind, but that was the
way he was and, besides, it was true. "Do you remember her
at all?" Verna asked. "How old were you, anyway, when your
father came for you?"

Romy shrugged. "Maybe three? I don't know. Four? I
can remember her singing us to sleep. As for how she looked,
I have an image in my mind of her, but I don't know if it's
an actual memory or a photo I saw. There were some. Not
many, but some. I found them when I was a kid, tucked
away in his drawer. Dad's drawer. They were kind of fuzzy.
She looked fuzzy."

"She was fuzzy," Verna replied. "Not in a bad way. At
least, that's the way I remember her. She was in a sort of soft
focus most of the time. I don't know how she managed it.
Like one of those Impressionist paintings. Maybe it was her
hair. Does that make any sense?"

"I guess," said Romy. "So, how did she die?"

Verna paused, wondering, but really for just a moment,
whether she should tell Romy the whole truth — what she
had to date not told another living soul, that Fern's cancer
had most likely been precipitated by the all-out attack upon
her immune system by the Human Immunodeficiency Virus
— or the authorized, pasteurized version. *But, no,* she told
herself. *You asked the doctor to keep Fern's HIV status confi-
dential for a reason. To spare Donald the embarrassment and
the shame. To spare yourself. What possible good would it do
Romy to know such an unsettling thing about her mother? Cui
bono?* So, in the end, "cancer," was all she said. "Cervical
cancer," adding, "although the immediate cause of death
was sepsis. Sepsis caused by the cancer."

"What's 'sepsis'?" Romy asked.

"You don't want to know."

"Try me."

"Oh, no. Trust me."

"No, I mean it. Go ahead. Try me."

"Putrefaction," replied Verna. "It means putrefaction. Sepsis. It's from the Greek."

Romy shuddered. "Okay, you're right. I don't want to know."

"I didn't think so," said Verna with grim satisfaction. Then, a moment later, "It didn't have to be that way, you know. Fern was such a goddamned hippie. She believed in magnetic bracelets. In crystals. She didn't believe in doctors. As a result the cancer went undetected until very late, too late." Culminating in a death, Verna thought, that was both messy and spectacular. Like her life.

Romy shook her head and sighed. "What a tragedy!"

Verna scowled. She hated it when people described Fern's death as a tragedy. It wasn't a tragedy. Not in her books. In her books it was equal parts carelessness, stupidity, and stubbornness.

"So where did she die?" Romy asked. "In Toronto?"

"Here, actually," Verna replied. "In her bedroom. Upstairs. She lived here, you know? The last few years of her life, at least. From ninety-eight until she died." And, with those words, a can of worms exploded open.

"Here? Really?" Romy looked around. "How come?"

Verna panicked. She did not want to go down this road. *Prevaricate*, she told thought. "Oh, well, she liked it here, I suppose," she waffled. "Nature. And so forth. And the rents in Toronto — through the roof."

The truth was that Fern lived in the cottage because her impromptu sexual trysts with randomly encountered males made their aging father too anxious to put her up at the house on Indian Crescent for more than a couple of weeks at a time. He was never sure of what he would walk in on. As for why she couldn't live with Verna and her husband, well …

"Who was with her when she died?' Romy asked. "Were you with her?"

Verna paused. She hated being asked this. It was the worst question and everybody asked it. She swallowed, then told the truth. "She died alone."

"Alone? That's terrible," exclaimed Romy.

"Yes, well … we'd had a falling out, she and I. We weren't talking. And she didn't let on how sick she was. Made light of it. If we had known, if we had had even an inkling, we would have come collect her, or Dad would have, at any rate, but, you see, we didn't. Know, that is."

"Was it over a man?" Romy asked.

"What?" Verna felt herself flushing.

"Your falling out. Because my Dad said she was a tramp."

"Well, your Dad's a dick," retorted Verna. *Settle down,* she advised herself. *Remember that we're talking a long time ago. A long, long time.*

"I know that," replied Romy. "But still. Was it over a man?"

1988. Seventeen years ago. Fern had just left one of her several husbands and was "getting herself back on her feet!" Again. A self-styled artist, Fern threw pots and knotted macramé hangings and tie-dyed T-shirts — all badly. Her pots were misshapen, her hangings lumpy, and her T-shirts bled like scalp wounds. She nevertheless remained maddeningly, inexplicably optimistic that she would be able to sell her artistic spew on consignment. This, of course, never happened, and, during those brief interludes between men, the chances that she would turn up at either her father's or her sister's door were very good. So Verna had agreed to let her live with them until such time as this theoretical getting-back-on-her-feet had transpired. Her sister had not been with them two weeks before Verna walked in on her and Bob in an untidy heap on the guest room bed, limbs tangled, clothes everywhere.

Verna had comported herself with a chilly dignity that surprised even her. The truth was that she was probably just a little drunk. Just enough to take the edge off, and, who knows? Perhaps she had known this would happen all along. Perhaps there had been signals between the two of them that she had read and recognized, but had somehow failed to compute. Then again she knew her sister and she knew her husband. They had propensities, the two of them. Perhaps it was just an accident waiting to happen ... one that the clock had run down on.

"Everybody out of the pool!" That's what she had said — what lifeguards at public pools say at the sound of distant thunder.

"I can explain everything," Bob had said.

But Verna had shaken her head. "Uh-uh. Nope. Not interested."

"I was upset ..." Fern had insisted. "And Bob, he ..."

"Oh, Fern!" Verna had scoffed. "Do I look like I just fell off the turnip wagon?"

"It will never happen again," Bob swore.

Where had she heard that before? Oh, yes. Only semi-annually for the past number of years — for Bob had hardly bothered to hide the string of affairs that had begun shortly after their eighth wedding anniversary and that were to continue for the years that remained to him. Only when he decided to ditch the current girlfriend and move on would he confess to Verna and pledge life-long fidelity. This had happened not once too often, but five times too often. The charade sickened her. Girls from the office, seeking advancement. Surely they could not have found Bob appealing, with his thick, Coke-bottle glasses in Elvis Costello frames and that really big ass — like there had been a landslide in his pants. But that Bob had proven successful in his career was both maddening and indisputable. Verna had only ever made it to manager, a hike in status that had brought with it a modest salary increase and a cubicle overlooking Bay Street, as opposed to one without windows. Bob, however, had risen quickly through the bureaucratic ranks until, at the time of his death, he was serving as senior policy advisor to the minister. This was thanks in large part to his lubricity, to the fact that he could slide into any social situation, and, like a slug exuding slime, ooze enough sloppy bonhomie to grease the wheels of any project or program of measure that was his to secure or undermine or promote. After all, the ministry was nothing if not an Old Boys' Club and Bob had been nothing if not an Old Boy. And Old Boys played around. All right. Okay. That she got. But not with their wives' twin sisters.

"Pack your things, Fern," she had told her. "You're going to Daddy's. I'm calling him now. Bob, you're driving. Put some clothes on." A dazzling display of sangfroid. Where had all that stiff upper lip come from? More to the point, where had it gone?

So Fern moved in with their father on Indian Crescent Road, then left with her next inamorato, then moved in again, and so on.

"You shouldn't be too hard on her," Donald told Verna. "She feels just terrible."

"I bet she does," Verna had replied.

"She didn't mean any harm by it. She hasn't a malicious bone in her body. You know how she is — emotional, impulsive. She doesn't think."

"'Feckless' is the word."

"Yes," her father agreed. "That's what she is. Feckless."

Thinking back on the affair now, Verna wondered why hadn't it mattered really? Or did it? Fern had been her sister.

At some point she must have loved her. She was sure of it. And then things changed. Not overnight, but gradually.

"She just ... she had this way about her," she struggled to explain to Romy. How had Carmen put it? That's right. "She exuded pheromones. I don't think she could help it. She didn't mean to steal men. It just ... happened. Really, I shouldn't have been so angry with her. In retrospect, I mean."

"You shouldn't have been so angry about *what?*" Romy wanted to know.

"Shit!" A cry from the roof. Cedar shakes rained down onto the lawn.

"Are you all right?" Verna called up.

"You're going to need some new shingles!" cried Winonah.

Jude emerged from the lake and trotted up from the beach. He stood at the porch door and yelped.

"No way. Not until you shake," Verna told him.

"About *what?*" Romy persisted.

"About nothing. None of your business. A long time ago. Believe me, you don't want to know," Verna replied. "Shake, Jude! Shake! Come on, boy!"

Romy shrugged, unwillingly relinquishing that particular line of inquiry. "What should I call you. You're the only one I have — aunt, that is."

Verna winced. "How about 'Verna'?"

"How about Auntie Verna?"

"I guess," said Verna, distracted by the dog, now pawing insistently at the door and yelping. "Jude! You heard me. Shake! Shake!" She half stood and imitated shaking. Jude stared confusedly at her. She sat back down.

"I just checked out of the Birches," Romy informed her. "God knows where Dad is these days. Well, actually, he's out in B.C. On some island with Nora. On *Salt Spring* Island with Nora. That's his new wife. It's disgusting. He's all old and fat and she's like twenty-six years old — only five years older than me! I haven't heard from him in months. Well, two weeks at any rate. He's busy. He's happy. I'm going to have a baby brother or sister in late August. Whoopee. So I took the train into Toronto and I looked up Grandfather in the phone book — see! I didn't have any problem finding him — and I went to his house. That's when I found out about Mom. The lady next door told me he had died and that you had come up here to scatter his and Mom's ashes. Mrs. Somebody."

"Mrs. Rothman," Verna supplied the name. Standing, she crossed to the door and let Jude in.

"She looked Jewish."

"Who did?"

"Mrs. Rothman ..."

"Jude!" squawked Verna.

But it was too late. Jude was shaking.

"Damn, it, Jude!" Verna protested.

"You got Mom's cremains all wet!" cried Romy.

"Oh, shit!" said Verna. "Don't worry," she told Romy, "They're in a plastic bag. Inside the box, I mean."

"Stupid dog!" Romy complained. Then, after a moment during which the two women wiped up, "Don't you want to know why I was in the Birches?"

"I don't know." Verna was distracted. All this talk about Fern. She had come here to divest herself of the past — of the cottage itself, of Bob, of Donald, and, especially, of Fern. Instead, she seemed to have walked into a time warp in which all three of them were vying for her attention. And now this — a niece. "What's the Birches?"

"It's in Guelph. It's like rehab. An addiction treatment facility."

Verna turned to look at her. "You're a drug addict?"

Romy shook her head. "Nope. I'm an anorexic. It's what they call a process addiction."

Verna peered at her. Of course! That explained the downy hair that carpeted her bony face, the visibly swollen glands. "You look like an anorexic."

"Well, thanks," said Romy huffily. "You don't look so hot yourself."

Verna took a few moments to absorb this information. Then, surprising herself, she said, "I'm an alcoholic. I think. A highly functional one, mind you." *And how not*, she asked herself. In the several years leading up to Bob's death, she had felt that she was just going through the motions. It was as if everything was swathed in cotton batting. How could she have not been glum? And bitter. Let's not forget bitter! But mostly bored. And just a little tipsy. Not that anybody noticed. It was remarkable what you could get away with, what people would not notice. Then again, she had never let herself get sloppy. She kept a tight rein on things, on herself. Well, maybe not so much now.

Romy shook her head. "Thanks for sharing, but that won't work for me. Too many calories in alcohol."

"There are always diet mixers," Verna pointed out. "Vodka and diet tonic. Rum and Diet Coke."

"I never thought of that!" Romy seemed faintly intrigued.

"So, are you cured?"

Romy shrugged. "Maybe. Sort of. A little."

"Because, if you don't mind me saying so, I'd guess no. You look pretty sick to me. Sort of like the walking dead, actually."

Romy shrugged. "I got fed up with it. Everybody watching you like a hawk. Silly group meetings. All those snacks."

"And your father…?"

"Oh, he'll be pissed when he hears, but he won't cut me off. If that's what you mean. It's not like it hasn't happened before."

"I see," said Verna, wondering what she should be doing under the circumstances. Should she call Paul? Probably. On the other hand, the girl was twenty-one, presumably capable of rattling around on her own recognizance. Did she really want to get involved in a struggle between her former brother-in-law and her obviously problematic niece? They sat for another few minutes, saying nothing, rocking, then Verna remembered. "I was a bed wetter. For years and years. Age seven to ten. God, I'd forgotten that! Every frigging night. I couldn't have sleepovers. I couldn't go to sleepovers. That's probably why I'm such a disaster. I wasn't socialized properly. Like a bad dog."

"And I," said Romy ruefully, "was a biter."

When Winonah came down from the roof, they had soup for lunch. Campbell's Cream of Tomato soup, several cans of which had over-wintered in the pantry. They would have had barley, beef, and vegetable — Donald's penchant for preparedness meant that the shelves of his pantry were piled high with canned goods and supplies. As it turned out, however, Romy was a vegetarian. They would have made the soup with milk instead of water, however, as it also turned out, Romy was lactose-intolerant.

Winonah had taken an evident dislike to Romy, which Romy reciprocated. After watching the girl idly trail her spoon through the soup, back and forth, back and forth, in a figure eight, the handywoman pushed herself back from the table and said, "If you're just going to play with that soup, you could have at least let us mix it with milk!"

Romy looked at Winonah, cocked her head, and licked the spoon. The gesture was both insolent and defiant. Verna noted that the girl's head looked too big from her emaciated body. She resembled one of those lolling bobble-head dolls.

"You're a picky eater," Winonah grumbled.

"I'm not a picky eater. I'm an anorexic."

"Anorexics are just glorified picky eaters."

"Are not!"

"Are so!" said Winonah. "Any minute now you'll be telling us you have Sprue. 'Guess what, Auntie Verna, I have Sprue!' Because Sprue would fit right in with that list of yours, eh? Wouldn't it?"

"What list?" Romy turned to Verna. "What's Sprue, Auntie Verna?"

"That list of what you can and cannot eat," Winonah told her. "And she's not telling you what Sprue is, because, if she does, you'd get it, eh, and then we'd all starve to death!"

Romy turned to Verna. "Auntie Verna," she repeated, "what's Sprue?"

Verna winced. "I don't know!" The word "Auntie" coming out of Romy's mouth made her squirm. Set her teeth on edge somehow. "Something to do with gluten. Could you call me 'Aunt Verna?' 'Auntie' sounds, well …"

"Affectionate," Winonah finished the sentence for her. She turned back to Romy. "Do you eat fish?" she asked. "Because some vegetarians eat fish. I guess they haven't noticed that a fish isn't a vegetable, eh? Too weak from hunger to tell the difference."

"I don't eat anything with eyeballs," Romy defended herself. "Fish have eyeballs."

"What about the fish that live at the bottom of the ocean where there's no light? They don't have eyes. Would you eat them?"

"Do they have eye buds?" Romy asked.

"How should I know?"

"Because I don't eat anything with eye balls or eye buds."

"I don't think I've ever seen anything with eye buds," Verna reflected. "Not that I was aware of."

"Worms!" Winonah said. "Eh? What about worms?"

"Worms?" Romy looked to Verna for assistance.

"Worms don't have eyes," Verna said. "They do have photoreceptors."

Winonah turned to her. "How do you know that?"

Verna shrugged. How did she know that? "I come from a long line of naturalists?" It's not that she had looked or anything.

The handywoman turned back to Romy. "So, worms don't have eyes. Would you eat worms?"

But Romy held her ground. "I don't eat anything with eye balls or eye buds or photoreceptors."

Winonah eyed her. "What you don't eat is anything. Period."

"You could be a little nicer to me," Romy pointed out. "I just found out my mother is dead."

"Kitchi Manitou has given his people all this good food to eat and what do you do? Turn up your nose. You should be grateful. You know what my granny had to eat at No-Talking-Indian School?"

Romy turned to Verna. "Itchy who? What's she talking about?"

"The Great Spirit," replied Verna. "Winonah's grandmother went to residential school."

"She had to eat green liver and rusty bacon and meat boiled in the laundry pot so that it tasted of soap and mush with grasshopper legs in it and mouse droppings!" said Winonah. "That's what she had to eat."

"So your grandma's school cafeteria sucked," said Romy. "What's that got to do with me?"

Verna decided to change the subject. "I'm assuming you'll want to stay the night," she said to Romy. "Do you have a suitcase?"

"In *her* car." Romy pointed a bony finger at Winonah.

"It's unlocked," said Winonah. "If you're not going to eat that soup, pass it over."

"What's her problem?" Romy asked Verna.

"Children starving," Verna speculated. "Third-world countries. Soup kitchens."

"Whatever!" Romy fumed. "At least I don't look like a beach ball." She looked pointedly at the round Winonah.

"Is there a reason all the doors are shut?" Romy asked. She and Verna stood at the head of the stairs.

"Didn't you ever see the *Mickey Mouse Show*?" Verna asked. Then, remembering that her niece was born in the 1980s, "Oh, sorry. I guess not. No. No reason. Well, yes. Privacy?"

"But you're the only one here."

"Yeah, and …?"

"I like doors to be open," Romy informed her. "So I can see what's behind them."

"Ah, well, that's where we differ, you and I," said Verna. "I prefer *not* to know what's behind them. So what'll it be? You could stay in my old room, if you wanted. Or your mom's …"

Apparently her attempt at nonchalance failed to fool Romy. The girl looked at her with eyes narrowed in suspicion. "Where are *you* staying?"

"In your grandfather's room."

"And why is that?"

"There were sheets on the bed."

"There weren't sheets on your bed?"

"No. But I could find some. Probably."

"I thought you said you were a bed-wetter?"

Verna winced. What had prompted her to tell the girl that? Donald had known, of course, and Fern and Bob, because Fern told Bob. And, also of course, everyone that

Fern and Bob had told. Lest we forget! Just one of the many reasons why Verna had been angry … *was* angry with Fern. "It's a new mattress … or it was a new mattress forty years ago. I was fourteen. I'd stopped wetting the bed by then!"

Romy wasn't buying it. "And are there sheets on my mother's bed?" she asked.

Verna shrugged. "Don't know."

"Did you look?"

"No," Verna admitted. "To tell you the truth, I haven't actually been in her room. Yet," she added.

"Why? What's wrong with her room?"

"Nothing's wrong with her room."

"Then why haven't you been in it?"

"I just haven't gotten around to it."

"What else have you been doing?"

"Unpacking," said Verna. "Napping."

"I want to see her room," Romy insisted.

"Fine. Go ahead. Be my guest."

Romy sized up the door. She swallowed. "I want you to come with me."

"Why?"

"I just do."

"Why?"

"Because she died in that room."

"Exactly!"

"What do you mean, 'Exactly'?"

"Exactly the reason I haven't gone into her room yet. She died in there. You may be her daughter, but I'm her sister, her *twin* sister for crying out loud, and she *died* in there. It freaks me out, if you want to know the truth."

"Then we can both go in together."

"Or we could do it later. For example, we could do it tomorrow. When you've had a good rest. When you've come to terms with the fact that she is … you know."

Romy reflected on this. "It won't be any easier tomorrow."

"But some terrible accident might befall us during the night," Verna argued, "and kill us and then we wouldn't have to ever open the door."

"Are you expecting a terrible accident to happen to us? Is there something you know that I don't?"

"Of course not. But that's the thing. You don't know. You never know. Your Uncle Bob's SUV got creamed by a train. I didn't see that one coming. And that's only one example."

"Really?" Romy was amazed. "By a train?"

Verna nodded solemnly. Two years ago, a passenger train on its way to Montreal had plowed into Bob's new Ford Escape at an intersection. This particular intersection was legendary: like a bloodthirsty Aztec deity, it seemed to require periodic human sacrifice. Concerned citizens had been circulating petitions calling for gates or warning lights for years. Verna had even signed one once. Still nothing was done to halt the carnage, and, over the decades, the deadly crossing claimed a baker's dozen lives. The lives in question belonged, for the most part, to drunken teenagers or to the aimless homeless seeking direction. With the advent of cell-phones, however, a whole new class of victim emerged. Train 75 had caught Bob mid-harangue on his Nokia; he had been chewing out his admin assistant, Maureen, when suddenly ...

"How could you not know a train was about to hit you?" Verna had asked Maureen as she was cleaning out Bob's desk at the ministry. "I mean, it's not like they sneak up on you or anything."

"There was a lot of static on the phone," Maureen told her.

"How much static can there be?"

Verna suspected that Bob's demise was almost as great a relief to Maureen as it was to her. Not that the poor woman would ever have owned up to it. In fact, Verna had to give the admin assistant high marks for her excellent impersonation of someone reeling from the shock of losing a beloved boss. Even then, a full ten days after they had managed to scrape what remained of Bob from the mangled Escape and the blunt nose of the train (not much), Maureen was still making a show of grief. Inside she must be singing a *Te Deum*, Verna thought, watching carefully as Maureen dabbed at red eyes with a wad of gray Kleenex. She must be thinking, *Hallelujah and thank you, Jesus! The son of a bitch is dead!* For Bob's replacement, poor, sweet Peter Orser, was ever so much nicer than Bob had ever been. That's when Verna had asked her what Bob's last words had been. After all, she had been the one talking to him when he died; it seemed like a reasonable question. "What were his last words, Maureen? Other, I mean, than, *'Aaaaghhh!'*" The look on Maureen's face! But then the assistant had glanced from side to side to make sure no one else could hear, leaned toward Verna and hissed, *" 'Fucking bitch!' *Those were his last words! *'Fucking bitch!' "*

"I'm so, so sorry, Auntie Verna," Romy apologized now.

"*Aunt* Verna. Don't be," said Verna. "Best thing that ever happened to me." And it had been. One moment she had been contemplating divorce and the inevitable financial fallout of that. The next she had found herself the sole beneficiary of mortgage insurance, Bob's term life insurance, his pension, his RRSP, the Cocoa Beach condo, and a modest, but tidy estate.

"Really?"

"Really."

"In that case, did you have to identify the body? What did it look like?"

"You mean, did I have to identify, 'the smithereens'?" Verna asked. "Because that was pretty much what was left of him. Oh, and his wedding ring and his U of T ring. And a few odd teeth."

"Ooh," said Romy. Then, undeterred, "Come on now. Open the door."

Verna sighed. She shut her eyes. She took a deep breath. She took the door knob in hand. "Are you sure?" she asked.

Romy set her clothes-hanger shoulders and swallowed visibly, her Adam's apple goiter huge in contrast to her stringy neck. "I'm sure!"

Verna closed her eyes, turned the handle to the left, and pulled.

Nothing happened.

She tried again.

Again, nothing.

She rattled it and tried again.

A third time: nothing.

Astounded, she turned to Romy. "I can't believe it!" she said. "It's locked!"

"What do you mean: it's locked?" Winonah asked.

"As in 'you can't open it; because it's locked'," explained Verna. Now all three women were standing in front of Fern's door.

"It can't be locked," Winonah said. "Who would have locked it? It's stuck, eh? The wood's probably swollen. You just have to give it some muscle ..." Planting her feet, the handywoman took hold of the door knob, twisted it one way, then the other, and yanked with all her might. Then she kicked the door once for good measure and tried the door knob again. No luck. "Okay," she conceded. "It's locked."

"Who?" Verna wondered. "Who would have locked it?"

"And why?" asked Romy.

"It's an old lock," said Winonah. "That means what we're looking for is a skeleton key."

"A *skeleton* key?" Romy was intrigued. "What's a skeleton key? Does it have a skull or something on it?"

"Are you that young that you haven't heard of a skeleton key?" Verna asked. "God, I must be old."

Winonah organized the search. "Let's divide up. Verna, you look in your dad's room. Look in the dresser drawers, eh? If you don't find it there, look in his study. In the desk. Stick Girl, you look in all the keyholes. If it was a skeleton key, it would have fit all the doors, not just this one. Then check the kitchen drawers. I'll check the shed and the boathouse."

"Slow down. Hold on," Verna was desperate for a reason to call off the search. "Have you ever thought that the door might be locked for a reason and that maybe, just maybe, we should respect that reason and not try and find the key?"

"What?" Romy was incredulous. "Are you crazy? How can you stand not knowing?"

"Not too many white people buy cottages with locked bedrooms, eh? Not that other white people have gone and died in," Winonah pointed out.

"What?" Verna turned to Winonah. "How did you know I was thinking of selling the cottage? Did Carmen tell you that?"

"Wait a minute," Romy interjected. "Hold on! You're selling the cottage?"

Verna was flustered. "Probably. Maybe. I haven't decided."

"Hey!" Romy objected. "Don't I get a say in this? Isn't it my cottage, too? And what about my brother and sister? Wherever they are!"

Verna winced. She leaned against the doorframe. In her head she could hear her father's querulous voice. *If Parsley or ... any of the others surface, you'll help them out, won't you?* "Yes, well, I didn't exactly know where you were," she told Romy. "Now I know. Okay?"

"So, you're not selling the cottage."

"I didn't say that. Look. We'll talk about it. Maybe I'll sell it and give you a share of the money. We'll make an arrangement."

Winonah crossed her arms over her chest and shook her head dolefully.

"What?" Verna demanded.

"Bad idea," said Winonah.

"Why?"

"You have your own lake."

"Yes. And? What am I going to do with a lake?"

"You got to think outside the box," Winonah told her. "Besides, the Manitous ... they would be some pissed if you sold this lake."

"Who is she talking about?" Romy tugged at Verna's sleeve. "Are they any relation to Barry Manilow? Isn't he some old guy?"

"*Manitous*," Verna corrected her. "Not Manilows. *Manitous*. They're like gods."

"Gods?" wondered Romy.

"Spirits," clarified Winonah.

"And, anyway, what do the Manitous have to do with anything?" Verna turned back to Winonah.

"They have everything to do with everything," said Winonah. "That's why they're Manitous. And they gave this land to your grandfather and his descendents. That would be you." She looked at Romy and her eyes narrowed. "And her."

"Right!" said Romy. "And I say let's find the key." Off she wobbled on her stick legs.

Verna looked hard at Winonah. "What's going on? First Carmen — a *real-estate* agent for crissakes — tells me not to sell and now you? I mean, this would probably be your land if my ancestors hadn't cheated you out of it. Doesn't that make you angry?"

"It was our land," said Winonah. "Still is."

"Well, if that's the case, why should you worry about what white person thinks they own it — me or the guy I sell the cottage to? I don't understand. Am I missing something? Are you being cryptic or are you just acting all inscrutable like an Indian or something? Because if you are, it's working. I'm just not getting it."

Winonah met her gaze steadily, inscrutably. "We prefer the term 'First Nations,'" was all she said.

Half an hour later, the women reconvened in the kitchen. No one had found *The Key*. Or anything remotely resembling *The Key*. They had found all sorts of other keys mixed into the chaotic landfill of the house's various drawers: skate keys, luggage keys, tiny keys that had once locked diaries and unlocked jewellry boxes, extra keys to the Indian Crescent house, keys to a car long since discarded, an Allen key, the keys to a file cabinet, a Phi Beta Kappa key, and what appeared to be the key to some safety deposit box somewhere. They found nothing, however, of such a shape and size that it could be inserted into the keyhole of Fern's door and turned to unlock it.

"There's only one thing we can do," Winonah said.

"What?" asked Verna.

"Climb up onto the roof of the back porch and go in through the window."

"Won't it be locked?"

Winonah brandished a hammer.

"You're going to break the glass?" Verna asked.

"You got a better idea?"

Verna trawled for a reason why not and came up empty. "No."

"Come on, then," said Winonah.

They went out back. Verna and Romy helped Winonah

position the ladder against the back shed. "Can I go up?" Romy asked. "Please?"

"Knock yourself out," Verna replied.

"What about the hammer?" Romy asked.

"Get up there first and see if you can get the window open just by lifting," Winonah told her. "If you can't, we'll pass you the hammer."

The girl clambered up the ladder and crawled up the roof pitch to the window.

"Go on. Try it," Verna called.

"I don't need to," Romy called back. "It's open."

"What do you mean, it's open?"

"It's open," the girl repeated. "Like a whole inch or so. Open."

Verna turned to Winonah. "That's strange," she said. "Dad wouldn't have left the window open all winter."

"He wouldn't have locked the door, either," Winonah pointed out.

"I'm going to try opening it all the way!" Romy called.

"Be careful!" Verna cautioned.

"There," Romy called. "Wow!"

"Wow, what?" Verna cried in some alarm.

"I'm going in!" Romy advised.

"Romy! Romy, be careful!" Verna cried as the anorexic disappeared through the window.

A moment later, she poked her head out of the window and triumphantly brandished something. "I found the key!" She looked like an emaciated elf, all ears and transparent skin under which the blue veins bulged.

Romy unlocked the door from the inside. Verna hung back in the hall for a moment, filled with ... what was that she was filled with? Dread?

Romy was impatient. "Are you coming?"

"I'm working my way up to it!"

Steady, now, Verna told herself. *One. Two. Three.* Lifting her right foot so high that her knee was cocked at nearly a right angle, she dangled it in the air for a moment before executing a Mother-may-I-size lunge over the door sill and into the room. *There*, she congratulated herself as foot met floor. *That wasn't so bad, now was it?*

No.

Wait a minute.

Hold on.

Winonah and Romy seemed to be talking, but Verna could barely hear them through the plush, absorbent silence that was pouring into her head through her ears. Her stomach flopped inside of her like a fish on a dock. The room started to tilt and then — even worse — to rotate slowly. *Glub*, she thought, slumping back against the wall, her throat constricted and her vision edged with ragged black.

Then Romy was kneeling beside her. "Are you all right?"

"No. I mean, yes. Give me a moment."

"Put your head between your legs," Winonah advised.

Doubling over, Verna rested her elbows on her thighs and let her head dangle.

Romy turned to Winonah. "What's wrong with her?"

"She feels guilty," Winonah replied.

"I do not!" Verna objected.

"She feels guilty, but she won't admit it."

"I don't feel guilty!"

"See?"

Verna slid her butt carefully down the wall until she was sitting, back pressed against the tongue and groove. She wrapped her arms around her knees and peered about her, shivery and blinking. Her old bedroom had looked pretty much as she remembered — just smaller and shabbier and sad somehow. Like the room of a child — any child — who disappeared one day, decades earlier, whose milk-carton photo had long since been replaced by that of another such child, and another, then another. The room's rag-tag collection of castoffs from more proper houses elsewhere had pre-existed her — the old spool bed, the wobbly rocker, the tilting bookcase. They had a permanency she lacked.

Not the case with her sister's room. Much of its original furnishings had been replaced with trophies of Fern's various failed unions. Or loot, depending on how you looked at it.

For example, that bedside table crafted from the root ball of a burr oak — that was courtesy of Ben, Paisley's father, the one who salvaged waste wood to make tables and chairs and beds. Ben and Fern had stood up for Verna and Bob at their City Hall wedding, which took place at high noon on a sultry day in mid-July. Bob's side of the wedding party had consisted of his aggrieved mother, who complained throughout of heat rash and the fact that Ben was wearing paint-stained jean shorts and Jesus sandals.

Then there was that Indian bedspread patched together from antique wedding saris ... well, technically it was a tapestry, but Fern used it as a bedspread. That had come from Tai's father, the brown one. Jag something. Jagadeesh? A sweet boy, quite clueless, very young. How momentarily elated Donald had been to see his daughter putting into action the Canadian principle of multiculturalism. Then the boy's uncle arrived at the Indian Crescent house to reclaim the tapestry, a family heirloom as it transpired and not Jag's to bequeath to some white trollop. Fern, however, forewarned, whisked the treasure away, and, all these years later, here it was, its mirrored disks randomly bouncing light from the window off the ceiling, scintillating and chaotic. Had Fern ever felt guilty about it? Probably not. She had been drawn to shiny things.

And finally Romy's father, Paul, a painter. His portrait of a young woman meant to be Fern hung over the bed in which she had died. Rendered in awkward dabs, it was perhaps best viewed at a distance. Seen up close, it portrayed its subject as deficient in edge, lacking in boundaries or margins, as something gaudily coloured in the process of melting.

Romy followed her gaze. "That's one of Dad's."

Verna nodded.

"Of Mom?"

"Yeah."

"He totally sucks."

"Yeah." Verna agreed. "Does he still paint?"

"Yeah," said Romy. "Stupid Canada Council!"

In the corner was a rattan peacock chair piled high with clothing. The door to the closet was ajar; more clothes huddled behind it, jammed onto hangers. Clothes littered the floor in bright disarray. Fern could not resist buying clothes or be persuaded to give them up once acquired. As she had made her way through life, moving from man to man, size to size, she had dragged behind her an ever increasing supply of clothing as though it were a swollen tail.

"How are you feeling now?" Romy asked.

"Better," replied Verna. "I felt faint, that's all."

"It must run in the family," said Romy. "I faint at the drop of a hat. Like one of those fainting goats."

"You faint because you're hungry." Taking the icy hand Romy extended to her, Verna allowed herself to be hauled to her feet.

Downstairs, Jude barked to be let in.

"I'll do it," Winonah said. "Might as well trough the eaves seeing as the ladder's out." She left.

"Mom wasn't very tidy," Romy observed, taking in the dusty jumble of crystals, geodes, incense burners filled with ash, fibre lights, wads of Kleenex, and bottles of pills that littered every available surface — the bedside table, the chest of drawers. Under the ornate Indian spread the bedclothes were rumpled. Pillows lay here and there. Waste baskets and ashtrays overflowed.

"She was a pig," Verna agreed.

Romy turned on her. "Why are you so hard on her? She's dead, you know."

"I'm not being hard on her," Verna defended herself. "I'm just … making an observation. I've known parrots that were neater than Fern and they shit everywhere whenever they feel like it. It's not like I'm judging her."

"Oh, sure!" Romy retorted. "First you said she was a pig. Then you said she was a parrot."

"She was like a tornado passing through a trailer park. There! Is that better?" Verna demanded. "A force of nature. That about sums her up." She paused. "Do you even remember her?"

Romy sighed. "No," she admitted. "Not really. A little." She walked over to the dresser and picked up a dusty green bong half filled with murky fluid and sniffed it. "Oooh," she said. "Mould." She began rummaging around in the clutter, picking up objects, looking at them, then setting them down: a pack of dog-eared tarot cards; a Tibetan meditation bowl; a battered dream catcher with a frayed, purple feather; an origami crane; a rhinestone tiara. Romy picked up the tiara, examined it, then perched it on her head. She surveyed herself in the mirror and adjusted its position.

"Oh, that." Verna remembered. "Fern used to go traipsing around the house in it whenever she felt an excess of *duka*."

"What's *duka*?" Romy asked.

"The human condition," replied Verna. "Suffering."

"I'm keeping this," Romy decided. "I've got lots of *duka*."

"You and me both," said Verna. She crossed over to the chair, scooped up its contents, and dumped them onto the floor. She sat down.

But Romy was busy rooting around in the clutter. "Hey!" she exclaimed. Reaching deep into a pile of discarded tissue, she extracted an amber plastic bottle of prescription pills. "Is this what I think it is?"

"What?" asked Verna.

Romy read the label. "It is! It's OxyContin!"

"Oxy-what?"

"OxyContin, hillbilly heroin, poor man's heroin, oxy, OC, otherwise known as 'kicker' … You know!" Romy was plainly excited. "It's pain medication. For people with cancer."

"Pain medication? You're kidding me. Fern?"

Romy handed her the bottle. "See for yourself."

"Willis Pharmacy in Beverley," Verna read aloud. "Dr. Lefevre … Fern Macoun." She sank down onto the platform bed. "It's dated to the week before her death. Jeeze." She shook her head. "The last thing I heard she was taking some powder made up of crushed bloodroot and wild yam and that was somehow going to cure her. She was so afraid of muddying her aura, of messing with her chakras …" She returned the bottle to Romy.

"How cool is this?" Romy raved. "OxyContin!"

"I don't know. What's the big deal?"

"You can get really stoned on this stuff."

Verna eased herself down onto her back. "So, let me get this straight. Not only are you an anorexic, you're also a drug addict." Placing her hands on her belly, she stared at a mobile dangling from the overhead light fixture: more origami cranes. The certainty that Fern had been in terrible pain toward her lonely end closed around her like a fist, making it hard to breathe.

"My friend's grandmother died of cancer a few years ago," Romy told her, "and, when no one was looking, she snuck into her room and took the rest of her OxyContin. All the grownups were drinking in the kitchen. They never noticed it was gone."

"That's awful!"

Romy shrugged. "Why? Her grandmother didn't need it. None of the grownups wanted it. They would have flushed it down the toilet when they got around to cleaning up her grandmother's room. They would have wasted it. As it turned out, Becca and I were stoned for a week."

Verna considered her options: come down hard on the girl or let go? She decided to let it go. Romy was a grown woman, sort of, and it was hard for an alcoholic, however functional, to take the high road in cases involving substance abuse. "What's it like?" she asked.

"Peaceful," Romy replied. "You feel peaceful."

"That doesn't sound like much fun."

"Don't knock it 'til you've tried it." Romy slid the bottle of pills presumably into a pocket located somewhere amidst the folds of her voluminous drapery.

"So Fern took painkillers!" Verna marvelled. "Mind you, she smoked like a chimney and that didn't seem to mess with her chakras too much. 'Oh, I'm going to stop,' she would say and then wouldn't. Or would, but only for a while. She was very inconstant, your mother." Reaching out, Verna plucked a half-empty pack of cigarettes from the slice of tree that topped Ben's bedside table and stared at them. "This is weird."

"What?"

"These cigarettes. They're Camels."

"So?"

"Fern didn't smoke Camels."

"That's right." Romy remembered. "She smoked Virginia Slims."

"How can you remember what cigarette she smoked when you can't remember what she looked like?"

"I always associate the jingle — that 'You've come a long way, baby' jingle — with her," Romy replied.

Verna shook her head. "Camels? I just can't see her smoking these. She was so particular and these are so … nasty."

"And bad-tempered, I hear," replied Romy. "She probably ran out and somebody gave her a pack of theirs. It happens. Smoking is an addiction, after all. You're not going to turn down a cigarette if you're desperate, even if you don't like the brand. Trust me. I know."

"And how would you know?"

Romy plucked the pack of cigarettes from her and slipped them into her invisible pocket along with the OxyContin. "I figured out long ago that smoking keeps you thin," she replied. At Verna's disgusted expression, "What?" she defended herself. "So I smoke. Big Deal! You're an alcoholic!"

"Oh, please!" Verna moaned. She clambered to her feet. *Why did I tell her that?* she chided herself. *What was I thinking?*

"And a bed-wetter!"

"Enough!" cried Verna, fleeing.

Later that afternoon Verna drove into Greater Gammage to hit the ATM for cash to pay Winonah and to pick up some groceries at the Pump and Munch — a combination gas bar and convenience store where locals could purchase white bread, cigarettes, and lottery tickets and where hunters and fishers could stock up on canned goods and tackle, propane and bait. Romy went along for the ride.

Greater Gammage had started life as Gammage's Trading Post on a steep bluff overlooking the Black River. Once track had been laid for the Temiskaming and Northern Ontario Railway from North Bay to Cochrane, a ragged community of sorts began to accumulate around the post, and, later, across the river. Those who lived on the bluff called their community Greater Gammage (it being the original settlement and higher in altitude), while those residing on the opposite shore had to settle for Lesser Gammage, scorn and condescension and a certain amount of seasonal flooding.

Over the decades that had intervened since Verna had last been north, Greater Gammage had begun to describe itself in a hopeful, yearning way as a destination for outdoor enthusiasts, fishermen, and hunters. Throughout most of its history, however, its chief claim to fame had been its propensity to catch on fire — and this to such an extent that, in the course of not quite a century, Greater Gammage had burned down and been rebuilt a total of five times. Moreover, when Greater Gammage wasn't burning down on its own, it burned down in conjunction with other hamlets, as it did in 1916, when 244 people died in a fire that swept through not only Greater Gammage, but also the villages of Beverley, Kelso, Val Gagne, Porquis Junction, and Iroquois Falls. Low-lying Lesser Gammage, on the other hand, not being situated on a bluff, had more immediate access to the river, not ideal during the spring thaw, but handy when one had a raging fire to douse.

It all came to a head in 1932, when a lightning strike ignited a ground fire on the outskirts of Greater Gammage. This was in the process of boiling through town when the severely undercut bluff on which Greater Gammage was poised suddenly gave way and tumbled fifteen metres into the river, taking a good deal of the upper town with it. Those denizens of Greater Gammage who survived the double disaster were forced to acknowledge that, despite its lowliness and soggy cellars, Lesser Gammage appeared to have something of an advantage over Greater Gammage as far as staying power went. They relocated to Lesser Gammage, which promptly became Greater Gammage.

"This is a pretty poor excuse for a town," Romy observed, as they drove past the four or five boarded-up storefronts that constituted the outskirts of Greater Gammage and pulled into what passed for the Pump and Munch's parking lot.

"It's not a town," Verna replied. "It's more like a hamlet."

"Well, it's a pretty poor excuse for a hamlet."

"Fern and I used to call it 'Hoserville.'"

"Hoserville," Romy repeated with relish. "That's a good name for it. *Hoserville*."

"Just don't say it too loud," Verna warned her. "Hosers tend to be thin-skinned."

While Verna shopped, Romy, wraithlike, ranged the five aisles of the Pump and Munch, gawping at the cans of beans and soup and dusty candy bars as though she were at a carnival freak show. "I've never seen so much disgusting food in one place," Romy told her in a stage whisper. "No wonder the locals are so *massive!*"

"*Shhh!*" warned Verna.

"No, seriously, you should see the one who just came in. She's gigantic!"

Verna looked up to see Carmen standing in the gas bar's door wearing a gravy-stained peacock-blue caftan and bright white, high-topped running shoes.

"What? Is she, like, *Moby Rapper?*"

But before Verna could respond, "Hey, Verna!" the realtor was calling. "I thought that was the Volvo!" She waddled their way, as wide as the aisle.

"You *know* her?" Romy gasped.

"*Hush!*" Verna warned. "Carmen! How are you?"

"Out of breath and out of smokes, that's how," replied Carmen. "In other words, in desperate straits, but not for long. Mind you, at these prices … forty-nine bucks a carton!" She shook her head. "Talk about sin tax! How are things up at your dad's place?"

"Good," said Verna. "I wanted to thank you for sending Winonah along to me. She's been a godsend."

"She's handy, all right," Carmen agreed. "Handy with attitude. God knows she's handier than poor Lionel ever was. All thumbs, that boy, plus not a great gag reflex. That reminds me, maybe you could ask her to bring me a couple of cartons of smokes from the rez. This should cover it." She gave Verna a twenty, a ten, and a toonie. "The butt-legged ones were going for around sixteen bucks the last time I bought from her."

"Butt-legged?" Verna wondered.

"Sixteen bucks?" Romy was interested. "That's cheap!"

"And who's this?" Carmen asked.

"Oh, I'm sorry," Verna said hastily. "Romy, this is Carmen. Carmen, this is Fern's daughter, Romy. The baby."

Carmen peered at Romy. "The baby, eh?" she shook her head. "Not much of a resemblance."

"What do you mean?" Romy asked.

"Too thin," Carmen replied.

"'You can never be too rich or too thin,'" Romy retorted.

"Oh, yes, you can," said Carmen smoothly. "Too thin, that is. I don't know about the too-rich part." She laughed. "Probably never will the way I'm going." She glanced at Verna's shopping basket. "You might want to stock up on some Off," she advised. "Blackflies should be starting up any time now."

Verna moaned. "Blackflies! Oh, Jesus! I'd forgotten about the blackflies!"

"What are blackflies?" Romy asked.

The two women stared at her.

"Are you serious?" Verna asked.

Romy blinked back at her.

"You're serious," Verna concluded. "And what country are you from again?"

The wizened crone perched atop the high stool behind the cash register burst, apparently spontaneously, into a cackle of song: *"Always the blackfly, no matter where you go/I'll die with the blackfly a-picking my bones/In North On-tar-i-o-i-o, in North On-tar-i-o."* Then, as suddenly as she had begun, she stopped, and, once again folded in on herself like a collapsed bat.

"I'm off," Carmen told Romy and Verna. "Don't forget about the smokes!" Turning, she lumbered back to the counter. "Pack of Du Mauriers, Darla," she told the cashier.

Romy tugged on Verna's sleeve. "Who is Lionel? What was that about his gag reflex? Do you think Winonah would pick up some of the cigarettes for me? Could you ask her because I don't think she likes me."

When they arrived back at the cottage, Winonah was sitting on the hood of the battered Buick, whittling. Verna recognized the stick. It was the one Lionel had been whittling when she saw him from her window that morning, the one he had abandoned on the stone wall, the one which she had retrieved to show Winonah and Romy.

"Wow!" said Verna. "You whittle!"

"Of course I whittle," replied Winonah.

"I knit!" declared Romy, not to be outdone. "They make you knit at the Birches. Keeps you from running around. Calms you down. Once I knit a scarf. It was very long."

Winonah looked at her, shook her head and turned to Verna. "No'okomiss is waiting. You can pay me now."

"Who's No'okomiss?" *Really, Romy is like a toddler*, Verna thought, *all questions.*

"Winonah's granny," Verna told her.

"The one who had to eat grasshopper legs?"

Verna ignored her. "Oh, and before I forget, Winonah, we ran into Carmen in town and she gave us some money to give to you — for two cartons of reservation cigarettes."

"*Butt-legged* cigarettes," Romy clarified.

As Verna counted out first Carmen's money, then an additional ten twenties into the handywoman's palm, she debated with herself: *should I ask her to come again tomorrow?* On the one hand, Romy was here, which meant that she would not be alone, should the spectre of Lionel happen to rematerialize. On the other hand, Romy probably weighed ninety pounds soaking wet. Yes, she was nervy and presumptive in a Jack Russell terrier sort of way, but wasn't Winonah's unflinchingly stubborn orneriness a safer bet when it came to fending off threats, real or surreal? Besides, Lionel was the round woman's brother, the twin with whom she shared a psychic bond. Presumably such a twin could sway the spirit, were suasion required. That cinched it. "Can you come again tomorrow?" she asked.

Winonah blinked at her. "Why?"

"There have got to be things that need fixing. It stands to reason."

"Such as ...?"

"I don't know. The dock? It's looking kind of twisted. The boathouse? God knows what's up with that. And what about vermin? There was mouse dirt in my old bed ..."

"You didn't tell me that!" Romy fumed. "You wanted me to sleep there."

"We would have brushed it off," Verna defended herself.

"Okay. Sure. I'll come." Winonah slid off the hood of the car, tossed the stick she had been whittling aside, and pulled car keys from her jeans pocket.

Suddenly Verna remembered Lionel's cremains on the front porch. Maybe if she sent them home with Winonah, Lionel would not reappear. After all, hadn't his spirit explained its presence in Donald's room by saying that it was too crowded downstairs? Maybe spirits require more *Lebensraum* than live people. Or maybe that was just Lionel: "Give me land, lots of land, and a starry sky above!" Like the old Cole Porter song. On second thought, *Lebensraum* might be the wrong word for it. "Wait!" she told Winonah. She turned to Romy. "Romy, run and get the cremains on the front porch. Not your mom or grandfather. The other cremains."

"The *what?*" Romy asked.

"The ... you know! The cremains! The *ashes!*"

"*Cremains?*" Romy repeated.

"Don't bother ..." Winonah began.

Romy was puzzled. "What kind of a word is '*cremains*'?"

"A stupid, made-up word," Verna snapped. "No, really, Winonah, you should take them with you. Romy, please!"

"*Oooh!*" Romy was reluctant. "How will I know which one to get?"

Winonah finished her sentence: "... 'cause I'm just going to bring him right back here tomorrow."

Verna wheeled around to face the handywoman. "What?" she demanded. "Do you just carry him around with you? What's that about? Don't you think that's a little ghoulish?" To Romy she said, "The cartons are labelled. Get the one that says 'Lionel.'"

"He gets carsick," said Winonah. "He's a bad passenger. Better he stays here."

"Hey, wait a minute!" said Romy. "Lionel? Isn't he that dead guy?"

"They're all dead!" cried Verna. "Romy, get the carton."

"But ...!"

Winonah closed the car door and put her key in the ignition. "I told you. No'okomiss don't like dead people in the house."

"Neither do I!" Verna said. "Run, Romy, run! It's exercise. You'll burn calories! Hurry up now!" Really, she would have done it herself, but she felt far too rickety at the moment what with having breached Fern's bedroom.

Too late.

"Bye! See you tomorrow!" Winonah leaned out of the car window to shout as she drove off down the laneway.

"Damn!"

"What is it with you?" Romy asked. "What's the big deal?"

"Oh …!" Verna toyed momentarily with the idea of telling Romy about her visit with Lionel, or, to be more precise, his visit with her, but dismissed it as too risky. What would be the point? The girl would just think she was crazy, and, who knows? Maybe she was. She picked up the stick Winonah had been whittling and noted that the handywoman had taken up where Lionel had left off — her buck knife had coaxed from the curve of peeled wood at the stick's end the sleek head of a water bird. "What kind of a bird do you think this is?" she asked.

"Auntie Verna! Don't change the subject!"

"It's nothing," Verna replied. "'Nothing you'd understand, at any rate."

Romy was undeterred. "Try me."

But Verna only scrutinized the carving, turning it this way and that. "I think it's a loon," she decided. "Look. See. There's its eye."

Romy and Verna sat on the screened-in porch, watching the sun ease itself, like a tentative bather, into the lake's western end, taking with it that meagre allotment of vernal warmth it had afforded during daylight hours. Jude lay on his side by the front door, humid and dreamy, in what Donald used to call his beached-whale pose. Verna glanced at Romy, who was white around the gills and shivering. "Cold?" she asked.

"And you're not?"

"Not so much, but I'm menopausal. I've got the thermostat to my central heating cranked up high."

"Not me! Everything in me is turned way down low."

Verna stood. "I'm getting a drink. I'll fetch you a jacket. There's a pile of them in the mudroom." She returned with a vodka and tonic, a tricolour Hudson's Bay blanket coat for Romy, and, for herself, a heavyweight black-and-plaid flannel shirt — not dissimilar to the red-and-black one sported by Winonah and by Lionel's apparition. "Here." She handed Romy the blanket coat.

"Thanks," said Romy, slipping it on. "What's the lake's name? It does have a name, doesn't it?"

"Marguerite," replied Verna. "Lake Marguerite. After my aunt. Margie for short."

"Your Aunt Margie had a lake named after her?"

"Well, my grandfather ... your great-grandfather, that is, discovered it," said Verna, remembering what her father had said on the subject: "A lake has to be called something. A topographical feature on a map, once noted, cannot go unnamed."

"How did he discover it?" Romy asked.

"He was a geologist and a cartographer with the Bureau of Mines," Verna replied. "George Dewey Macoun. His map of northeastern Ontario — the Macoun Map it was called — formed the basis of all future maps of the area."

"Wow." Romy was impressed. "So why do you call it 'the lake'? Why don't you call it Lake Marguerite?"

"Because my grandmother forbade it."

"Why?"

"Because it upset Aunt Evelyn."

"Who was Aunt Evelyn?"

"Your grandfather had four children," Verna explained. "George Junior, Evelyn, Dad. Margie was the baby."

"So Evelyn was jealous of her sister."

"Apparently."

"What happened to them all — your aunts and uncles?"

"Uncle George died on August 31, 1944, in the battle of Pozzo Alto Ridge, a lieutenant in Lord Strathcona's Horse," Verna recounted. "He had been working as a geologist at the Athabasca oil sands out in Alberta when he enlisted. As for Aunt Evelyn, she married an American and moved to California. Salinas, California. There were children — a boy and girl, cousins we never met. I can't remember their names now. Strange, American non-names. Tracy? Chip? Up until 1996, Dad always got a Christmas card from her, then nothing. When he finally checked into it a year or two later, he found that she had been diagnosed with Alzheimer's and put into a home. As for Marge, she killed herself in the late eighties." A pang of pity for the only one of Donald's siblings that Verna had actually known. Verna shook her head. Once her father's darling, Margie had become a soft, spongy, middle aged woman whom her husband — Uncle Phil — would discard along the way. When Donald called Verna to tell her of the suicide, this was how he put it: "Your Uncle Phil had a midlife crisis from which your aunt never recovered."

"Oooh!" crooned Romy. "How did she do it?"

"Carbon monoxide poisoning," Verna replied, remembering with a flash of pride, that, when it had come right down to it, Margie had proven herself not only more resourceful, but also far more vindictive than anyone would have given her credit for. On Day Two of Phil and his impossibly young bride's honeymoon — a ten-day cruise down the Mayan Riviera — Marge somehow managed to break into the garage of the newlyweds' Etobicoke side split. There she hot-wired the girl's sporty new Suzuki Samurai, climbed inside, and curled up on the back seat as the garage filled with exhaust. By the time Phil and his bride returned home eight days later, Margie had managed to go very badly off indeed, ruining the car's interior, and, as Donald could not refrain from observing, "reeking a good deal more than havoc!"

"That's not very exciting," Romy complained.

"Oh, trust me," Verna assured her, remembering the note Marge had left on the new bride's dashboard, "it was plenty exciting." The note had read: "Loons mate for life."

"I can't imagine Aunt Margie breaking into a house," Verna had said at the time.

"Never mind that," her father had replied. "Where did she learn to hot-wire a car?" *Secret lives*, she thought. *We all have them.*

"So, Auntie Verna," Romy's next question muscled its way into Verna's consciousness. "What are your feelings about popping an Oxy?"

"What?" Verna asked, then, remembering Fern's painkillers, "No. Absolutely not. And you shouldn't 'pop' one, either." Setting her drink on the Queen Anne table between the Heywood rockers, she pulled on the flannel shirt and sat down. "Honestly!"

Romy shook her head. "I hate to inform you of this, but you are *so* not the boss of me. I can do whatever I want." As if to illustrate this, she produced a cigarette from the depths of her clothing along with a Zippo lighter.

"Oh, no!" declared Verna. "No, you don't! You are *not* going to smoke that foul cancer stick on this porch!"

"Oh, yes, I am," replied Romy. "And I'm going to have an Oxy, too. If I want." She lit the cigarette and took a deep drag on it. "Come on, Auntie Verna! What's the harm? So my mother's dead! So, these pills are, like, her gift to me, her legacy."

"Her *legacy*? For cripes' sake! Her *legacy*? You do know, Romy, that it's not fair to me, you smoking in my vicinity. Haven't you ever heard of second-hand smoke? People die from it."

"Yeah, yeah." Romy dismissed her concern. "And people drink themselves to death, too. As for the Oxys, what do you want to do with them that's so frigging noble? Drive to Timmins and give it to homeless people with cancer? You'd flush it down the toilet. That's what you'd do. And then what would happen to all the fish in the Great Lakes? Stoned out of their gourds! And you thought mercury was bad!"

"Hah!" Verna was triumphant. "Gotcha! We're north of the Arctic Watershed."

Romy blinked at her. "What?"

"You flush a toilet here, it drains into the Arctic Ocean, not the Great Lakes."

Romy recalibrated her argument. "Polar bears," she said. "Polar bears would be stoned out of their gourds. And you thought global warming was bad!" Retrieving the bottle, she shook it. "Oooh," she exclaimed. "Lots!" Then she peered at the bottle's label in the fading light. "Eighty milligrams. Wow!"

"What do you mean — 'wow'?"

"As in 'wow,' that's a lot of milligrams. This is the good stuff."

"As opposed to …?"

"Forty milligrams, twenty milligrams." Romy opened the bottle and shook a pill out into the palm of her hand. "You really should reconsider," she told Verna, popping the pill in her mouth. "It would calm you down. You're, like, a total stress puppy."

"I'm not a stress puppy!"

"Yeah, right!"

"I'm not!"

"Think about it. You're old. You've got nobody. And you have no idea what you're going to do with the rest of your — excuse me for saying so — but your miserable life."

How do you know that? Verna wanted to ask. She didn't, however. She took a sip of her V and T instead. "My life's not so miserable. Well, maybe a little."

The women sat in a silence for a few moments. Romy butted out her cigarette and lit another. "Did you think when you were a little girl that you were going to grow up to be an alcoholic, Auntie Verna?"

"Did you think that you were going to be an anorexic?" Verna countered.

"It wasn't an aspiration, if that's what you mean," Romy replied. "I mean, in retrospect, it makes sense."

"It's strange to be something and know how you got to be something without realizing that you actually are, in fact, something," Verna mused. "Do you know what I mean?"

"Absolutely."

"I think I will try one of those pills." Verna decided. *Why not?* she thought. *What difference does it make? Maybe it will make me not see Lionel. Maybe it will make me less fragile, more resolved.*

"Excellent!" Romy produced a second pill from wherever she had stashed the bottle and handed it to her. "You have to chew it," she told her. "Otherwise it's time-release."

"Time-release?" Verna asked. "That's an interesting Germanic word construction — two nouns sort of mushed together to create an adjective. Really it should be 'timed release.'"

"Auntie Verna." Romy sighed. "Nobody cares. Chew."

Some time later (it had grown quite dark), Verna realized that someone had joined them on the screened-in porch.

This realization was gradual. A dawning, really. Well, sort of. *Oh!* She thought. Then, *I wonder!* A few moments later, she whispered, "Who's there?" Whispered, because what need was there to raise her voice? Whoever it was — he or she or possibly even it — was right there beside her.

"Pardon?" This from Romy.

"No. Not you," Verna told the girl. "Lionel? Lionel, is that you?"

Oh, it was Lionel all right — a little blurred around the edges as befitted something ectoplasmic, but Lionel nevertheless. All she had to do was turn her head ninety degrees to the right to sort of see him sitting cross-legged on the floor beside her. "Indian-style," was what they used to call it. So politically incorrect, really. When you thought about it. Wasn't everything these days? Bob had thought that this was a bad thing — people were too bloody sensitive; grin and bear it; suck it up and choke it down; put up or shut up. He might as well have been an American, a Republican American. Donald, on the other hand, had thought political correctness a good thing — according to him, inclusiveness was the watermark of an enlightened society. How could she have married a man so different from her father? Why had she made so many bad choices?

"You don't have to sit on the floor, you know," she told Lionel. "You can sit on the settee."

No reply. Lionel stared out towards the lake. *He is implacable*, she decided. *Implacable? No, that wasn't right. Inscrutable.*

"Be that way," she told him. "Be inscrutable." Closing her eyes, she allowed herself just to float. *I am a beautiful water lily*, she told herself, *and my legs are hollow stems anchoring me to my underwater rhizomes, my creeping root stalks ...*

Despite her whispering it, Romy's question barged into Verna's subaqueous reverie like a policeman breaking up a fight: "Are you talking to cremains?"

Verna was startled. "No, actually. Well, sort of. I was talking to Lionel."

"Lionel?" the girl asked.

"Yes, Lionel," she replied.

"If you're going to talk to Lionel, I'm going to talk to Mom!" Romy's tone was both defensive and defiant

"Sure. Right. Go ahead. I'm cool with that," Verna told her. Remarkably, she was. Cool with that and so many other things, now that she thought about it. Floating on a sea of tranquility. *This Oxy, this hillbilly heroin,* she thought, *is outstanding.*

"There's so much I want to say to her," Romy explained.

"I understand," Verna assured her. "Oh, believe me, I understand! My mother — your grandmother, that is — she died when I and your mom were born. We killed her, Fern and me. Yep. Oh, it was an accident. Of course we didn't mean to. We were ... like ... newborns. Happened all the same. So, yes. Once upon a time I, too, had so much to say to my mother, but now ... well, whatever it was I had to say, I've forgotten." She paused, and, in that moment, noticed that she was sinking down, down, down into some place she hadn't been for a very long time. Someplace dark and hollow where unseen fingers played an electric arpeggio down her spine. She shivered and drew the bulky flannel shirt close around her, "So, be my guest. Talk to your mother," she told Romy. "Just don't expect me to."

"Why?" asked Romy. "Why don't you want to talk to her?"

"It's complicated."

"Not wanting to talk to your own sister — that sucks."

"Yeah," Verna agreed. "It does suck. I still don't want to talk to her."

"What could she have done to you that was so terrible? Did she steal your boyfriend or sleep with Uncle Bob or something?"

Verna must have looked funny, because Romy's jaw dropped. "Oh! She did! She slept with Uncle Bob, didn't she? She did!" The girl shook her head. "Wow! That *is* bad. No wonder you were mad at her."

"Yeah. Well, I was. Am. Sort of. Not so much now."

"But you still don't want to talk to her?"

"No. That would be stressful."

"Okay. That's fair, I guess." Romy hesitated, then said, "I've never slept with anyone. I guess that means I'm a virgin."

"In most universes."

"I don't even have a period. That is, I had it, but then I lost it."

"Hey!" said Verna. "Easy come, easy go."

"Auntie Verna?"

"What?"

"Do you think it's … like … whacked to talk to her?"

Verna considered this for a moment, before countering with, "Do you think it's whacked for me to talk to Lionel?"

"Yes, actually. But, no, it's okay. If you must." Reassured, the girl retrieved the carton of Fern's ashes from the floor by her rocker and set it on her lap.

A long moment ensued. "Well …?" asked Verna.

"I'm collecting my thoughts."

"Be spontaneous," Verna advised. "Say whatever comes into your head."

"I guess you're right," said Romy. "Mom? Is that you? Are you there? It's me, your Little Roo."

"Little *Roo*?"

"Don't laugh!" Romy warned her. "That's what she used to call me. Like Baby Roo in Winnie the Pooh. At least that's what my Dad told me." She hesitated, listening for a moment. "Auntie Verna, did you hear that?"

"What? No."

"She said, 'Yes.'"

"Sure she did!"

"Actually, she did," Lionel piped up.

Verna turned to him. "What? So now you talk!"

Lionel shrugged and returned his gaze to the lake.

"What? Did Lionel say something?"

Verna considered her response, then said, "Oh, to hell with it! If you must know, he said that your mother said 'yes.' That he heard her."

"Really?"

"Yes, really."

"And you heard him say that?"

"Uh-huh."

"I didn't hear him."

"But I did."

"And you didn't hear Mom, but I did."

Verna's heart felt like a stone hitting the water's surface and then skipping. "You h*eard* her? As in actually *heard* her?"

"Yes."

"As in 'with your ears' heard her?"

"Yes."

"Really? Her *voice?*"

"Well, I assume it's her voice!"

A moment passed, no, floated downstream. In its wake the porch seemed to lose its form, its definition — to melt and slip away. It became a kind of panic room, one with walls not of screen or plaster or stone, but night and distance.

"This is super weird," Romy managed from her very small place in the chair.

"You're telling me!"

"It must be the Oxy."

Verna debated mentioning her earlier, non-drug-induced encounters with Lionel and decided: *Best not.* "Yeah," she agreed.

"Maybe we've entered another dimension," Romy speculated.

"Who knows? Anything's possible. On second thought, is it?"

"I think I'd better go to bed." Romy decided.

"And leave me here with the dearly departed? Thanks!"

"No, really," Romy insisted. "I feel ... woozy."

"Are you a fainter?" Verna asked. "Oh, yes. I remember. You said so. Earlier. Which makes sense, because Fern ... she was a fainter."

"Should we leave the cremains out here?" Romy asked.

"I think we'd better," said Verna.

"They won't get cold or anything?"

"They're dead."

"Yeah, well." Romy stood, a slow racheting upright. Her ascent more closely resembled that of an arthritic old woman than a girl in her early twenties. "Winonah said that Lionel's got carsick."

"Do you get carsick?" Verna asked Lionel.

"No," replied Lionel. "I used to."

"Will you be cold?" she asked.

He shook his head.

"He says 'no,'" Verna told Romy. "They won't be cold."

"Well, then." Romy wobbled toward the front door, negotiating the air between her chair and it was though she were striking out across a marsh through tall grasses. The door opened and into the house she fell.

While this was going on, Verna's thoughts fell like a gentle rain — *pling, pling*. It wasn't until she heard the squeak of her niece's running shoes on the stairs that she snapped out of whatever idyll she had, for the moment, been, well, idling in. "Romy!" she called after her, "Where are you going to sleep? You can sleep in my old room! There are sheets." *And mouse droppings*, she thought. *Could be worse. Could be ...*

"Sleep in a bed-wetter's bed, steeped in urine? I'll sleep in my mother's bed, thank you very much ..."

... your mother's deathbed.

A distant click — Fern's door being closed. Verna sank back into the rocker and closed her eyes.

After a moment: "Eh, Verna, what you doing?" This from Lionel.

"Contemplating my navel," Verna said, not opening her eyes. "Metaphorically speaking."

"You and the big words."

"Me and the big words," Verna agreed. A wave of sadness rolled over her, swept her away. Inexplicably she began to cry — little catlike yips.

"What's up?" Lionel asked.

"What do you mean, what's up?"

"Why are you crying?'

"Because I'm old," she blubbered. "And I've got nobody. And I have no idea what I'm going to do with the rest of my miserable life, not that there's much of it left. Oh, Lionel, I've ruined everything!"

"Hey! How do you think I feel?" Lionel asked. "I choked to death on marshmallows."

"And that's supposed to make me feel better?"

"Well, yeah," said Lionel.

They lapsed into silence. Verna wept quietly, making snuffling noises like a mole nosing its way underground.

"I know," said Lionel after a few minutes had elapsed. "You could jump in the lake."

This startled Verna. "Excuse me?" she asked.

"You could jump in the lake," Lionel repeated.

"Why?"

"It would make you feel better."

"How?"

"Refreshed," replied Lionel.

"Frozen is more like it," Verna told him. "Do you know how cold that lake is?"

"I didn't mean now, eh? I meant tomorrow."

"I've been in the lake on May 2-4," Verna informed him. "It's frigging freezing."

But Lionel was undeterred. "The *Nebaunaubaequaewuk* who live in the lake. They will give you a nice scalp massage. Foot massage. All-over body massage. Like one of those fancy spas."

"The ... what?" Verna asked. "Did you say 'nematodes'?"

Lionel shook his head. "The Nebaunaubaequaewuk," he corrected her. "Female manitous that live at the bottom of the lake. Half human, half fish."

Verna giggled. Extracting a Kleenex from her jeans pocket, she wiped her streaming eyes. "Oh, Lionel, are you actually telling me that there are mermaids in the lake?" She blew her nose loudly.

"Of course there are," Lionel replied. "There are Nebaunaubaequaewuk in every lake and stream and river. Nebaunaubaewuk, too. Male manitous. But you don't have to worry about the Nebaunaubaewuk. You are too old and stringy for them."

She laughed. "Thanks a lot!"

"No, no, you should be glad," Lionel assured her. "How there get to be Nebaunaubaequaewuk in the first place is the Nebaunaubaewuk see a pretty girl on the shore or playing around in the water and they grab her, drag her down to the bottom of the lake and make her into a nebaunaubaequae. It's a real concern for parents. But you — you are old enough to be No'okomiss. Nebaunaubaewuk honour No'okomiss. Steal only young girls."

"Will they steal Romy?"

Lionel appeared to consider this for a moment, then shook his head. "No," he said. "She is also too stringy."

"Well, that's certainly a relief," said Verna. "Knowing that neither Romy nor I will be abducted by lascivious Indian mermen if we should decide to swim in the lake."

"We prefer the term 'First Nations,'" Lionel reminded her.

At that moment, Jude lurched to life. First he lifted his head. Then he sniffed the air and cocked his ears. Then he rolled over, stood, and stretched. He shook and loped over to the carton containing Donald's cremains. As Verna watched, he applied his nose ravenously to the box before yelping — the sound made her jump — and wagging his tail.

"Shit!" she breathed, shaken.

"What?"

"Shit, Lionel, is my *father* here?"

Lionel shrugged. "Sure. Of course. What do you think? They're all here. Everybody's here. Everybody who belongs to the lake."

"And Aunt Margie?"

"And your grandfather."

All of a sudden Verna remembered Bob — Bob, who, to the best of her knowledge, *Resquiat in pace* in a Dumpster on the way to Greater Gammage. "But not Bob?" she begged him. "Tell me Bob's not here."

"Who's Bob?" asked Lionel.

Verna let out a sigh of relief and cast her eyes heavenward. "Thank you, Jesus!"

"He's not here, either," Lionel told her.

"I'm talking to dead people," Verna marvelled. "Which leads me to my next question: am I going insane?"

Lionel shook his head. "Nah," he assured her. "After a certain age, everybody talks to dead people. Just because people are dead doesn't mean you don't talk to them."

"Oh, yes, it does," Verna countered. "Crazy people talk to dead people. Sane people —"

"— do it when nobody's listening," Lionel finished her sentence.

"The difference is: the dead don't talk back," said Verna.

"How do you know?" Lionel asked.

Trumped, Verna stood. "I'm going to bed," she announced. "I'd say good night, only you're dead, so you can't hear me."

"Okay," said Lionel.

"Fern and Dad aren't here, either, so I won't bother saying goodnight to them."

"Suit yourself."

"And, while we're on the subject, how come I can see you, but not the others? It's not like I knew you or anything. I mean, when you were alive."

"All I know is I heard somebody say my name and, all of a sudden, here I was," replied Lionel. "Don't ask me to explain it. I'm new at this myself."

"Okay," said Verna. "I guess. Well, I'm off. Come on, Jude." She took hold of his collar; he was reluctant to go. "Come on, boy," she insisted. "Time for bed! Come on, boy." *Don't worry, Jude. He'll be here tomorrow. Right here. I promise. Come on. Time for bed.* She dragged him by the collar to the door, opened it, and shoved him inside. As she closed the door behind them and turned the key in the lock, she heard Lionel softly say, "Yes, it is. A beautiful, starry night."

Then, "Yes, me too."

Friday, May 20, 2005

The third night in her father's bed was dreamlike, due, she suspected, to the narcotic effects of the OxyContin. Well, how not? Typically Verna did not waft, but she had that night. Wafted upstairs. Wafted out of her clothes. Wafted into bed and into sleep, where she had bobbed upon a sea of dreams until twittered awake by tightly wound warblers already busy about their day. Hell, she had even wafted awake! Actually, *materialized* was more like it — a gentle marshalling and then a commandeering of those vibrant molecules that added up, in this particular configuration, in this particular dimension, to Verna Macoun Woodcock.

A scratching sound. She turned her head on the pillow — a larch clawed at the window. *I'll have to speak to Winonah about trimming that back,* she thought. *Is she even coming today? Did we make arrangements? Oh, yes. We did. That's right. That's good.* Verna had difficulty remembering past the previous evening, spent in a distinctly altered state on the screened-in porch with Romy and Lionel and Jude, of course, always Jude, but possibly others, as well. Not Bob, however. Thank God for that. Lying there in the belly of the bed, she felt a momentary pang of guilt at having disposed of her husband's … well, his "cremains," so cavalierly. Or maybe it was indigestion that she felt. In any case, it passed quickly. She sat, stood, and, floating over to the window, peered out past the insistent larch towards the lake, which exhaled mist like frosty breath into a sky of heartbreaking blue, its wind-rumpled skin cerulean.

"Perfect morning for a swim," she announced. Then, realizing what she had just said and the fact that she had spoken earnestly rather than sarcastically, she clapped her hand over her mouth. "Where did that come from?" Was she channelling someone? Her father? Because that was just the sort of crazy thing he would have said on a brisk May morning when jumping into the lake was like jumping into an ice bucket. And then he would have done it — jumped in. He had always maintained — not with an air of superiority, but with a grateful wonder — that he owed to this regimen his longevity and general good health and, indeed, he had remained more or less hearty until death had flipped his switch at eighty-three. "This is getting creepy," she told Jude. "Am I becoming my father?"

The dog blinked up at her from his dugout on the rag rug.

"And look at me! I haven't changed my clothes since Tuesday morning. My *underwear* is three days old, Jude. Do you know how disgusting that is?" In fact, now that she thought about it, she had yet to do anything beyond splashing water on her face since she had set out from Toronto. What must Carmen have thought when she saw her at the Pump and Munch? She looked like a homeless person. Mind you, Carmen had looked like she'd had a serious run-in with a plate of poutine, but Verna was reasonably sure that the realtor was wearing cleaner underwear than she was. "I am so going to the dogs," she told Jude. "No offence, but I've got to get cleaned up."

Jude thought this was a good idea. He beamed, then panted, the big pink triangle of his tongue lolling.

Verna picked her jeans up off the floor and hung them over the back of the rocking chair. She pulled off her T-shirt, bra, underwear, and tube socks, balled them up and threw them onto the seat of the chair. Then she dug into her suitcase and extracted a pair of overalls, an orange T-shirt (overalls ≠ bra), and a fresh pair of pitters, which she laid out on the counterpane. "But first a bath," she told Jude and, taking from its hook on the closet door Donald's old flannel bathrobe — muted browns and grays embroiled in plaid (she sunk her nose into it — wood smoke) then put it on and tied the sash. She opened the door to the hall and peered down it to the bathroom at its end.

The door to Fern's bedroom was open. Was Romy still asleep? What time was it, anyway? Didn't young people sleep ridiculously late? She had heard they slept until noon sometimes. Would she wake her by sneaking past her door? Did she care?

Jude, however, had his own agenda. Coming up from behind, he squeezed past her into the hall, scrambled towards the stairs, and then toppled headlong down them in a barely controlled fall.

Verna winced. Of course. He needed to be let out. He needed to be fed. She tiptoed gingerly down the hall, making a wide arc in front of Fern's open door and deliberately not looking in, lest eye contact be made with a possibly awake niece, sparking a conversation that Verna, at this early hour, did not feel remotely up to. Not yet. Not without serious reinforcement and certainly not without coffee. She found

140 • Melissa Hardy

Jude looming over his dish in the kitchen, every fibre of his being taut with anticipation. Below his juicy muzzle, a sea of drool expanded across the linoleum squares.

"Pavlov's dog had nothing on you," she informed him, picking up his dish and measuring out three scoops of kibble from the bag of Iams. "I don't suppose there's any point in suggesting that you chew." She replaced the dish on the floor, closed her eyes and counted: "One-Mississauga! Two-Mississauga ..." At "Six-Mississauga," she heard the slurp of water — he was done. "Okay," she said. "Let's go jump in the lake." Wait a minute, she thought. Jump in the lake? Why was that ringing a bell?

In the meantime, Jude, his eyes straight ahead and his expression fixed, was slowly backing his way out of the narrow passage created by the juxtaposition of table and counter. It was like watching an eighteen-wheeler cautiously negotiate a tricky reverse. *Beep. Beep.* Once in the clear, he wheeled around and bolted for the hall. Verna followed. She found him before the front door, vibrating. What was it that Donald used to say about dogs?: *They have a great capacity for joy.* "Your enthusiasm comforts me," she told Jude, unlocking the door and pushing it open. She followed the Lab the length of the porch and opened the screen door. Jude burst out, ricocheting from one edge of the lawn to the other, his leg hiked, until, a bladder's worth of urine spent, he bounded over the rock wall and into the lake.

"I really should go for a swim." Verna spoke the words out loud to see how they sounded — crazy or not so much? It was the Friday before the May 2-4 weekend, after all. Official start to summer. *And how long has it been since I've swum in a lake? Years, probably. Years? Has it really been that long?* Oh, she had been in the ocean down in Florida, but that was different. Lakes are different. Lakes stay put. Oceans are always coming in or going out: they are here and there all at the same time. Lakes, on the other hand, are predictable. And she had always liked them. That was right. She had. Had liked slipping into them like one slips into satin pajamas. Had liked the feeling of being enveloped. How had it happened that she had forgotten that? For what had she set that pleasure aside?

Letting the porch door close behind her, Verna wandered out onto the lawn in her bare feet. The grass was wet with dew, the ground beneath, spongy. Jude barked as if to say, "Come on in! The water's fine!" She laughed for no reason at all. No, there was a reason. It was the dog's joy. It was infectious.

"It's too cold!" she called out to him, making her way across the lawn to the low stone wall separating the lawn from the cobble beach. Of course, her father and grandfather always used to swim in the lake at this time of year. And what about all those crazy people who belong to Polar Bear Clubs, who swim all winter long in freezing waters? "Okay, okay," she told the dog, "I'll stick my toe in. Test the waters. I'm not promising anything!" Verna negotiated the two-foot drop from the top of the wall to the beach and picked her way between the cobbles to the water's edge. Crouching down, she trailed her fingers in the water — velvety, cold. What was it? Five degrees Celsius, maybe. Too cold? What was it Dad used to say? "Cold is just a feeling!"

To which she and Fern would say, "Yes, a really, really bad feeling!"

"Oh, what the hell!" she said. The only person in a five-kilometre radius was Romy and she was probably still asleep. And even if she wasn't ... Verna turned back to the lake. What *is the best way to go about this, she wondered — by increments or all at once?* She decided in favour of all at once. In for a penny, in for a pound.

She walked down the beach, climbed the two steps up to the dock, and made her way to its end. She slipped off her father's bathrobe and was about to hang it over the back of the splintery Muskoka chair, bleached the colour of driftwood by decades of exposure to the elements, when she saw a battered leather case on its seat. She recognized it immediately — Donald's prized German binoculars. He must have forgotten to take them inside when he had closed the cottage the previous autumn. Odd. Donald had been always so careful with his things. Then again, he had been forgetful towards the end; he had been an old man, after all. She picked up the case and opened it. There they were — the Carl Zeiss binoculars that had passed down from her grandfather to Donald — lightweight, brass under the finish, with a times-eight magnification. She held them up to her eyes and, turning, surveyed the lake's opposite shore, a football field away — the view they gave her was sharp and clear. She could even make out what she thought must be lakeside daisy and Indian paintbrush dotting the alvar pavement. She replaced the binoculars on the chair and told herself that she must remember to bring them in with her when she went. She turned back to the lake. A slight breeze played idly with its surface, causing her to erupt in goose flesh. Hugging herself tightly, she closed her eyes and reeled off to one side and into the water like a gyroscope toppling off its axis.

The moment in which the lake absorbed her body was an attenuated one, a drawn out "now" in which she temporarily dangled, suspended, like a chunk of canned pineapple in one of poor dead Aunt Margie's infamous molded salads. The water seemed thick, somehow, gelatinous; it solidified around her, holding her in place. Then, time reasserted itself (no dallying; now she must kick her feet to stay in place), and, with it, sensation: cold! However, she mused, now that it contained her wholly, it was both colder than she had imagined and less cold than she had feared.

She kicked her feet once, twice, and surfaced. There was Jude, chugging laboriously toward her, his head lifted so that his chin just grazed the surface. He was a tugboat, not a diver; he only put his head underwater to retrieve. When he was within two metres of her, however, he did an abrupt about-face and headed toward the lake's eastern shore.

"Hey! Where'd you think you're going?"

Ducking underwater, she wriggled after him through the azure haze. Lake Marguerite was what geologists call a blue lake, not green with marl or stained the colour of tea by leached tannins. More light filters through a blue lake than a green or brown one, and to greater depths, making for an abundance of aquatic vegetation. Verna remembered the summer Fern and she campaigned for weed removal — their twelfth, when they became convinced that, if only the lake's bottom were not so weedy, cute boys might come to swim. To no avail. Donald would hear nothing of raking or herbicide, not even if it promised to improve his daughters' love lives. "Fish have to have something to eat, somewhere to hide from bigger fish," he had reminded them. As if the needs of fish mattered.

She came up for air and saw that Jude was heading toward a patch of shallow open water just a little deeper than she was tall, over which a colony of bullhead lilies was in the process of extending itself — a floating canopy made up of heart-shaped lily pads thrusting compressed balls of yellow bud up to heaven. This was about ten metres up lake from the dock. "Where do you think you're going?" she cried. Then, when he persisted, "Crazy dog! You're going to get yourself all tangled up!" Ducking underwater again, she snaked after him toward the forest of swaying root stalks. She had just about closed the distance between them, when, once again, the Lab did a one-eighty and veered off the lily-pad colony and back out into open water.

"You're leading me on a wild goose chase!" she yelled after him. "That's it. I'm getting out!"

She was about to turn around and swim back to the dock when it occurred to her that she hadn't peered at the underside of a lily pad colony for over forty years, not since she and Fern had played at being mermaids in the forest of wavering root stalks — those long, hollow tubes through which oxygen flowed from the lake's surface to the fleshy rhizome anchoring the lily to the silt bottom. She ducked underwater, and, reaching into the tangle of stalks, parted them. A rush of tiny fish blew past her like scattering wind. Dog-paddling, she peered around her. It was just as she remembered: the water was different here than in other parts of the lake — not blue, but green and slippery with nutrients. Sunlight flowed through gaps in the pad canopy, illuminating the hazy underwater world, showing her the thickly veined underside of the pads, the adventitious roots below the leaf base to which other rhizomes — these ones creeping and horizontal — clung to form a loose, vegetative weave. The veins were burgundy-coloured; the stalks smooth, a burnished gold. She was thrusting her face farther into the forest of root stalks when, suddenly, she came eye to eye with a huge walleye. Startled, she retracted her head and the fish exploded past her into open water. She surfaced, and, treading water, gazed around her at the expanse of floating leaves, the yellow buds as tight as fists. *Beautiful*, she thought. *Peaceful. Not cold at all. Well, not so much.* Closing her eyes, Verna allowed herself to float on her back, there among the lilies. The velvety water caressed her. It buoyed her up. With its fingers it stroked her hair — far more tenderly than any lover ever had, which was to say Bob, because there had never been any other. Lover, that is. Sad. That's what that was. Just sad. Well, that part of her life was over and weren't bullhead lilies supposed to be good for something? Some ailment? Oh, yes. Donald used to rub thin slices of its root on her and Fern's childhood scrapes and cuts, saying, "This is how the Ojibway treat their wounds." *I am so out of my element*, she thought. *Floating. Floating ...*

Her reverie was shattered by a shrill screech, "Auntie Verna! Omigod! Help! Help, somebody, help!"

Verna's eyes snapped open. She craned her head to look down lake in the direction of the dock. There stood Romy, Donald's binoculars hanging from their strap around her neck; she was wringing her hands and baying like a beagle. Verna squinted. Was Romy wearing sleepers with feet? She was — pale blue ones screen printed with white woolly lambs and crescent moons. What grown person wears sleepers with feet? "Romy! What the ...?" she began.

Romy gasped. "Auntie Verna!" She clapped her hand over her mouth. "Omigod, you're alive!"

"Of course I'm alive. Did you think I wasn't?"

Romy nodded, gulping. Her eyes and nose were red, her yellow skin blotchy. "I thought you were dead. That you had drowned yourself. Like Virginia Woolf. She put stones into her pockets and walked into an oozy river."

"It was the River Ouze," Verna corrected her. "And don't be silly. Why would I want to drown myself?"

"I don't know. Maybe because of what I said last night. About you being old and alone and all. And what about your Auntie Margie? She killed herself."

"Yeah, but I'm not my Aunt Margie." Verna said. "At any rate, not to worry. I'm not wearing anything with pockets." Righting herself, she began to wade through the lily pads toward the open water separating the colony from the dock. She felt like Godzilla with heat-rash chafed thighs — ponderous and clumsy. The lake bottom was gooey; she could feel with her toes the water lilies' knobby rhizomes poking through the silt.

Woof! Woof!

Jude paddled out to meet her. *My trusty dog,* she thought. "Hi, there, Jude! How's it going?"

Extracting herself from the forest of root stalks, she stepped out into open water a little higher than her waist.

"*Eeuw!*" Romy cried. "Auntie Verna, you're naked! Totally gross!" She turned away, snatching up the binoculars and pressing them to her eyes.

Verna chuckled darkly — cackled, actually. "Have I got news for you, kiddo! One day you're going to look like this!" *If you live long enough,* she thought. *If you don't blow away.*

No doubt about it. Verna felt great. Better than she had in a long, long time. She stretched out her arms, making a V-for-Victory shape with them. She lifted her chin and thrust out her chest so that there was an arch in her lower back. She felt better than she could remember feeling for … well, forever, maybe. No mutinous knee twinges, no sulky stomach steeped in vitriol, no clicking, clanging jaw hinge or aching gums. An early morning swim in a cold lake. That was the ticket.

"Anyway," she said, "except for you and Jude, there's no one around to see."

"Oh, yeah?" Still holding the binoculars to her eyes, Romy pointed toward a stretch of dusky woods on the lake's opposite shore. "What about *him?*"

Twisting to look in the direction where Romy was pointing, Verna shaded her eyes with her hand and squinted. She could just make out something that might be a person — or possibly a bear — silhouetted against the green backdrop of balsam fir and white spruce on lake's opposite shore; the distance was too great for her to be able to discern anything further. She ducked down to cover her nakedness. "What is it?"

"It's a man," replied Romy. "A creepy-looking man."

"Creepy? What do you mean 'creepy'?"

"Sneaky. Jumpy. Creepy."

"Well, don't just stand there," Verna said. "Get my bathrobe! There on the dock. That plaid thingy."

Jude, picking up on their agitation, went to bark and inhaled a big gulp of water instead. This made him hawk, *"Aagghhh! Aagghh!"* Verna grabbed the dog by his shoulders, turned him around, took hold of his hindquarters and pushed him, honking, ahead of her as she duck-waddled toward the dock.

The sound of a car rattling loosely down the rutted laneway, its emphysemic muffler wheezing as it pulled into the parking space — unmistakably Winonah's decrepit Impala. "It's all right, Auntie Verna," Romy informed her. She lowered the binoculars. "He's gone."

"Gone? Good!" Verna shoved Jude, still making elaborate retching noises, towards the shallows and clamored onto the dock. She took the bathrobe Romy handed her.

"Who was that total perv?"

"I have no idea." Verna slipped on the bathrobe and tied the sash around her waist. It had never occurred to her that she and Romy might not be perfectly safe in a house five kilometres from the nearest other human habitation, surrounded by dense northern Ontario woods ... or even that they might not be alone. The realization that they were not was not a comforting one. "What did he look like?"

"I don't know. Flannel shirt. Baseball cap. This gingery beard."

"Gingery? You mean red?"

"Gingery — kind of an orange red."

"How old was he?"

"How should I know? Old. Not as old as you, but old."
She shivered. "He gave me the willies!"

"Yeah, well …" *Me, too*, thought Verna.

They looked on with relief as Winonah rolled from her
car and trundled across the lawn in their direction. Verna
stepped off the dock onto the lawn. "Are we glad to see
you!" she told the round little woman.

Winonah looked wary. "Why?"

"We saw a strange man in the bush!" Romy exclaimed
breathlessly.

Winonah snorted. "Welcome to my life!"

"No, really! We did! Over there! Through these binoculars" She pointed towards the lake's opposite shore. "And
Auntie Verna was *naked!*"

Verna flushed. "I was skinny-dipping, okay. I didn't
know there was a guy in the woods."

"Ack! Ack! Ahhhh-ack!"

Winonah glanced at Jude. "What's with him? Trying to
cough up a kidney?"

"Granddaughter!" A shrill caw from the Impala. "Granddaughter! Come over here and help me out!" The Impala's
passenger side door creaked open and a wooden walking
stick emerged from it and waved in the air like the rattle of
an eastern Massasauga.

"It's my no'okomiss," Winonah explained. "Just a
minute! I'm coming!" Crossing around the front of the
car to the passenger's side, she pried the walking stick
away from its brandisher, leaned it against the side of the
car, then bent down. A scuffle ensued, at the end of which
she resurfaced with a tiny wizened nut of an old woman
— no more than four feet ten inches tall — with patchy

white hair and a pronounced dowager's hump. The crone was clad in a faded calico duster held together with two buttons and a series of safety pins — its colour was indeterminate — grey or toast or mauve. Over this she wore a stretched-out-of-shape formerly yellow cardigan of the sort affected by Mr. Rogers. She looked like a cantankerous apple doll. Grabbing the walking stick from Winonah, she stumped bow-legged up to Verna and stared fixedly up at her with eyes as bright and as fierce as a ferret. "Uh?" she grunted.

Verna was at a loss as to how to respond. "Uh … hello," she stammered. "Winonah's granny … we've heard a lot about you. I'm Verna Macoun."

"I know who you are," grumbled the old woman, who then fixed her beady gaze upon Romy. "Who are you?" she demanded.

"Romy," the girl replied, sliding behind Verna as if for protection. "She looks like a really scary gnome," she whispered to Verna.

"Shush!" Verna hissed back.

"These two just saw a man in the bush," Winonah told Granny. She spoke slowly and loudly. Apparently Granny was deaf.

"Eh?" The old woman cocked her head.

"A-man-in-the-bush," Winonah repeated.

Granny scowled, shook her head. "That's no good. Man in the bush. What kind of man? White or red?"

"White," replied Romy.

"That's bad," said Granny. "White man in the bush. What was he up to? Nothing good, probably. Doesn't look good. Not good at all. Give me a smoke, Granddaughter."

Winonah extracted a cigarette from the unmarked pack in her pocket and handed it to Granny along with a Zippo.

"Can I have one, too?" Romy asked.

"Romy!" Verna looked daggers at her niece. To no avail.

"Please!" Romy begged. "I want to try a butt-legged cigarette."

Winonah shrugged. She removed two cigarettes from the pack and handed one to Romy. "Your ancestors gave our people blankets infected with smallpox," she told Romy. "We gave you tobacco." Granny passed the lighter to Romy who lit her cigarette, then passed it to Winonah.

"What did this white man look like?" Granny asked, puffing away at her cigarette like the little engine that could.

"He was wearing a flannel shirt." Romy remembered. "And a baseball cap."

"Great," said Winonah. "You've just described every man within a five-hundred kilometre radius of here. How old was he?"

"Old," replied Romy. "Maybe forty."

"Anything else?"

"He had a beard. Kind of a reddish colour."

"A red beard," said Granny. "Not good news. Means he has a temper. A bad temper. I knew a priest had a red beard. He used to bugger all the little boys at school."

"Ooh!" Romy breathed.

"Nothing else?" Winonah asked.

Romy shook her head. "It was like a minute and then he was gone."

"Probably just some hoser wandering through," concluded Winonah. "There's some that live in the bush all year round. Hermits, like."

"Or a windigo. Or a blood stopper. Or a bear walker," said Granny.

Romy tugged at Verna's bathrobe. "What's a windigo? What's a bear walker?"

"You don't want to know," Granny assured her. "It would scare the shit out of you. You would never go outside again."

Lionel's occasional woolly manifestation may have ceased to unnerve Verna; not so the flesh-and-blood presence of a strange man at the lake's shore. Suddenly it seemed more imperative than ever to keep the formidable Winonah close at hand even if it meant inventing tasks for the handywoman to do. Accordingly she marshalled her forces. "Say, Winonah, now that you're here, I mean, I noticed that the larch outside Dad's window needs cutting back. And wouldn't it be a good idea to caulk the windows and doorsills?"

"Maybe tomorrow," Winonah told her. "Today Granny and I are going to return my brother's ashes to Mother Earth so that his spirit can begin its journey to the Sky World." She sounded oddly formal.

Finally, thought Verna, relieved and, at the same time, slightly saddened by the thought of Lionel wending his way to some Happy Hunting Ground, never to be seen again. She had grown to enjoy their little brushes and certainly he had given her some good advice. "You've come to pick up Lionel's cremains, then?"

"Shhh!" Granny hissed, putting a bony finger to her lips and wagging her head. "Don't say his name, Verna. If you say his name, he might think you want him to stay. He's been around too long as it is."

"Since the Spring Pow Wow. Two months," Winonah confirmed this. "Way too long."

"Usually, it's ten days, eh?" Granny said. "For our people. But the stupid white undertaker guy in Beverley, he made a mistake."

"Two mistakes," Winonah clarified.

"Two mistakes," Granny agreed. "First mistake is he goes ahead and cremates him without even asking us."

"Ojibway, we bury our dead," explained Winonah. "Not burn them in a big old oven."

"Second mistake is he loses him," Granny continued. "The cremains, that is. Only turned up over the weekend. In some shed out back."

"Just a minute." Romy was incredulous. "The undertaker lost Lionel's cremains?"

"Shhh!" Granny warned her. "No names!"

"If he's even in that box," said Winonah. "And not somebody else they're pawning off on us."

"Oh, I'm pretty sure it's him," Verna said.

Winonah looked at her strangely.

"What?" Verna asked.

Winonah frowned. "We need to borrow your dad's canoe."

Verna was puzzled. "Sure, but why?"

"So we can get to the glen."

"Why do you want to get to the glen?"

"That's where we're scattering his ashes."

"I'm sorry," said Verna. "You're talking about our glen? The one on the other side of the lake?"

"I'm talking about the glen that was an old Ojibway burial ground a long, long time before your grandfather came here," Winonah reminded her sternly. "Yes. I'm talking about *our* glen."

"Gee!" exclaimed Verna, her mind in sudden, headlong freefall. The stranger had been on the southern shore of the lake, right where they would have to land to reach the grove. Maybe splitting up wasn't such a great idea. "I have an idea!" She hadn't, but she felt one coming on. "Wait! Wait!" She held up her hand, squeezed her eyes closed, and furrowed her forehead, forcing the thought front and centre. "Here it comes! I've got it! Why don't we make an outing of it? All go together. Kill three birds with one stone? I mean, we've got to scatter Dad and Fern's ashes sometime. Why not today?"

"Yay!" cried Romy.

Winonah was less than enthusiastic. "Not a good idea," she warned. "A bad idea." To her way of thinking, the scattering of Lionel's ashes should be a private affair with only her and her grandmother present. There were aspects of the ceremony that Romy and Verna would not understand, that they might possibly mock afterwards, when they were alone together — the speeches that would have to be made so that Lionel's spirit might be released from its duties on earth and given sanction to move on to the Sky World, the burning of tobacco, the invocation of the four directions on the medicine wheel. The thought that they might mock this set her teeth on edge.

But Romy was not to be deterred. "Come on!" she cajoled the handywoman. "It'll be fun."

In the boathouse they found a cottonwood canoe slung from the ceiling and a small skiff — a flat-bottomed rowboat with a pointed bow and a transom stern — bobbing sluggishly in one of the two slips. Donald had steadfastly refused to own any watercraft equipped with an outboard motor. He didn't like fiddling with machinery (he wasn't good at it), but mostly it was the noise — like a bone saw jangling through cartilage and gristle he said. And, in truth, the lake was not so big that getting from one end of it to the other was arduous.

Verna had forgotten about the boathouse. She had forgotten how it smelled — of water as thick as soup and sodden pilings shaggy with rot. She had forgotten the way it sounded — creaky and reverberant with the reflected sound of water lapping against the pilings and the skiff's straight sides. She had even forgotten the way the air bottled up inside of it felt — moist and sticky with cobweb that draped down from the ceiling beams to graze her as she passed below, to briefly cling to arm and face — the boat-house was an arthropod paradise, teeming with expectant spiders. *Best not to mention that to Romy*, Verna thought. She was bound to be terrified of spiders. What Verna did recall was how spooked she and Fern had been of the boat-house when they were younger, scared to go into it on their own, but not because of spiders. No. They had been convinced that some monster — some thing of death by drowning — lurked in the murky water below the jumbled floor. *Mishepishu*. That was its Ojibway name — the unpre-dictable one, the one who pulls boaters and swimmers to their deaths, the hidden form beneath the ice. Looking around her now, she thought that perhaps they had been right, that it had been some thing of death by drowning that had come in the night to take Fern that bleak October four years earlier; that even now was biding its time. She repressed a shudder. *Don't be silly*, she told herself. *It's an old, smelly boathouse. End of story.*

While Granny sat in the old Muskoka chair at the end of the dock, chain-smoking and muttering incantations as she crumbled loose tobacco into the lake — offerings to the mishepishu and whatever other manitous might inhabit its depths — Winonah, in some dudgeon, pre-pared for the short journey across the lake to the glen. First she hauled up the boathouse door. Then she took down the canoe, and, with Verna's help, lowered it into the second slip. Next, she removed a paddle from its hook on the wall and put it, along with the sturdy plastic LCBO bag containing not only Lionel's cremains, but Fern's and Donald's, as well, in the canoe's hull. "Are you ready?" she asked Romy and Verna. She sounded grumpy. She was grumpy. Not only had she not wanted the white women's company in the first place, she and Granny had ended up having to wait for an hour while Verna bathed and Romy agonized over what to wear to what was, after all, the next best thing to her own mother's funeral. She finally settled on a baggy black dress that made her look that much more ill. And that made Winonah angry. It exasperated her. Why in a world of trouble someone would not eat seemed perverse to her, fundamentally ungrateful. "Coming?" she repeated fiercely.

Romy, chewing hungrily on her middle finger, eyed with trepidation the canoe, twenty feet long with a shallow arched hull, a rockered bottom, and a moderate degree of tumblehome. "We're not going in *that*, are we?"

"You have a better idea?" Winonah growled.

Romy appealed to Verna. "It looks tippy. Don't you think it looks tippy?"

"It's a canoe," said Verna. "That's how canoes look. And it's not just any canoe. It's the canoe my grandfather — your great-grandfather — paddled all over this part of north Ontario when he was a surveyor for the Crown."

"So it's not only tippy," said Romy, "it's *old*. Really *old*."

"Look, it wasn't my idea to make this a party," Winonah intervened. "If you don't want to go in the canoe, fine. Go some other time. Walk. It's no skin off my nose."

"There's nothing wrong with this canoe," Verna attempted to reassure Romy. "Dad had it restored a few years ago. I remember him talking about it. Some place up on Lake Temagami."

"It's too small," Romy objected.

"Don't be silly," Verna told her. "It used to hold all Granddad's gear." Her father had kept all of George's instruments — his Dollond's sextant with the ten-inch radius, his artificial horizon, his solar compass, his micrometre and aneroid barometers, his brasses ... beautiful things, really. She wondered how much they would fetch on eBay. "He could get his camping equipment into it along with

156 • Melissa Hardy

three months' worth of provisions. It'll sit four easy with room for the dog."

"The *dog?*" Romy asked.

Winonah had had enough. "Come on, Granny. Let's get going."

"No, wait," Verna implored her. She turned to Romy. "If you don't want to come, you can stay here. I can scatter Fern's ashes."

"But I do want to come! I do! I just don't want to go in a canoe. Can't we go in that rowboat thing?" She pointed to the skiff.

"*Clang! Clang! Choo-choo!* All aboard!" Granny announced, imitating, Verna could only imagine, a railroad conductor. "*Woo! Woo!* This train's leaving the station, eh? All aboard!"

Winonah helped Granny into the canoe, steadied it while the dog clambered in, then climbed in herself. Picking up the paddle, and, without a backwards glance, she brought its blade forward along the side of the canoe, dipped it into the water, and drew it straight back, propelling the canoe out of the boathouse and into open water.

"Great!" Verna was exasperated. "Now we have to use the skiff."

"The skiff! Hooray! But you'll have to row, Auntie Verna. I'm feeling kind of lightheaded or something."

At some point the skiff sprang a leak. Unfortunately for Verna and Romy, they did not discover this until they were in the middle of the lake. Verna because she was still fuming — paddling the skiff solo was far more work than paddling the canoe in concert with Winonah would have been; only half way and already her shoulders and upper back had started to ache; her hands, too, unaccustomed to gripping oars;. As for Romy, she wiggled and squirmed and nattered nervously on and on about this and that: "Oh, it's so beautiful here, Auntie Verna! What would you call that colour that the lake is? I would call it 'midnight blue.' Do you see the clouds reflected in the water? What kind of clouds are those? Are those nimbus clouds or cumulus clouds? Auntie Verna! Is that a dragonfly? Why do they call it a dragonfly? It doesn't look like a dragon." When she did pause to catch her breath and glance at the bottom of the boat, she gasped with horror. "Omigod, Auntie Verna! What is that?"

Verna, disgruntled, followed her gaze. Water was pooling at the bottom of the boat. "What? What do you think it is? It's water."

"I know it's water. Do you think I'm an idiot?" (*Well, yes,* thought Verna unkindly.) "What I want to know is what's it doing on the bottom of the boat?"

"There must be a leak. Don't worry. Boats leak. It'll be fine."

"What if it isn't fine?" Romy demanded. "What if the boat sinks?"

"It's not going to sink."

"But what if it does?"

Honestly, Verna thought. "Romy! It's only a little water."

"Oh, yeah? It's more now."

"No, it isn't."

"Yes, it is. Look!" And she pointed.

She was right. The bottom of the skiff was now covered with water an inch deep. Verna could feel it start to seep through the canvas of her sneakers. *Don't overreact,* she told herself. *Go into downplay mode. Otherwise Romy will go ballistic. She's teetering on the edge as it is. She's always teetering on the edge. What is wrong with her, anyway? Doesn't she realize that youth is everything, that she's obsessing away the years that matter? That, in the end, this is what you're left with: only this. For example: me. I am left. And it's not bloody much, not at all.* "Remember Archimedes' principle of buoyancy." A clumsy attempt to dampen the girl's evidently escalating panic — one which turned out to be entirely unsuccessful.

"*What?*" Romy made a horrible creaking noise.

"'A body immersed in a fluid is buoyed up by a force equal to the weight of the displaced fluid.' You know, Romy. The principle of buoyancy. *Archimedes.*"

"Archie *who?*"

"Oh, Jesus, never mind! Look, all I'm saying is that, as long as we don't take on too much water, we'll stay afloat long enough to get to shore. Worst comes to worst, we come back in the canoe. Or walk."

"What if we don't *get to* shore?"

"What if? What if?" Verna closed her eyes. God, what an exasperating child! "Why are you such a Chicken Little all the time? 'Oh, Auntie Verna, the sky is falling, the sky is falling!' The sky is *not* falling and this skiff is *not* sinking. And, even if it is, — and I'm not saying it is — we just swim to shore."

Romy wrung her hands. "But I can't!" she bleated.

"Can't *what?*"

"*Swim!*"

Verna blinked. "What do you mean you can't swim? Everybody can swim."

"Not everybody!" Romy insisted. "Me, for example."

"Your father — that Paul guy — he didn't teach you how to swim?"

"No!"

"What kind of a father is that?"

"The kind that doesn't teach his kid how to swim."

"My dad taught us how to swim. Hell, it was practically the first thing he taught us."

"Well, my dad didn't. He was too busy chasing tail."

Verna shook her head. "Well, all I can say is that if he had left you with your mother, you would have known how to swim. Fern was a beautiful swimmer. She swam like a goddamned mermaid. Both of us. Like mermaids."

"*Oooohhhh!*" Romy wailed, pointing to the bottom of the skiff.

Sure enough, the water was continuing to rise. They weren't going to make it to shore. Not at this rate.

"Okay," Verna told Romy, "I can get us both to shore. But you have to promise not to panic. Do you promise?"

Romy moaned and shook her head. Closing her eyes, she hugged herself tightly and began to rock back and forth.

Verna reached over and took hold of her forearm. She shook it. "Romy, Romy, listen to me. You've got to promise not to panic! I can't save you if you're freaking out. You've got to trust me! Do you trust me? Romy, do you trust me?"

An eerie wail. *"Aaagghhh!"*

Apparently not. Laying down the oars, Verna took stock. The water level had risen to about six inches now — fully a third of the skiff's depth — and the lake's southern shore was still half the lake away. Should they bail now? The last twenty feet or so would be in shallower water. All she had to do was get Romy from here to there. From there they could walk to shore. She leaned forward, and, prying Romy's arms open, gripped her forearms. "Okay, Romy," she said. "Open your eyes. Open your eyes, now! Look at me!"

Romy opened her glaucous eyes and blinked wetly. She looked terrified.

"Listen closely," Verna told her. "I'm going to drop off the side into the water and then you're going to climb out after me and hold on to the side of the skiff. I'll come up behind you. Then, when I tell you, I want you to let go of the boat and float on your back. I'm going to hook my arm over your chest and sidestroke us into shore. But I can only do this if you stay calm. Do you understand?"

Romy just stared at her, stricken.

"Do you understand?" Verna repeated.

Romy gulped, then nodded.

"Okay," said Verna. "I'm going in."

She had just started to rise from her seat when, "Auntie Verna, don't leave me!" Romy cried and lunged for her.

"Romy, no!" cried Verna. Too late. The boat tipped over, dumping them both into the lake. No sooner had Verna registered that she was in the water than Romy tackled her full-on, shrieking like a banshee and wrapping her arms around her neck. It was like being tackled by a skeleton swathed in sackcloth — four metres of black crinkle-cloth swirled around them. "Romy, stop it!" Verna gasped, dog-paddling to stay afloat as she flailed at the buoyant dress, trying to beat it down. "You're going to drown both of us!" Romy, however, was too busy trying to climb on Verna's head to pay much heed. In desperation, Verna reached out and grabbed hold of the first piece of the capsized boat that came to hand — the stern — and held on. "Romy," she managed. "Romy! Hold on to the skiff!" With her right hand, she shoved Romy away from her and toward the boat's gunwhale at the same time as she wrenched herself free, and, twisting, dived downward into the lake.

For a split second, relieved at having escaped her niece's frantic clutches, she continued to bore downwards, the light disappearing one wavelength at a time as she pushed toward the lake's ink-blue bottom. Then, just before she was due to run out of air, she detected movement in her peripheral vision — the heave and pitch of what must have been the silvery tail of a very big fish — a fish bigger than any she had ever seen in fresh water. She turned to look after it and found herself gazing, instead, into a pair of round fish eyes. Then adrenaline ripped through her like a chainsaw. She twisted away and shot back to the surface, coming up this time on the opposite side of the capsized skiff. She grabbed hold of the gunwhale and gasped for air, her heart racing. *Jesus!* She thought to herself. *What the hell kind of fish was that? It was the size of a porpoise!*

"Auntie Verna! Is that you?"

"Yes. Yes. Just let me catch my breath." *Thank God*, Verna thought. *She hasn't drowned. Not yet, at any rate. Don't mention the giant fish. That will only freak her out more. If that's even possible.*

"Auntie Verna, I'm so cold! I don't think I can last much longer."

"Oh, for God's sake, Romy! Buck up!"

"But ...!"

Woof!

There was a huge splash toward the bow, out of which Jude emerged in an explosion of water drops. Romy and Verna looked up to see Winonah pulling up alongside them in the canoe. She poked the skiff with her paddle. "I guess that patch didn't hold," she said.

"What patch?"

"There's a hole in the keel. I told my brother duct tape's no good for fixing boats."

"*Duct tape?* He patched a hole in the skiff with *duct tape?*"

"That boy!" Granny cackled. "He was a rascal, all right! Not too bright."

"You knew that there was a leak in the skiff and you let us take it anyway?" Verna demanded.

Winonah shrugged. "It might have worked. You can never tell. Actually it worked pretty good. Got you all the way to the middle of the lake."

Verna was on the verge of saying something tart, but stopped herself. No point alienating the handywoman, especially not in the middle of a lake with a capsized boat, an anorexic who couldn't swim, a strange man lurking in the bush, and some monster fish swimming around in the waters just below them. She made do with, "Here, you grab her arms and pull while I push. Romy, being catatonic is not helping the situation!"

"Hee! Hee!" Granny laughed at the sight of Romy in her wet weeds. "Looks like Old Crow fell into the mud puddle!"

It was one o'clock. While Verna, Granny, and Winonah sat at the kitchen table eating Campbell's beef and vegetable with barley soup, Romy lay curled up in a tight ball on Fern's bed, under a heap of covers and wearing a musty-smelling pair of her mother's oversized flannel pajamas. She said she was cold. She actually was — too cold. Spurred on by some atavistic quasi-maternal impulse, Verna had insisted on taking her temperature. Ninety six degrees. No wonder the girl's teeth were chattering and her hands and feet felt like ice.

Two hours had transpired since Winonah had returned Verna and Romy, soaking wet, to the dock. While they had dried themselves off and changed clothing, Granny had curled up like an old cat on the living room sofa under one of Frieda's afghans and napped. In the interim, the indefatigable Winonah had towed the capsized skiff back to the boathouse and hoisted it up onto the dock. She seemed in altogether better spirits than previously. Possibly the capsizing of the skiff and the dunking of its two occupants had provided her with a measure of cheer.

"Do you think we should go out again?" Verna asked distractedly. "Maybe while Romy's asleep?" She was having difficulty getting the image out of her mind of a near-naked Romy, glimpsed through a half-closed door as she stepped out of her sodden widow's weeds and into Fern's pajama bottoms; of her naked back, all shoulder blades and bumpy spine, with her two flat pancakes of deflated buttock riding atop broomstick legs. Indeed, Verna had been so shocked that she had pushed the door to Fern's room shut — ostensibly out of respect for Romy's privacy, but really to spare herself the sight. The girl looked like a walking skeleton. She had no subcutaneous fat. None whatsoever. Of course, she had looked thin to her from the get-go, even ultra-thin, but not this thin. Not *uber* thin; not Auschwitz poster-girl thin. Suddenly Verna understood the reason for Romy's layered look, the baggy style she espoused. She chided herself: *Why did I so blithely accept her statement that she had "checked out" of whatever the name of that rehab facility down in Guelph was and that that was all right? What kind of an aunt am I?* She knew the answer to that question: a bad aunt. A really, really bad aunt. Just like she had been a really bad sister.

Granny shook her head. "Unlucky," she said, sucking broth. "Tomorrow we'll try again. The Nebaunaubaequaewuk, maybe they're trying to tell us something, eh?"

"The who?" The word rang some kind of distant bell in Verna's memory. "Are you talking about the mermaids? The ones who live in the lake?"

Granny looked up from her soup and squinted quizzically at Verna.

"How do you know about Nebaunaubaequaewuk?" Winonah demanded.

It was on the tip of her tongue to say, "Lionel." Instead Verna muttered. "I don't know. Maybe Dad?"

"They look out for us, the Nebaunaubaequaewuk," said Granny. "It is wise to listen to them."

Winonah pushed her empty bowl away from her and stood. "So, Verna, you wanted me to do something today?"

"Huh?" asked Verna. "Oh, sorry!" She rooted around in her brain for the tasks she had come up with earlier to keep Winonah close at hand. "Something ... doors and windows ... Maybe we should recaulk ... and, oh, I know, the larch, the one outside Dad's window. I noticed this morning that the branches are scraping at the pane."

"We'll need sealant, then." Winonah decided. "And a caulking gun. The one in the tool shed is pooched. And we could use some real food. I'm tired of soup. What about some wieners?"

"How about fish sticks?" said Granny.

"Baloney is good," said Winonah.

Verna sighed. She had thought to get by largely on what Donald had left in the pantry, supplemented by small purchases at the Pump and Munch, but along the way she seemed to have collected additional mouths to feed — apparently Granny Madahbee now numbered among these. Romy, on the other hand ... what had the girl actually eaten since she had arrived yesterday morning? A few spoonfuls of soup? *I have to make her eat*, she decided. She tried to imagine Winonah holding the girl down while she wedged gelatinous chunks of Spam into her protesting mouth. Winonah would enjoy that.

But, of course, that wouldn't work. How can you force someone to eat? Especially someone as determined not to as Romy. *But you could entice her*, she thought. *Get foods she would like. What do anorexics like, anyway? Carrots? Celery? Clear broth? Boiled eggs?* "Okay," she agreed. "I guess it's time to do a proper grocery shop. Is there still a grocery store in Beverley?"

"There's Wenger's," said Winonah. "I'll come with you. We can pick up sealant and a caulking gun at the

Home Hardware. And I can show you what Granny and I like to eat."

"But ..." Verna lowered her voice. "What about Granny?"

"What about her?"

"Doesn't she ... want to go home?"

"No," replied Winonah.

"But what about Bingo?"

"Bingo's on Wednesday. Today is Friday. There's no Bingo on Friday."

"But I thought she didn't like white people ..."

"She likes it here," Winonah said. "She told me. This is a good place, she says. She will sit on the porch and watch the lake while we're gone. She will watch out for your niece." Verna must have looked doubtful, because Winonah added tartly, "No'okomiss raised six children and sixteen grandchildren by hand. She has strong dreams, my grandmother. That skinny white girl could do worse than be left with her."

"The lake is better than TV," Granny observed with satisfaction. "So much going on."

Before setting out for Beverley, Verna checked in on Romy. Curled up into a ball of jutting bones under the purloined Indian tapestry, she appeared to be sleeping, albeit fitfully. Across her downy, sunken face expressions ranged confusedly — she twitched, eyes rolling under the nearly transparent lids; she sucked her breath in short gasps, in hiccups; pieces of her jerked — a broomstick arm, a shrivelled leg. Even in repose the girl seemed uneasy, preyed upon.

Standing there in Fern's room looking down on Romy with Jude at her side, Verna experienced what might be described as a Lassie moment. "What's she dreaming about,

boy?" she whispered to Jude. "Is she dreaming about rabbits?" Then, "Stay with her, boy. Keep her safe."

Jude panted in apparent agreement. She patted him on
the head and went downstairs. He followed.

"Will you at least guard the house?" she asked.

But Jude, restored by his recent nap, wriggled around
her and headed for the lake.

"Are you coming?" Winonah sounded impatient. She
was down by the Volvo, ready to go.

"On my way!"

Then, just as she was closing the front door behind,
"Auntie Verna!" A querulous cry from upstairs. "Auntie
Verna, if you're going into town, could you pick me up
some cigarettes?"

"No way!" Verna shouted back.

"Virginia Slims!"

"You heard me!"

"What's the biggest lake fish you've ever seen?" Verna
asked Winonah on the drive back from Beverley. "I
mean, not ever, but from this part of the country." She
was thinking about the monster fish she had encountered
while diving to escape Romy's clutches that morning.
Behind her on the back seat were bags of processed food
and various petroleum by-products — Cheez Whiz and
head cheese, potted ham and Pop-Tarts. Just looking at
it would probably catapult Romy into a full-scale panic
attack; Verna had been close to one herself as the cashier
had rung up the contents of her cart — each additional
item another nail in the coffin of nutrition. Truly, it was
a measure of her desperation to keep in Winonah's good
graces that she was willing to ply her with a mountain of
crappy food.

"I saw a walleye your dad fished out of this lake that was going on ten pounds," replied Winonah. "And a four-foot long muskie, but that was from the river."

"Four feet, eh?" Verna asked, chewing on her lip. That didn't sound nearly big enough. The fish that she had encountered that morning must have been five feet long at the very least. Or six. But was it a fish? That was the real question.

"Why do you ask?"

Should she tell the handywoman that she thought it was possible — just possible — that she might have had a brush with a local mer-person that morning? What would Winonah think? Would she think she was crazy? She chickened out. "Oh, nothing," she said. They rode on in silence for a few minutes.

"We need to stop in Greater Gammage," Winonah informed her. "I want to give Carmen her cigarettes."

"Oh, all right." Verna was reluctant. She did not feel quite up to Carmen's over-the-top ebullience at the moment; the largesse of her. Not without a stiff drink. "But let's make it quick, okay? I don't want to leave Romy for too long. This low body temperature thing of hers has got me worried." She pulled up in front of Black River Realty. To her relief, the storefront was dark. "She must be closed," she concluded gratefully.

"Oh, Carmen never closes," replied Winonah, retrieving two cartons of unmarked cigarettes from under her seat. "She hibernates sometimes. In the winter." She got out of the car, crossed the sidewalk, and rattled the doorknob. "Carmen? Carmen, are you there?"

"Come on in!" came a voice from within — unmistakably Carmen's, throaty and rippling with twang.

Winonah pushed the door open. The office exhaled a brown cloud of cigarette smoke out onto the street.

"Hey, Winonah, is that you?" cried Carmen. "And Verna! Verna, are you trying to hide?" Verna had ducked down behind the steering wheel; now she re-emerged, mortified. This seemed, however, to in no way faze Carmen. "Come on in, you two," she called cheerfully. "Help me celebrate."

"Okay," Winonah agreed and trotted into the office.

"Verna!" yelled Carmen. "Get in here!"

Verna sighed and got out of the car. She crossed to the office doorway and peered in. The feature-sheet-encrusted front window provided scant natural light; by it she could just made out the imposing heap that was Carmen, piled onto her chaise lounge with a Tim Hortons double-double in hand. On either side of her was a round side table topped with overflowing ash trays; on one of these sat a bottle of Tia Maria. Tia Maria. Things were looking up.

"Here are those smokes you wanted." Winonah handed Carmen the two cartons of butt-legged cigarettes.

"Outstanding," said Carmen, setting them down on the floor beside her. "Would you two ladies care to join me in a celebratory drink? I just sold the old Gauthier place and this here's what you might call my victory dance." Clearly Carmen's victory dance was a sedentary affair, more metaphorical than literal, although she did look festive in a hooded purple *jalaba* trimmed in gold braid — like a large and colourful hobbit.

"Sure," said Winonah.

"I'd like that," said Verna.

"Get yourself a couple of glasses, then. If you don't mind a few random germs." Carmen pointed to a jumble of coffee mugs and glasses on the shelf on top of a file cabinet. "To my way of thinking, people are way too paranoid about germs these days. All these wipes and gels — wipes for this and gels for that — and sneezing into your elbow instead of your hand ... what's that all about?"

"The elbow is the new hand," said Winonah.

"You got to eat a peck of dirt before you die," said Carmen.

Verna fetched two dusty tumblers sporting ancient lipstick stains on their rims — one coral, the other vermillion. Fishing around in her overalls, she retrieved the tail of her T-shirt and discreetly wiped the insides of the glasses before pouring each of them a drink. "Cheers!" She raised her glass.

"Cheers!"

"Cheers!"

They drank.

"Why do you have the lights off?" Verna asked.

"Saving on electricity," Carmen explained breezily. "Saving the planet. Meditating. Actually I don't want to blow a fuse while I'm test-driving my new smoke eater. The electrical in this building isn't exactly what you'd call up to code."

Verna listened. From somewhere within the shadowy confines of the office, an air purifier hissed; the stench of tobacco that dominated the room was edged by the metallic smell the purifier exuded.

"Doesn't it do a great job?" Carmen was enthusiastic. "It arrived yesterday from down south. Some outfit in St. Catharines. The things they can do these days! I tell you! Technology. But, hey!" She snapped her fingers. "I almost forgot. There was somebody come by here looking for the cottage, Verna. Yeah. About an hour ago. I was busy presenting the offer, so I just gave him directions."

Verna was puzzled. "I wonder who that could be. Nobody knows I'm up here. Except for Dad's next-door neighbour in Toronto." *Nobody knows because there is nobody to know,* she thought ruefully. *I could be the sole survivor of a nuclear holocaust and I would not be more alone than I am now. Sad, but true.* "Did he give a name?"

Carmen shook her head. "Nope," she said. "He was driving a pick-up, though. Sort of a dark green."

"Hey, I wonder if it's that guy you saw this morning."

"What guy?" asked Carmen.

"A guy snooping around the lake."

"Wow! You think?" Verna turned to Carmen. "Was he wearing a flannel shirt?"

"Maybe."

"And a baseball hat?"

"Definitely."

"What colour was the shirt?"

"I can't remember," said Carmen. "To tell the truth, I didn't pay much attention to him. Just told him how to get to the cottage and that was it."

"Oh, my God," cried Verna, panicking. "Romy and Granny! Winonah, we have to get home!"

As the Volvo emerged from the laneway, they spotted the mud-encrusted hunter-green truck parked next to the Impala at a slight angle. In its cargo compartment was a jumble of tools and equipment — spreaders, aerators, and seeders, and a lawnmower — against which were piled shovels, spades, and rakes of various descriptions. Winonah read aloud the decal on the tailgate: GOOSEN'S ORGANIC LANDSCAPING. RECOMMENDED BY MOTHER NATURE.

"That's a late-model Toyota Tacoma," Winonah observed admiringly. "Nice ride."

"Goosen," fretted Verna. The name pricked at her memory like a tickle in the throat — a small, but compelling irritant. "Goosen — why do I know that name?" Pulling the Volvo up alongside the truck, she threw it into park and climbed out, followed by Winonah. "Hello," she called, coming around the front of the truck. She half-walked, half-ran to the steps leading to the cottage, followed by Winonah. "Granny, are you there? Romy?"

Jude exploded into joyous barking from the screened-in porch. She heard the scramble of his claws across the wooden floor.

"Hey, Jude!" Verna bounded up the steps, Winonah on her heels, and flung open the porch door. A second later, eighty pounds of enthusiastic, wet dog hit her square in the kneecaps. Knocked off balance, she staggered back into Winonah, causing the handywoman to pitch backwards. Twisting to one side to avoid coming down on her tailbone, Winonah came down hard on her knees instead. Then Verna toppled on top of her. Winonah collapsed under her weight and the two of them lay there for a moment, Winonah face down, Verna face up, while Jude, delighted, pranced about the resulting heap.

The floor creaked. The sound of footsteps.

"Are you all right?"

Verna cranked her head to the right: scuffed work boots with steel toes and the frayed bottoms of faded blue jeans. She looked up — a lanky, boyish-looking young woman wearing a blue baseball cap and a faded green-and-navy Maine guide shirt came into view. Her tanned face was devoid of makeup, her dark, thick eyebrows appeared never to have been plucked, and the hair that poked out from under her cap was short, dirty-blond, and choppy.

"I think so," Verna managed.

"Speak for yourself!" Winonah fumed. "I'm suffocating!"

"Oh, stop complaining!" Verna rolled off the handy-woman and onto the grass.

"Here," said the stranger, squatting down and extending a hand to her. It was her left hand, rough, calloused, and soil-stained, the fingernails chewed short and dirty. Verna took it gingerly and allowed herself to be pulled to her feet.

Winonah climbed up on her knees. "Geeze, Verna, how much do you weigh?"

"How much do *I* weigh?" Verna snapped. "That's the pot calling the kettle black!"

"Verna! Winonah! Stop your fighting! We got company." The ragged voice of Granny from somewhere within the bowels of the porch. "Go on, girl. Tell her who you are. I forget."

"It's Paisley," the girl said. "Paisley Goosen."

It was as though the name had thrown a spanner into Verna's works and sent her into sudden cognitive arrest. Her faculties, such as they were, came screeching to a screaming halt. She stared at the girl, dry mouthed and gawping — gawping again! — like a fish on a dock.

"You know, Auntie Verna," the girl said, her brow furrowed, her dark, small eyes — the colour of blueberries — pleading. "My mother was your sister."

"I came across Granddad's obituary in the *Globe and Mail*," Paisley explained. She and Verna sat on the porch drinking coffee. After putting away the groceries, Winonah decided that Granny had had enough excitement for one day and that she was taking her back to the rez. This was not, however, until after they had prepared for themselves a small feast of fish sticks, beans and wieners, and Eskimo Pies.

"See you tomorrow!" Granny called gaily.

Verna winced at the mention of Donald's obituary. One of his former students, now a distinguished professor at the University of Toronto, had written a glowing tribute to Donald that had appeared in the *Globe and Mail*'s "Lives Lived" feature in the week following his death. "A beloved teacher who had communicated his passion for Canadian history and the Canadian wilderness to generations of high-school students, blah, blah, blah ..." Mrs. Rothman had rung up to ask whether Verna had seen it. In fact, she had missed it entirely. She had skimmed that day's paper as she always did. She had even skimmed the section of the paper in which it appeared. But her eyes had bounced off her father's obituary like a stone skipped across water. It had not occurred to her that the individual described as "Inspirational teacher" and "Authentic Canadian" might be so humble and unimportant a man as her father and so she had not registered the name "Donald Macoun" when it appeared in conjunction with these tributes. By the time Mrs. Rothman called (and to her shame), Verna had recycled that issue of the paper, so her neighbour cut it out and left it for her in her father's mailbox.

"Ah, yes," she said now. "The obituary."

"Actually it was my partner who spotted it," said Paisley. "The obit."

"Who?" asked Verna.

"My partner."

"Your partner in the landscaping company?"

"No, my life partner."

Life partner, Verna thought. *So that was what they were calling them these days.* She wondered what sort of man would be attracted to a woman so, well, androgynous as Paisley. And it was not just her appearance. It was her manner, as well — how she walked with just that hint of low-slung swagger, the way she was sitting at that very moment, her knees falling casually open, feet planted, sharp elbows on her thighs, and rough hands clasped as she stared out at the lake; the matter-of-fact way she smoked (another smoker!) and cracked her knuckles and her neck. It was easy to see how Carmen had mistaken her for a man.

"It was a great tribute," Paisley ventured. "Even though I didn't really know him ... I don't know. It made me feel proud to know that he was my grandfather."

"Me, too," said Verna. "That he was my father." In fact it had surprised her, or, to be more precise, surprised *and* saddened her — that someone she did not know, someone who claimed to speak for many others whom she also did not know, had felt so strongly about her father. She had found Donald's preoccupation with history tiresome, his fascination with the natural world nerdy in the extreme. What others perceived as positive attributes, she had seen as foibles — sometimes charming and endearing, more often annoying.

"I mean, I sort of knew him," Paisley continued. "I have a dim memory of him."

When would she have last seen Donald? Verna wondered. Probably the same time Verna had last seen the children, before Fern took off out west. That would have been back in '85 or '86, before the various fathers of Fern's children had begun to pick them off, one by one, starting with Tai. She peered at Paisley and thought for the first time that she saw in the rangy young woman — all elbows and hipbones, all collarbones and knees and shoulder blades — the forthright tomboy she had been. Defiant and very dirty. Fern had not been a big believer in baths.

"I remember you, too," said Paisley resolutely, forging ahead. "I remember you yelling at us for walking on the furniture."

"You were little savages," Verna told her. *After all, why lie?* "And I had just had those chairs re-caned at very great expense. Your father ... that was Ben, wasn't it? Ben the woodworker?" She had been turning that one over and over in her mind — whose daughter Paisley was. Because Fern had had so many men — not just the fathers of her children, but others, as well, tucked into the spaces in between. After a while, last names just dropped off and Fern's men had become for Verna and Donald, "Ben the Woodworker," or "Paul the Painter," or "Hindi Jag," or "Kenny, the Jesus Freak," or "Brian, the Waiter." "How is he anyway? Ben?"

"He died last year," said Paisley. Verna could see that she was a solemn young woman. There was a heaviness about her, as though she carried around with her invisible items of great weight. "M.S."

"I'm so sorry," said Verna.

Paisley shrugged; she looked anguished. "He had a good life. Except for the last couple of years. They were pretty crappy." She blinked back tears and rubbed her nose and then her eyes with her sleeve. "He was a good father though. I'm grateful for that."

"There's a table he made upstairs," Verna remembered — a feeble effort to cheer the girl up. "A beautiful one carved out of oak. Maybe you would like it."

"I have a whole house full of beautiful furniture that he made out of oak," Paisley told her dejectedly.

"Well, of course you do."

They sat silently for a moment. Verna stroked Jude's bumpy head, her mind stuck in cognitive malfunction, gears grinding, while Paisley stared intently out at the lake as though she expected it to do something. Then the girl cleared her throat. "And Mom?" she asked. "The obituary said that Granddad was survived by you. Just you. It didn't mention her. It didn't mention any of us ..."

Here it comes, Verna thought. *What I've been waiting for. What I've been dreading. The* mea culpa, mea maxima culpa. *Again.* She reminded herself of a dung beetle, only her ball, the one she rolled through life, that seemed to be getting bigger by the day, was a stinking aggregate of remorse. She sagged into the chair, closed her eyes, took a deep breath, and hopped aboard a whole new groundswell of freshly minted guilt. "Your mother died four years ago," she said. "Cancer. Cervical cancer." She waited a beat, then launched into her apology, "I'm so sorry, Paisley. We didn't know how to get in touch with you. We should have tried harder. *I* should have tried harder. I feel just terrible about it." Why did the words sound so hollow, as though she were shouting them through cupped hands from the bottom of a well? What was it Donald used to say? "When it comes to children, you pay now or pay later. You never *don't* pay." Well, she was paying now and they weren't even her children. And wasn't that just typical — Fern skipping out and leaving her to pick up the tab?

"I know she's dead," Paisley told her. "My partner looked online on the government site — the public records site."

Verna opened her eyes and stared at her. "You can do that?"

"Well, you have to buy a subscription," Paisley replied glumly. "So I drove to Toronto and went to the house on Indian Crescent and knocked on the door. A neighbour heard me and came out."

"Mrs. Rothman?" *Mrs. Rothman*, thought Verna — *a Jewish version of the Greek chorus who greeted visitors to the Indian Crescent house with a doleful, "Lo! She has gone to northern Ontario to scatter the ashes of her sainted father and prodigal sister! You wouldn't believe how much that dog eats."*

"She told me that you had come up here, that you were going to scatter Granddad's ashes. And Mom's. That's why I came. Dropped everything and came north. I remember this place, you know. I was here a couple of times when I was a kid. I knew it was just outside Greater Gammage and that I could ask once I got that far. I thought I might be in time."

"In time for what?"

"To scatter her ashes," Paisley replied. "And to get some answers."

"Well, as it turns out, you are in luck," said Verna. "At least as far as the ashes go. Granny didn't tell you?"

Paisley shook her head. "She was on about something. Her school days, I think. Something to do with kids getting frostbite and having their toes cut off. To be honest, I couldn't follow it. And I was ... you know ... nervous about meeting you, about being here again after so many years. I was pretty distracted."

"We were going to scatter them today, but there was an accident and ..." Suddenly Verna remembered Romy. "Heavens!" She clapped her hand over her mouth.

Paisley looked startled. "What?"

"Romy! I forgot all about Romy!"

"Romy?"

"Your little sister Romy."

Paisley looked stricken. "Don't tell me she's dead, too!"

"No, no! Of course not," Verna assured her. "Well, not yet anyway. No, she's right upstairs. Sleeping. In your mom's bedroom. She sort of fell in the lake today. Long story. "

Paisley blanched. She swallowed. "Really?" she said, sounding a bit strangled. "Romy's here? Little Roo?"

Verna winced at Fern's nickname for Romy. "She arrived yesterday," she said. "I know! Let's go wake her up!"

Verna paused just outside of Fern's bedroom door. Taking hold of Paisley's arm and drawing her close, she whispered, "I have to warn you. She looks pretty ... you know ... terrible."

Paisley stared at her, confused. "What?" she whispered back. "Terrible? Why?"

"Are you talking about me?" A voice from within the room. Apparently Romy had awoken from her nap. She sounded weak and aggrieved.

Verna grimaced at Paisley, shook her head, neutralized her expression, and opened the door. There was Romy, huddled in the rattan Peacock chair with the heavy Indian tapestry wrapped around her. "You're up!"

"Duh!" Romy replied listlessly. She peered past Verna into the hall where Paisley, suddenly shy, was hanging back. "Who's that?"

Verna took Paisley by the arm and steered her into the room. "It's your sister," she said. "Your sister Paisley. Come up from ... where have you come up from, Paisley?"

"Port Hope."

"Port Hope," Verna repeated.

"My sister?" Romy blinked. She looked bewildered. "Really? My big sister Paisley?"

Paisley took a step forward, then halted — it was as if she wanted to rush to Romy and embrace her, but was unsure what the occasion required, what would be allowed her. Instead she wrung her hands. "Yeah," she croaked. "Do you remember me?"

Romy gulped and shook her head. She drew the Indian tapestry tighter around her, up to her chin. "No," she said in a small voice. "But I've thought about you. I've pictured you."

"I remember you," said Paisley. "You were — what? — four when I last saw you. Little Roo. Mommy's Little Roo." A lone sob escaped her — *"Yeep!"* — and dangled potently on the air. She lumbered across the room and awkwardly gathered up the bundled-up bones that was Romy in a big bear hug.

"*Ooph!*" managed Romy.

"Now, isn't this a nice surprise?" asked Verna. She sounded like somebody's grandmother, maybe, but definitely not like herself. She sat down on the bed, feeling extraneous.

Contact having been achieved, Paisley released Romy and stepped back. Her expression turned solicitous; doubtless she had been able to surmise that the body beneath the tapestry was little more than skin and bones. "Are you all right, Little Roo?" she asked. "Because you don't look so good."

In fact, Romy looked ghastly. Her skin was the faintly bluish-white resembling the colour of whey; her eyes the slippery colour of boiled eggs on the verge of going bad.

"All right?" Romy laughed weakly. "Well, if you want to know the truth, not really. My electrolytes are unbalanced and it's making my heart act all funny."

"Your heart?" demanded Verna.

"Funny?" asked Paisley. "What do you mean — funny?"

"Flip-flopping," said Romy.

"Your heart?" Verna repeated. "Flip-flopping?" That didn't sound good. In fact, that sounded really bad.

"As in … what?" Paisley knelt beside the chair. "As in palpitations?"

Romy gulped. She nodded. "Yeah. And I feel kind of dizzy."

"Oh, my God!" Verna cried. "She's having a heart attack. Twenty-one years old and she's having a bloody goddamned heart attack!" Fragments of a song popular in her youth burst out of locked storage and into her consciousness. Something about white lace and promises. Who the hell had sung that? The Carpenters? Of course, it was the Carpenters — Karen and Richard. Karen Carpenter — an anorexic icon, an anorexia role model, a pioneer on the forefront of eating disorders. Karen Carpenter, who died at a ridiculously young age of a heart attack. *What to do? What to do? Oh, right: call 911!* "Paisley," she croaked, "call 911!"

"No!" Romy protested, grabbing Paisley by the hand. "Don't, Paisley, please. It's just my electrolytes. It's happened before. It happens all the time. Really! Don't call 911. I'm just shaky."

"You're having heart palpitations," Verna said. "That's not the same thing as 'shaky.'"

"You don't understand!" Romy pleaded. "All I need is a Diet Coke and a banana. It'll fix me right up."

Verna and Paisley stared at her.

"Trust me!" Romy insisted. "Diet Cokes and bananas are high in potassium. If I get some potassium, I'll be all right. Please, Auntie Verna, if you call 911, they're going to take me to a hospital and weigh me and put me on a drip and run all these tests and call in a psychiatrist and I'll have to stay in a ward with crazy people and ..." She looked terrified. Stricken.

Suddenly it became clear to Verna. "You've been admitted before for this, haven't you?"

"For what?" asked Paisley.

"She's an anorexic," Verna explained. "Romy! Come on now. You've been admitted before for this."

"Anorexic?" Paisley repeated. "Shit! Really? Roo? Well, she always was a fussy eater."

"This is beyond fussy. Romy!"

Romy cast her eyes down. She nodded.

"How many times?"

Romy shrugged, not meeting Verna's gaze.

"How many?"

Romy muttered something.

"Speak up!"

"Four times," Romy said. "All right? Four times before I went to the Birches."

Paisley turned to Verna. "What's the Birches?"

"A rehab centre," replied Verna. "In Guelph. She's supposed to be there right now, but she checked herself out."

"Roo!"

"Well, it was boring." Romy defended herself. "Snacks every five minutes and you have to finish them or else. And they watch you like a hawk. You're never alone: Not even in the bathroom. Always some gargantuan, sour-faced nurse watching, watching."

Verna stood and walked to the end of the bed. She took Romy's hand in hers — it felt like a dead fish. "Romy, you're sick," she said. "You look like hell."

"Yeah, well," said Romy glumly. "Tell me something I don't know."

"I'm worried about you," said Verna. "And I don't know what to do. My mother died in childbirth. I don't know how to be a mother."

Romy snorted. "You've got that right!"

"Are you sure that it's your potassium levels are causing this?" Paisley asked.

"Of course I'm sure. Like I said, it happens all the time."

Paisley turned to Verna. "Because a Diet Coke and a banana would fix that," she said. "I played basketball in high school and that was what the coach would give us if we got shaky."

"So you're absolutely, positively sure it's your potassium levels?" Verna asked Romy.

"One hundred percent. Scout's honor. So help me, God," Romy swore.

"And are you absolutely, positively sure that will fix it?" Verna asked Paisley.

"If it's her potassium levels, yeah, it will," replied Paisley.

"Well, okay," conceded Verna reluctantly. "But, if it doesn't work right away, we're calling 911. Deal?"

"Deal! Thanks, Sis! Thanks, Auntie Verna." Romy slumped back in the chair and closed her eyes. She looked both profoundly relieved and near to death, waxen.

"Damn!" Verna realized.

"What?" Paisley asked.

"We don't have Diet Cokes or bananas. And I just went to the bloody store."

"I've got to run out for cigarettes anyway," Paisley offered. "I can pick up a case of Diet Coke and some bananas while I'm at it. There was some convenience store I passed coming out of Greater Gammage ..."

"The Pump and Munch," said Verna. "That would be the closest place."

"Pump and Munch?"

"Cigarettes!" Romy remembered. "Did you get me any cigarettes at the store, Auntie Verna?"

"What do you think?" Verna asked. "Of course I didn't."

"Could you get me a pack, Paisley? Please! Please!"

"Sure," said Paisley. "What brand?"

"Mom's brand," said Romy. "Ultra-Light SuperSlim 100."

"Hey!" Paisley cried. "Mine, too!"

And the girls burst into a somewhat pitch-challenged rendition of the sixties jingle: "You've come a long way baby, to get where you've got to today; you've got your own cigarette now, baby, you've come a long long way."

"You remembered!" Paisley cried, rapturous.

"Of course!" said Romy. "How could I forget?" She turned to Verna. "Mom used to sing it to us at bedtime," she told her. "It was ... like ... her own personal lullaby."

"Good times," said Paisley.

"Good times," Romy agreed.

Half an hour later, Paisley returned from the Pump and Munch with a twelve-can case of Diet Coke, a bunch of bananas, and a carton of Ultra-Light SuperSlim 100s.

"Thanks for doing this," Verna said.

"She is my sister," Paisley pointed out.

Together they walked up the steps, across the lawn, and onto the screened-in porch. Opening the front door, Verna called up the steps to Romy, "The cavalry has arrived!" She turned to Paisley. "What are electrolytes, anyway? Are they related to phosphates?"

"Beats me," said Paisley.

"Better get some ice for that Coke," said Verna. "And a straw."

From deep within the study, the old English drop-dial clock told the approximate time — cottage time — in bongs; it was going on nine. Verna and Paisley sat on the porch, watching in stunned silence as darkness gathered over the lake, deepening its hue to sombre navy. To the west a band of orange edged the treeline — vibrant at first and pulsating, before fading to umber, then draining away entirely. Then colour began to desert the lake, like a crowd slowly dispersing now that the spectacle that was day had ended.

It was Paisley who broke the silence. "Who would have ever thought eating a banana was such a big deal?"

Verna shook her head. "It boggles the mind."

First there had been the lead-up: when presented with an actual banana, Romy revealed that it might not be possible for her to do such a thing as eat it. Yes, she knew she had *said* she would. She had *thought* she could. Honestly! But now ... now, she wasn't so sure. There were many reasons for this. Bananas had a lot of calories for a piece of fruit — one hundred and five for a medium! And this was a freakishly large banana. It was the biggest banana she had ever seen. To make matters worse she didn't like bananas. Never had. It was something about their texture. And what about those stringy things, the one between the banana and its peel?

"Phloem bundles?" Verna had asked.

"Yeah, those," said Romy. "They are really disgusting. They make me want to barf."

Then came the bargaining phase. Romy would eat a half the banana; surely half the banana was enough. It was after all a HUGE banana. No, Romy must eat the entire banana. What about a third of the banana? Romy! A deal was a deal. The whole banana.

Once Romy had, at last, accepted the necessity of eating the whole banana, she had to psyche herself up for it. This involved eying the banana as though it were an explosive device that might detonate at any moment — as though she were an unwilling, coerced suicide bomber. It entailed shuddering, gasping as though she were hyperventilating, and one ten-minute-long freak-out complete with sobbing, shrieking, and something resembling convulsions.

When that had run its course, Paisley tried another tack. "I know," she said. "We'll all of us eat a banana together. You, me, and Auntie Verna."

She and Verna each unpeeled a banana. Ate it.

"Ummm, good!" said Paisley.

"I'm not two!" Romy objected, sullenly.

"Well, you're acting like you are," Paisley shot back.

Finally Romy, having played all her various cards, began to eat the banana. Actually, she began to gum, suck, and nibble the banana. Very, very slowly. Every few moments, she would stop, moan, and slump to one side, eyes squeezed shut, as though overcome by the great effort she was expending.

In the end they had tussled over the last quarter of the banana, which Romy declared had a brown spot, rendering it inedible.

"Only because you squeezed it!" Paisley told her.

"Did not!"

"Did, too!"

"But I can't eat it," Romy wailed. "It's all mushy!"

It was when she began to make gulping, retching noises — *"Ba-lug! Ba-lug!"* — that Verna gave in and let her feed the rest of the banana to an enthusiastic Jude.

"Was that ever *weird*!" Paisley said now.

"Oh, yes," Verna agreed.

By the time the banana-eating exercise had been accomplished, it was nearly eight o'clock. The ordeal, start to finish, had taken upwards of an hour. Paisley had risen then, saying that she needed to make some phone calls, and gone downstairs. Verna had stayed with Romy until the girl had slid into a noisy doze, her breath rattling around in her boney carcass like an animal in a trap. It was only then, when Verna was relatively sure that Romy was down for the count, that she had gone rummaging in the girl's discarded clothes for the bottle of OxyContin. After tunnelling down through several sedimentary layers of clothing — first Fern's, then Romy's — piled onto the floor beside the bed, Verna had surfaced with the orange prescription bottle, which she had tucked into the front pocket of her overalls. Followed by the attentive Jude, she had tiptoed from Fern's room, leaving the door to the hall slightly ajar.

Verna roused herself. "Are you hungry?"

"Yes, no, maybe. Maybe a little something. You?"

"Not really. All those bananas." They had each eaten three to Romy's almost one. "But maybe we should."

"After what we just witnessed, I'd say so. Never before have I been so convinced that eating is a good thing."

"A very good thing," Verna agreed, thinking that drinking was also a very good thing — she was desperate for a cocktail. "Let's go inside and I'll heat something up. I'd light a fire, but I don't remember how."

"Oh, I can light a fire," said Paisley, brightening.

While Verna poured herself a hefty vodka and tonic in the kitchen (making up for lost time), Paisley crumpled up old newspaper that Donald kept in a twig basket beside the river-stone fireplace for the purpose and placed it under the grate. She selected kindling from a galvanized tin tub to one side of the basket, arranged it on the grate, and added some more newspaper. Then she picked up the canvas log tote and walked to the kitchen. "Where's the woodpile?" she asked.

"On the back porch," said Verna. "Just outside the door. Want a drink?"

"Got any beer?"

Beer? Verna thought. "I'm afraid not."

"Got some Coors in the truck," said Paisley. "I'll get one once I've got this baby going." Suddenly she exuded an air of breezy competence. Clearly things like starting fires fell squarely within her area of expertise, her comfort zone.

Verna opened a can of beef stew, held it upside down over a saucepan, and gave it a shake. A tube of congealed stew slid wetly into the pan. Paisley reappeared with the tote full of logs and headed back to the living room.

As Verna broke up, then stirred the gelatinous goo into something resembling stew, Paisley stacked the wood horizontally on the grate, leaving gaps for air to pass, and alternating the stacks so that the wood formed a mesh. She checked to see if the damper was open and the draft was moving up the chimney. Then she lit the kindling and the newspaper with her lighter, and, crouching in front of the fireplace with the poker, prodded the first small licks of flame into a bona fide fire.

She appeared once more in the kitchen door. "We're in business!" she announced. Crossing to the sink, she rinsed her sooty hands under the tap. "I'll get that beer from the truck. A cold one would go down good right about now." She left by the back door. Verna poured herself another vodka and tonic — a double this time — and slopped the stew into bowls. She put the bowls on a tray, together with her drink, a pile of paper napkins, and two big spoons, and headed for the living room. Setting the tray down on the coffee table, she stood for a moment, looking at the fire Paisley had built, marvelling at how it gave sudden life to the cavernous room, lit up its dark corners and made it a place you wanted to be. Paisley wandered in with her beer. "There's nothing like a fire," she observed.

Verna looked at her with surprise. "That was what your grandfather always said."

"Well, it's hardly profound."

"I guess not." Verna sat down on the sofa. "Who were you calling earlier?"

A little hesitation. "My partner," Paisley finally replied stiffly. She sat down in one of the armchairs. "To let her know I got here safely. You know."

"Her?" The pronoun just slipped out.

Paisley cleared her throat nervously. She leaned forward and picked up her soup bowl. She looked uncomfortable, anxious. "Yes, her," she said tensely. "Jill."

"Jill?" repeated Verna.

"Jill. That's her name."

"I see," said Verna carefully, not sure she did. She poked around in her stew in search of vegetables and dredged up the remains of a carrot and a drab hunk of potato. Then she got it. "You're a lesbian!"

Stew sprayed from Paisley's mouth.

Verna wadded up some napkins and handed them to her. "Here you go."

Then, as Paisley started mopping up the chunks.

"Why didn't you say so?" Verna asked. "Although I guess you just can't go up to someone and say, 'Hi, my name's Paisley and I'm a lesbian.' Except maybe in a bar. A gay bar." The real question was why Verna hadn't put two and two together earlier? The clothing. The mannerisms. *Beer.* On the other hand, it wasn't as if she had proven particularly intuitive over the years. "Still, I'm your aunt."

"Yeah, the aunt who yelled at me for walking on the furniture," Paisley pointed out glumly.

"Well, that's hardly the same thing, is it?" Verna said. "Sexual orientation and bad manners."

Paisley took a swig of beer. "I guess not. Still, I didn't know how you'd react. People can be pretty bloody narrow-minded."

"The way I see it, heterosexuality is no picnic. It's not like my marriage was anything to write home about."

"Was? So you and Uncle Bob are divorced?"

"Better than that," replied Verna with a blitheness that surprised her. "He's dead. And then some."

"Dead!" Paisley was awkwardly solicitous. "I'm so sorry, Auntie Verna!"

"Don't be," Verna told her. "The world is a better place for him not being in it."

"Well, he was sort of a prick."

"He was a HUGE prick."

"Yeah, he was," said Paisley. "Was he always that way?"

"Pretty much."

"If that was the case, why did you marry him?"

Verna laughed. "To get my M.R.S."

Paisley looked blank.

"My M.R.S." Verna repeated. "It's a joke. Men went to university to get a B.A. Women got their M.R.S." Then, when Paisley still looked blank. "You know. The honorific. The *title*. *Missus*. When I was a girl, you were expected to marry. Or, at least, *I* expected *me* to marry. So I did. The first person who asked me. To tell you the truth, I didn't have a lot of choice as to whom. I was hardly the belle of the ball. Not like your mother." This triggered a memory that yawned open like a sinkhole and into which Verna tumbled headlong: "The Boys of Summer." Boys on foot, on bicycles and motorcycles or in the family car. Boys from all over — from Beverley, Greater Gammage, Val Gagne, and Iroquois Falls, from Timmins and Cochrane, or on vacation with families from down south. And every one of them came for Fern. Not Verna. Fern.

"So how did Uncle Bob die?" Paisley asked. "When?"

"What?" asked Verna, distracted. "Oh. Bob. His SUV was hit by a train. Two years ago."

Paisley gasped. "Jesus! Really?"

Verna nodded.

"That's rough!"

"It was more surprising than anything," reflected Verna. "I wasn't prepared for such a thing to happen. I hadn't seen it coming because ... well, because there was no seeing it coming. Although I must admit: I had thought about it. Not the train-hitting-the-car-*POW*-he's-dead thing. Just what would happen if he suddenly up and died. I sometimes find myself wondering whether my thinking about it might have caused it to happen or contributed to it happening." She considered this for a moment, then shook her head. "No," she concluded. "I'm not that powerful. I was, however, lucky. Lucky in this one respect, that is. Not lucky in most respects. But lucky in this." She hesitated, then, "You know what I did with his ashes?"

"What?"

"I put them in a garbage bag and gave it to Winonah to put in the Dempsy Dumpster on the way to town."

"You didn't!"

"I did."

"Jeez, Auntie Verna," said Paisley. "That's pretty harsh. I wouldn't want to get on your bad side."

They sat for a moment in silence, poking around in their stew.

Then, "I asked Jill to marry me," Paisley told her. "A civil union. Now that we can do that in Ontario."

"Oh? And she said yes?"

Paisley sighed. It was a heavy sigh, phlegmatic. "Not exactly. She says I'm too conflicted. That I have to deal with my issues and get some closure before she'll marry me. She doesn't want somebody with so much baggage."

Verna blinked at her. "I'm sorry. Closure? Baggage?"

"Oh, come on, Auntie Verna!" Paisley sounded miserable and exasperated all at the same time. "What baggage do you think? Family baggage. Family issues. Mom issues. Romy and Tai issues. The way it all went down. The way everything came undone. The fact that we were lost and nobody came looking for us. That we were a family and then, suddenly, we weren't. The fact that Mom did things that put us at enormous risk and didn't stop to think of the consequences. And now I find, to top it all off, she's up and died. So I can't ask her why she did what she did, which means I can't forgive her. And I want to forgive her. I do. But I can't. Because she's dead. Why the hell else do you think I'm here?"

"I see," said Verna, suitably chastened. "That baggage. Of course." How much of this was her fault? she wondered. Surely she could not be held to account for Fern's mistakes. Still, hadn't she been glad when the children were taken away? Secretly. Seeing Fern get her comeuppance? She stared into her stew. She didn't feel very hungry. "Paisley," she ventured, "what happened? I know that Ben came and got you, but that's all I know. Romy can barely remember your mother and God knows where Tai is. What happened that split you all apart?"

"You never knew?" Paisley sounded surprised.

Verna shook her head. "Fern never talked about it. As a matter of fact, she refused to talk about it. 'Sunny side up!' she would say whenever you or the others were mentioned. 'Water under the bridge.' Then she'd change the subject. Fast." What Verna also remembered, but did not mention was the stab of pleasure she had always felt in seeing Fern flinch at the mention of her children's names, then turn away. What a monster she had been. It shamed her now.

"Wow!" Paisley was clearly taken aback. "I thought you knew. You really didn't know? You and Granddad?"

Verna shook her head.

"Okay, then." Paisley put her soup bowl on the coffee table and sat back in the big chair. "Tai was the first to go. That happened when we were in the Kootenays. The Patels came and got him in the middle of the night. Not Jag. The family. Or some of the family at least. A gang of them. All I know was that one minute we're asleep — Tai and I were sharing a bed — and the next minute I'm waking up to this jabbering sound — it sounded like a flock of seagulls had descended upon the bed. They had just swarmed us — a whole pack of them — and snatched Tai. We never saw him again."

"Jesus!" Verna murmured.

"It was terrifying," Paisley said. "And absolutely chaotic. Dogs were barking. Hell, wolves were howling from the nearby park. Mom and I were both screaming our heads off. Romy was bawling ..."

"How awful!"

"Apparently Jag's family had finally managed to talk him into an arranged marriage — some girl from India — and decided that she should raise Tai, not Mom, so they just came and took him."

"And Fern didn't call the police?" Verna asked. "Surely it was a clear case of child abduction."

"Ah, now there's the rub." Paisley laughed ruefully. "The house we were living in was a grow-op. We were living there for free in exchange for Mom tending the crop. She was what is called a *farmer*. So calling the cops in was not an option."

"I see," said Verna.

Paisley stood, crossed over to the fire, and, kneeling down in front of it, scrutinized it critically, her head canted to the right.

"So what about you? What about Romy?"

Paisley took a poker from the stand and prodded the fire experimentally. "Maybe a year after they snatched Tai, Mom met this guy, Diego. He was a real spiritual guy. At least he thought he was. And Mom thought he was too. She was pretty frigging gullible. And she was still pretty cut up about Tai. Depressed. You know. So the next thing we know we're off to Brazil with Diego."

"I always wondered how you ended up there. It was such a weird place to hightail off to — Brazil."

Paisley replaced the poker. She stood. "You don't know the half of it, Auntie Verna. It just so happened that Diego was a member of the Children of God."

"The who?"

"The Children of God," Paisley repeated, "C.O.G., aka the Family of Love, aka Heaven's Magic, aka the Family ..."

Verna interrupted her. "You mean the cult?"

"The cult." Paisley sat back down in the chair.

"Good Lord!" Verna considered this new information. "Fern joined a cult."

"She did," said Paisley grimly. "And it was a pretty freaky place. Lots of crazy shit going on, mostly having to do with sex. Not a good scene. I mean, I was just eleven, and I knew it was not a good scene."

Verna was dumfounded. "I guess not."

"So we had been in this commune in Saõ Paulo for maybe a half a year and then, one day, out of the blue, there's my dad and Romy's dad, Paul. They show up at the commune's gate with somebody from the Canadian consulate and the next thing I know I'm on one plane headed back to Ontario with Dad and my little sister's on an entirely different plane with Paul and headed for God knows where. It turns out that Dad had always kept tabs on me and when he found out where Mom had gone and with whom, he contacted Paul and together they flew down to Brazil to rescue us. Paul was sort of a self-centred flake and probably wouldn't have come if Dad hadn't guilted him into it — he left Mom before Roo was even born, just walked out. Which was the reason we ended up living in the Kootenays grow-op."

"Wow!" said Verna. "That's some story."

"They showed up just in the nick of time, too," said Paisley. "I was about to turn twelve in a couple of months."

Verna raised her eyebrows, questioning.

"According to C.O.G. rules of the road that's the age for sexual initiation," Romy explained. "When they can rape you with impunity, in other words. That was just about the time that sex with minors was forbidden — the leaders had taken a lot of heat on that issue — but, believe me, it was still going on."

"Oh, dear," said Verna. So the men had been right all along. Fern really had been an unfit mother. Of course, that

was also what Verna had always thought — that she was an
unfit mother, an unfit anything. Then why should it surprise
her to find out it was, in fact, true? Surprise and distress her?

"Yeah, so I was pretty glad to see Dad," concluded Paisley. "And grateful, too. I still am. For saving me. Only I
never saw my mother or sister again."

Verna remembered Fern returning from Brazil without the girls. She had stayed with Donald for some
months and would never say what she had been doing
down there or whom she had been with, but only that
Ben and Paul had come and taken the girls from her; that
they had called her an unfit mother and that she supposed
she was. She had been very subdued at the time. What
Verna had taken for blitheness, for insouciance, could that
have been despair?

"I made a second call when I came downstairs," said
Paisley.

"Oh?"

"I called Tai."

Verna looked up in alarm. "Tai?"

Paisley nodded.

"You know where Tai is?"

"Yeah," said Paisley evenly. "He's in medical school. At
Western."

"But … how did you find him?"

"I went online to 411.ca and searched Ontario for his
father. There were eighteen J. Patels. Then I called each of
them until I found the right one. Number Seven. He lives
in Brampton now. Jag, that is. Not Tai. His wife was pretty
pissed off. She didn't want Jag to tell me where Tai was. I
got the impression she hated anything to do with Mom.
Maybe she was jealous."

"Everyone was jealous of Fern," said Verna. "I certainly was."

"In any case, the two of them are having this big-ass fight on the other end of the line. She's screeching at him and he's yelling at her and the two of them are grabbing at the phone. But in the end he got it away from her long enough to tell me how to get in touch with Tai."

"Medical school," said Verna. Little, snivelling Tai, always hanging off of Fern like a little monkey. A cling-on, that's how Bob had described him. Contemptuously, of course.

"I think Jag still carries a torch for Mom," Paisley said. "When I told him that she was dead, I thought I heard him … you know … sobbing. It was hard to tell with all the noise his wife was making."

"Jag was a sweet boy," remembered Verna. "Awfully young."

"In any case," said Paisley, "He should be heading out about now. Driving through the night. He'll be here by morning."

"Who?" Verna asked. "Jag?"

"No. Tai."

"Tai? Tomorrow?"

"Driving up. From London."

"Whatever for?"

"To scatter Mom's ashes, of course! And to meet me and Romy. And you, Auntie Verna. He has to be back by Tuesday, so he thought he'd better come right away."

"Well," said Verna, her heart sinking. "The more the merrier."

"Hey, Verna!"

Verna's heart bumped once in her chest, then, "Oh, of course," she said. "Lionel! You gave me a start!" She had expected to encounter him, of course. That was why she had come downstairs, after all. Why, after she and Paisley had brushed the mouse dirt off her old bed and made it up with musty-smelling sheets that they found in the upstairs linen closet, Verna had not retired for the night, as Paisley had, but instead had gone downstairs, freshened up her drink in the kitchen, pulled on the black-and-white flannel shirt jacket she had worn the previous evening and wandered out onto the porch. To see Lionel, to get his take on things, maybe even, like Paisley, to get some answers. That she had expected him did not, however, seem to lessen the jolt she experienced upon actually seeing him. Encountering a ghost was probably never an easy thing, she reflected; it must always be more or less unsettling. She sank down into the Bar Harbor chair nearest to where he sat cross-legged on the floor, his broad back to her, his face turned in the direction of the lake. "It's been quite a day," she began.

But Lionel motioned her to be quiet. After a moment he asked, "There! Do you hear that sound? That hum?"

Verna frowned and leaned forward. She closed her eyes and listened intently. "That kind of high frequency hum?" she asked, isolating one strand from the bundle of night noises — the *jug o' rum* ... *jug o' rum* ... of frogs, the yodel of the male loon, the soft hooting of a grey owl. "Is that what you're talking about?"

Lionel nodded. "Know what that is?"

She considered this for a moment. "Nope. What?"

"Blackfly hatch."

Donald had been the resident expert when it came to blackflies. "Did you know that we have over seventy different kinds of mosquitoes in Canada?" he would ask the girls. "And one thousand different species of blackflies?" He made it sound like this was, if not a good thing, then at least a matter of some interest. According to Donald, a hatch was that interval during which blackfly adults, enclosed in air bubbles, escape from their underwater cocoons and rise to the surface of the lake with a resounding *pop*. If you could hear a hatch, he had told them, it meant that thousands, perhaps hundreds of thousands of flies were emerging from the water all at once. "Ooh! Disgusting!" they had cried.

"Great," said Verna. "First Romy. Then Paisley. And now Tai's driving up from southwestern Ontario. Through the night. *And* the blackflies are hatching."

"Do you know where blackflies come from?" Lionel asked.

"Hell?"

"Close," said Lionel. "My no'okomiss says that the first blackflies rose from the ashes of a windigo, a cannibal manitou who roams the forests in winter looking for human flesh to feed on. That is why blackflies are so hungry."

"I met your no'okomiss today."

"I know," said Lionel. "I was in the canoe."

They sat in silence for a few moments while Verna considered the pros and cons of asking him about the giant fish she had seen that morning. On the one hand, she didn't want to appear overly credulous in regards to the possibility of having encountered mer-persons in the lake (if, in fact, it were possible to appear overly credulous to a ghost); on the other, who else could she ask and not appear insane? "I took your advice. I went for a swim this morning. You were right. It made me feel better. Much better, actually." She reflected on this. Even now, hours later, she felt better than she had in ... well, years, maybe. "Then later, when the skiff had overturned and I was diving to try and get away from Romy, I saw something. Like a fish. Only it was too big to be a fish."

Lionel nodded. "A Nebaunaubaequae."

"A mermaid?"

"Sometimes they let you see them. Not always."

"Or it could have been a hallucination," Verna countered. "Me seeing things that aren't there. Like you."

"Could be," said Lionel. "Maybe. You never know."

Thursday, May 19, 2005

Tai arrived just as Verna was emerging from the lake. This time she had thought to wear a swimsuit for what she had determined the previous evening would be her daily morning swim. At least as long as she was here at the lake. It was an old suit — a purple Speedo. Portions of her shone whitely through the threadbare Lycra (she hadn't worn a swimsuit for oh, so long), but it provided more coverage than nothing at all and would presumably prevent her sister's children from being totally grossed out by her aging, sagging flesh. *Not that Fern hadn't skinny-dipped at the drop of anybody at all's drawers*, she thought, but she had been younger at the time and now, of course, she was dead.

On seeing the car — a late-model, champagne-coloured Toyota Camry — pull up, she had closed her eyes, taken a deep breath, and fiercely read herself the riot act. Romy and Paisley had surprised her. Caught her off-guard. But she had known in advance of Tai's coming and she was determined

— absolutely determined — not to be so … well, weird and hostile and defensive with him. And it would be good to have a young man around the place, wouldn't it? Given that menacing stranger she and Romy had seen just yesterday. And a doctor, too, or a medical student, at any rate — perhaps he could tell her what to do about Romy; point her in the right direction. *So get a grip, Verna*, she told herself sternly. *Suck it up. Tai's being here is a good thing and, besides, what choice have you? Pay now or pay later.* Wrapping a towel resolutely around herself, she strode along the beach toward the Camry, trailed by Jude. Jag must have done all right for himself, she thought, for his son to drive such a nice car — it was, after all, a doctor sort of car, the kind of car one expected a doctor to drive. The door on the driver's side opened and a young man slid out. Jude took this as his signal to bark riotously and bound toward the car, tail whopping back and forth like a *nunchakus*. The young man — Tai — shrank quickly back, interposing the car door between him and the dog.

"It's okay," called Verna. "He's friendly!"

Somewhat hesitantly, Tai pushed the door open again and braced himself. The Labrador lunged at him, then proceeded to sniff him up the way police pat people down, pinning him against the car, his hands raised and open in a gesture of surrender, his narrow shoulders hunched.

Verna grabbed Jude by the collar and pulled him back. "You mustn't mind him," she explained. "He's just … enthusiastic. About everything. You must be Tai. I'm your Aunt Verna." Funny, she realized, but she was starting to enjoy the sound of those two words together: Aunt and Verna. Auntie Verna not so much.

Tai blinked at her. He seemed taken aback. "Oh, yes. Hi. Sorry. It's been a long time since anyone called me Tai. Actually Paisley asked if this was Tai the first time she called me, and, for a moment, I thought she had a wrong number."

He started to extend a soft-looking hand to her, but aborted the mission when he saw that she was holding the dog back with one hand and her towel in place with the other.

"I don't understand," said Verna. "Tai's your name. I was at your christening. Or your 'wiccaning,' at any rate. I think that's what Fern called it."

"Yes, well," said Tai forlornly. "My family didn't approve. Well, my father didn't mind it, but Deepa Auntie — my step-mother, that is ... anyway, they always called me Kamal. After my paternal grandfather. I think they even had it changed ... you know ... legally." He pointed at Jude. "I remember that dog. That's Granddad's dog. His name is Cato, isn't it?"

Verna laughed. "Cato was three dogs ago. Don't worry. It's an honest mistake. Dad always kept black Labs and they do look pretty much alike. No, this one is named Jude and he's a good dog, isn't he? Aren't you, Jude? You're a good dog!" She paddled him on his rear end. For some reason it rankled her that Tai's family should have changed his name from the one Fern had chosen, this despite the fact that she herself had always made fun of it, saying that it was a hippie name. Well, it was a hippie name and what was wrong with that? And what kind of a name was Kamal, anyway? Oh, right. An Indian name.

"Hey, Jude," Tai greeted the dog. Then, getting it, "Granddad did that on purpose."

"Of course he did."

"I was sorry to hear that he died. From what I can remember, he was pretty nice."

"That he was."

"Kind of vague."

"That, too."

Now that she saw Tai in person, she dismissed the notion that he might provide any sort of muscle to their operation. He was diminutive — five foot five inches at the most, if that

— and very slight in build. His features were delicate — a pale, perfectly shaped mouth, a Grecian nose, a square chin and lustrous eyes fringed by very long, dark lashes. His hair was a sooty, soft black and his skin was a light, even taupe. He looked like Jag had as a young man, but prettier. That being said, he did not strike Verna as effeminate so much as careful, precise. But, no, she acknowledged, he was certainly no bruiser. The lanky, overgrown Paisley would afford more protection than him.

"So, are you ready to meet your sisters?" she asked gently.

He gulped and looked in the direction of the house. His face was drawn; he looked tired. *Well, he did drive all night to get here.* "I guess," he said, sounding unsure.

"Come on then," she said, releasing Jude's collar. Taking her nephew by the elbow, she steered him toward the cottage.

Several hours later Verna, Winonah, Granny, and the cartons containing the gritty quintessence of sister, father, mother, and brother skimmed across the blue face of the lake toward its southern shore. Winonah and Granny had arrived at the cottage shortly after ten o'clock. After a hearty breakfast of blueberry-syrup-drenched Eggos and sausage, purchased by Verna at the grocery store in Beverley the day before, they announced their intention to make another stab at launching Lionel on his path to the Sky World, and, once again, Verna and Fern's children — "the kids," as Fern used to refer to them — had opted to join them.

"The kids" had spent the better part of the past several hours in a huddle on the porch, speaking in hushed tones. Verna had thought it best to leave them to it; actually, she had gotten the distinct impression that Tai's arrival had closed some inner circle, leaving her on the outside looking in. And looked in she had — every half hour or so to see if

Paisley would like more coffee or if Romy was warm enough or if Tai could use a lie-down after his long drive. And every time the door creaked open and she stuck her head out, three heads swivelled in her direction and an awkward, sudden silence descended upon the group. Why was that? What were they talking about that they felt they must stop when she was within hearing? Were they talking about her? Blaming her? *But no*, she thought. *Stop being so paranoid. They are probably just being sad together.* Sad and happy — sad because of what they had lost — a mother, a family — but happy to be reunited and wary at letting others see this, particularly unsympathetic others, as she had certainly been. Had been to her shame, she realized now. She saw something else too. When she looked at them, together like this, Fern looked back. This, despite the fact that each of them individually resembled their fathers more than they did their mother. It was unsettling and wonderful all at the same time.

The kids had decided to walk to the glen, accompanied by Jude — this was driven by Romy's reluctance to commit herself to any more deeps. "I am never setting foot in a boat again."

Verna was concerned that the walk, given that there was no real path, might be too much for Romy, but she maintained that she would be fine, just fine. She was in excellent shape; didn't they know that she worked out constantly? Fortunately, her widow's weeds were still damp from her ducking the day before, so they would not have to contend with attempts to drag yards of black crinkle cloth through deadfall and bramble. The plan was to make their way along the west shore of the lake until they reached its southernmost point. There they would meet up with Verna, Winonah, and Granny and together, make the short trip into the bush and to the glen. The kids had set out about twenty minutes before the canoeists, since it took longer to reach the far shore by land than water and were just clawing their way out of a scramble of creeping juniper and sand cherry, bedraggled and covered with burrs, when Winonah ran the canoe up on shore and climbed out onto the rock barren dotted with lakeside daisies and Indian paintbrush that occupied the lake's southernmost point.

"Jeez!" Romy complained, swatting randomly. "What's with these horrible flies? They're eating me alive!"

"They're pickin' at your bones!" cried Granny gleefully.

"Sorry, guys," Verna apologized, standing up in the canoe and handing Winonah the LCBO bag containing the three cartons of cremains. She toe-heeled her way to the bow and stepped out onto the rock barren. "I forgot there was a big hatch last night. I should have told you to splash some vinegar on your faces before going out." That was what Donald had always suggested when she and Fern had complained about flies. It was a fix the efficacy of which he had remained utterly convinced his entire life; that was what he did and he swore by it. She, of course, had never done it, would have rather died than do it. Now, it struck her as possibly sensible.

But not Romy. "Sure!" she scoffed. "Next you'll be suggesting that we depilate with battery acid!" She turned to Paisley. "Do lesbians depilate?"

"Some do. Some don't," replied Paisley. "I don't."

"Ooh!" Romy grimaced. "Yuck."

"Look who's talking!" Paisley snorted. "I could b*raid* your facial hair!"

"Excess body and facial hair — that's caused by the anorexia," Tai explained shyly. He seemed both pleased and grateful that this esoteric medical information was his to impart. "It's the body's attempt to keep warm." Tai had a kind of sweet earnestness that reminded Verna of his father, poor, limp, clammy-handed Jag Patel. How wistful he had been. How hopeless a romantic. Well, actually more of a helpless romantic, unable, finally, to withstand the pressure placed upon him by his family to abandon Fern and live as they would have him. What might have happened had they not intervened? What kind of a life might they have had together? But Fern was inconstant by nature, headlong and random. Surely she would have abandoned Jag, given time. Just as she had Ben.

But was that true? Had Fern left Ben or the other way around?

Verna had always assumed that her sister had engineered the failure of her various unions, sprung herself from the traps she herself had set. On the other hand, she had always thought that Fern left Paul, when, according to Paisley, that had not been the case. *How much do you really know about your sister's life?* she asked herself. *How much is pure conjecture, rooted in malice and sustained by willful ignorance?* The idea distressed her; it hurt her heart. She dismissed it as best she could by turning to the task at hand — helping Tai and Winonah drag the canoe up farther onto the alvar in order to secure it.

With Winonah taking the lead, they picked their way across the limestone plain to the stand of Jack pines at its edge. Verna noted that, for a woman her age, Granny proved surprisingly spry, hopping from rock to rock like a bandy-legged toad, steadying herself, when required, with her walking stick. It was Romy who had the most difficulty negotiating the uneven terrain. There was no tone to her; everything about her was slack. Well, she was probably weak with hunger. Verna was relieved when Tai took Romy by the elbow to prevent her toppling over in a heap of layers. Her bones had to be as brittle as glass. One false step and she could imagine — *snap!* — an ankle broken. *Pop!* One of those jutting hipbones shattered into a million pieces, strewn like potsherds around an archeological dig.

Beyond the alvar lay a mixed wood, both coniferous and deciduous — this much Verna had remembered, but it was Paisley who identified the different kinds of trees for her as they went along — the black and white spruce, the Jack pine, the balsam and the fir, the tamarack and eastern white cedar, along with the poplars and the white birch.

Verna was impressed. "You really know your trees."

Paisley shrugged. "I was in the tree-care industry before I got into landscaping."

The tree-care industry? Verna thought. She had never known there was a tree-care industry. "Your grandfather liked trees, too," she told her. "Until you, he was the only person I've ever known who could identify so many."

To her delight, Paisley was also able to name the ephemerals dotting the forest floor — those wildflowers that must fulfill their biological imperative before the canopy overhead becomes too dense for sunlight to penetrate, that begin to fall even as they bloom. "Hepatica," the girl had told her, pointing. "Trillium. Trout lilies."

This much Verna knew: that in another week, this flurry of colour would be all but gone, leaving only the ostrich and the bracken and the maidenhair spleenwort ferns to unfurl in this shady realm. Their father had named Fern for this ancient plant form, which, not coincidentally, reproduces not through conventional means, but, like fungus, through the production of spores. Indeed, Fern had always been susceptible to fungus — to athlete's foot and then to toenail and fingernail fungus. She had shared a kind of affinity with it. The last time Verna had seen her, her thumbnails had looked like copper gone green with verdigris, fecund. Verna thought about mentioning this — Fern and her affinity with fungus — but thought that such an observation might be construed as criticism, as had been the case when she had compared Fern to a pig and a parrot and Romy had taken umbrage.

And then suddenly, up ahead, a gathering of birch around a clearing, a white verticality, shining through the deciduous gloom like a forest of bone. "There it is," she said to Fern's children, pointing. "There's the glen." At the sight of it, Verna's eyes welled up with sudden, ridiculous tears. She quickened her pace to put some distance between her and the others. She needed to regain some measure of control over her wayward emotions; the last thing she wanted was for Fern's kids to see her cry. She didn't think she could bear being comforted at this juncture and they might be moved to do so if they noticed her distress. How were they to know that hers were tears not of sorrow so much as remorse? Bitter, not sweet, and, therefore, incapable of being soothed away, but only endured. This hastening of her step soon landed her in the epicentre of the clearing known as the glen. Festooned with yellow violets and pink Lady Slipper orchids, it was delineated at its perimeter by rotting nurse logs, once giants twenty metres tall; saplings now clung to these, wavering greenly upwards. The cylinder of dusty light that bored through the canopy bathed her in a kind of mote-filled radiance.

"Beam me up, Scotty," Winonah said sarcastically.

Verna blinked back hot tears. Ignored Winonah. "Well, here it is. The glen. Your great-grandfather's ashes are scattered here and your great-aunt Margie's ... the lake was named after her ..."

"Lake Margie?" Tai asked

"Marguerite," clarified Verna. "Lake Marguerite."

"Margie was her nickname," said Romy. "She committed suicide."

But Verna was not finished. "And your grandmother, too — my mother, your mother's mother." She imagined her tearful father upending the urn in this very spot (they had returned a loved one's ashes in metal urns in those days, not in cardboard cartons; somehow that seemed more gracious), while, back at the cottage, she and Fern, infant matricides, lay howling in their cribs. Why was it that Donald had never remarried? Had he loved their mother that much? Or had he just been overwhelmed? Why hadn't she asked him? She should have. Now she never would. So much she didn't know about the people in her life; the thought oppressed her, weighed her down. "Oh, and our dogs," she added by way of afterthought. "Those that died in the summer. You don't want to be putting a Lab on ice for any significant period of time." She briefly considered, but thought better of telling them about Fern's "offerings to Gaia."

"Oh, and by the way, this is also an old Ojibway burial ground," Winonah piped up. "Not that my ancestors are as important as your family pets."

"Hey!" Paisley exclaimed. "What's this?" Her eyes had snagged on a blaze cut into two sides of a tree. She ran her hand over the tree's exposed inner bark. "I think these are fresh cuts."

Winonah appeared to have discovered something equally untoward. "Would you look at that!"

"What?" asked Verna, looking in the direction where Winonah was pointing. There, about twenty paces from the blazed tree, a wooden post a little more than a metre tall had been driven into the ground. "What's that?"

Winonah snorted. "Now we know what your Peeping Tom was up to."

"Peeping Tom?" Tai turned to Romy and Paisley. "What Peeping Tom?"

"It's a corner claim post," Winonah informed Verna.

"A really creepy one," Romy told Tai. "Auntie Verna and I saw him yesterday morning."

"I'm sorry, a *what*?" said Verna. "Can we all be quiet for a minute so I can hear Winonah?"

"A corner claim post," Winonah repeated. "Somebody must be staking a claim to this land. Or a piece of it, anyway.

See there? How the brush is cut back? And that stone cairn there. And there, that line post, the one with the red tag. Those mark the claim line."

Verna was confused. "But how is that possible? This is my land."

"Hey!" Romy said. "You mean, it's *our* land."

"Yeah!" Paisley asserted herself. "All of ours."

"Okay, okay, *our* land," Verna conceded. "How can somebody lay claim to our land?"

"Our people have been asking that question for years," said Winonah.

Tai crossed over to the post and hunkered down next to it. "J.R. Eubanks," he read the attached metal tag. He looked up. "According to this, he began staking at eight yesterday morning and finished at ten. There's a number, as well, but I can't make it out."

"Probably his licence number," said Winonah.

"Licence?" Verna asked. "What kind of licence?"

"A prospector's licence," said Winonah. "You need one of those if you're going to stake a claim."

"I don't care what kind of licence this jerk has!" Verna declared heatedly. "He has no business coming onto my ... onto *our* land and blazing our trees and ... I don't know. Piling up rocks!"

"Yeah!" Romy was aggrieved. "Those are our rocks!"

Winonah looked at Granny. "What do you think?"

Granny scrunched up her face in wrinkled contemplation, shook her head, and, without a word, she and Winonah turned around and started back towards the canoe.

"What? Stop!" Romy cried. "Where are you going?"

"Where does it look like we're going?" Winonah asked.

"We're going back to the cottage," said Granny.

"But what about ... you know ... the cremains?" asked Paisley. "Aren't we going to scatter them?"

212 • Melissa Hardy

Granny shook her head. "A guy with a truck comes in here, trenches the place out. All that digging ... that would make the spirits restless. All turned around. Not able to find their way to the Sky World. Then we'd never get rid of them, eh? They'd be always hanging around, bugging us."

They all began to talk at once.

"You mean they would haunt us?" asked Tai. "That's ridiculous. There are no such things as ghosts."

"Digging?" Verna demanded. "What digging?"

"But we've come all this way!" wailed Romy. "And it was such an ordeal! Those blackflies must have sucked a pint of blood from me! And yesterday I nearly drowned."

"How are we supposed to ever get closure if we can't lay our mother to rest?" Paisley asked.

Winonah held up her hands for silence. "Quiet! Quiet, now." When she had got their attention, she said, "Look, Macoun Clan, this is how it works. A white guy stakes a claim. Then he brings in a truck and starts to trench. The law says he can haul up to a thousand tons of earth out of a claim."

"That's a lot of Mother Earth," observed Granny.

"The law?" Verna demanded. "What are you talking about? What law?"

"And what about this beautiful stand of birch?" Paisley cried. She looked stricken at the thought of the grove's destruction.

"The Mining Act," Winonah told Verna. To Paisley she said, "The birch is a sacred tree to my people. For your people, it is the money tree that is sacred."

Tai rose to his feet. "I've got an idea. Winonah, you said that this was an old aboriginal burial ground!"

"Yeah," said Winonah guardedly. "And ...?"

"Why don't we play the old aboriginal burial ground card!" Tai said this in the same way he might suggest a game of shuffleboard or croquet. *Oh, God*, Verna remembered suddenly, he was the one who liked board games. She remembered him furiously hunched over a checkerboard, nose dripping green snot onto the checks.

"Never knew there was one of them," said Granny.

"One of what?" demanded Verna.

"An old aboriginal burial ground card," replied Granny.

"But, of course there is," Romy insisted. "If you mess with an old Indian burial ground, weird shit happens. Poltergeists and zombies. Everybody knows that!"

"Really?" asked Granny. "Well, that's good."

"Roo!" objected Paisley. "Come on! That only happens in movies."

"Yeah," said Winonah. "Otherwise every house in every suburb of this country would be haunted. The whole country is built on our burial grounds."

"I don't watch a lot of movies," Granny admitted. "Too many white people, eh? Can't tell them apart."

"What I'm talking about is the fact that, legally, you can't disturb a burial site," explained Tai. "Not without a lengthy process involving the police and the coroner. And right now Native burial grounds are a real flashpoint for the government. Rather than kick off another land claim, they might just say that this guy can't dig here."

"He's got a point!" Verna said.

"Well, sure he does," Winonah conceded, "if we could prove it."

"Prove what?"

"That it's an old burial site."

Tai blinked at her. "There's no proof?"

"No," Winonah replied.

"What do you mean?" Paisley muscled in. "No records?"

Winonah shook her head. "Oral tradition." She snapped her fingers in mock regret. "Gets us every time."

"Records are for keeping track of people," explained Granny. "Where are the people? What are their names? Are they dead? Are they a Status Indian? We're not so interested in those things."

"Tai's got a good idea," Paisley pleaded. "Let's not give up on this. We can do some digging ourselves. All we have to do is unearth some remains. How hard would that be? I've got spades and shovels in the truck."

"I hope you don't expect me to dig," said Romy. "Because I'm not a digger."

"That could be a pretty big job," Winonah warned. "Because the glen, eh, it don't stay put."

"What do you mean — it doesn't stay put?" Paisley asked.

"Birches grow old and die and topple to the ground, tearing a new hole in the canopy," explained Verna. "For a time, the ground beneath that opening is where the glen is. The centre shifts."

"Meaning ...?" Paisley asked.

"Those bones could be anywhere over a pretty large area," said Winonah.

"The glen is not so much a location with coordinates as it is a state of grace," Verna told her. Somebody had said that to her. Once. Long ago. Was it Donald?

"But surely there is something we can do?" Paisley insisted. "I know. We could tie ourselves to the birches. We could lie down in front of the bulldozer."

Romy tugged at the sleeve of Paisley's shirt. "I hope you don't expect me to lie down in front of anything. That's not my style."

"We'll do something," Verna promised, hoping to hell that she could come up with some sort of fix to save the glen from depredation — having worked in the Department of Agriculture for twenty-eight years, she knew full well that governmental bureaucracy was, at the same time, relentless and lugubrious. Her best chance was probably to throw some spanner in the works, something that would buy them time. "What I don't know, but we'll come up with something. As far as the cremains go, though, Winonah's right. Until we've got a handle of this thing, we'd better hang on to them."

"I'm hungry," announced Granny. "What's for lunch?"

"How about fish sticks?" asked Winonah. "There's baloney, too. And red-hot wieners."

"I hope you don't expect me to eat meat," said Romy. "Because I'm a strict vegan."

On the canoe ride back to the cottage, Verna suddenly thought of Carmen. Surely a real-estate broker would know about property rights and the laws governing them. Maybe she would have some advice or know how Verna could get more information. How she could fight this thing. With that in mind, the first thing Verna did when they arrived back at the cottage was to dial Carmen's office on the red wall-mounted rotary phone in the kitchen. She got a busy signal.

"You got any arrowroot biscuits?" Winonah asked Verna.

"Probably," Verna replied. Her father had always stocked up on arrowroot biscuits. It was the cookie he most admired. Born stale, it defied the passage of time. It was, as he used to say, incorruptible, pure.

"Where are they?"

But Verna was too preoccupied to want to think about the location of hypothetical cookies. "I thought you knew everything that Lionel knew."

"He didn't know where the arrowroot biscuits were," said Winonah evenly. "He didn't like arrowroot biscuits. He liked Fig Newtons."

"Look for a tin. A tartan tin," she told her. She redialled Carmen's number. Still busy.

"This tin?" Winonah emerged with a tarnished tartan tin.

"That's the one," said Verna. How had she remembered that Donald kept the arrowroot biscuits in a tartan tin? What minute wrinkle in her brain had that piece of data been tucked into all these many years? It was unfathomable, the way memories lurked in the shadows. "Give me one of those," she said. She took a cookie and tried the number again. Busy.

She stamped her foot peevishly. "What the hell is she doing?"

"Talking on the phone," said Winonah. "She is a person. She has a life."

"Yeah, well," said Verna. "I thought you were going to fix lunch."

"We're waiting for the kids," explained Winonah. They were due to arrive from their trek to the glen in another ten minutes. "When they come, we'll make lunch. This is a snack."

Verna glared at the phone.

"A watched pot, eh?" Granny reminded her. "Never boils."

"What kind of arrowroot biscuits are these?" Winonah asked. "Are they Nabisco? 'Cause they don't taste like Nabisco. They taste like President's Choice. Nabisco is better."

"How do I know?" asked Verna. "I didn't buy them."

"Got any condensed milk?" Granny asked. "Eagle's — that's the best, eh? Sweet."

"And tea," said Winonah. "Red Rose Tea."

"Nothing tastes better than a Nabisco arrowroot biscuit dipped in a cup of Red Rose tea sweetened with Eagle's condensed milk," Granny said longingly. It was a dazzling display of brand loyalty.

"Look in the cabinet," Verna told them. "Look in the pantry. I don't know what's in there." She tried calling again. This time, Carmen picked up. *Third's the charm, as Donald would have said.* "Hey, Carmen," she greeted the realtor. She could hear the air purifier hissing in the distance.

"Verna!" Evidently Carmen had Call Display. "How'd that thing of yours turn out?"

"What thing?"

"That guy. The one in the truck. You and Winonah left in an awful big hurry. Was everything all right back home?"

"Oh, that wasn't a guy. It was Paisley. You know. Paisley. Fern's oldest child."

"He's a she?"

"Yep."

"Could've fooled me. *Did* fool me. But that's good, isn't it? You've got the one niece there already and now the other."

"Actually all three of Fern's kids are here," said Verna. "The boy came up this morning. Tai."

"All three kids! Imagine that. I thought you said they'd disappeared."

"Well, they've reappeared."

"What did I tell you?"

Verna couldn't remember. "What did you tell me?"

"The cat comes back!" said Carmen triumphantly.

"I guess," said Verna, "but that's not the reason I called. I need to pick your brain about something."

"Pick away!"

"It seems that some guy's staked out part of our property. Actually, his name is Eubanks. J.R. Eubanks. Apparently he did it yesterday morning. We just found the corner claim post."

"Okay," said Carmen.

"He can't do that, can he? I mean, my grandfather bought that land from the Crown. He handed it down to my father and my father handed it down to me. We have first title. We've always had first title."

"Yeah," said Carmen, "but do you own the mineral rights?"

Verna was puzzled. "The *what?*"

"The mineral rights," Carmen repeated.

"I *own* the land," Verna said flatly. "Doesn't that mean I own the mineral rights?"

Carmen sighed. "Let me give you a little history lesson. Before gold and silver were discovered in these parts, people came and went as they pleased. Stayed, left, put down roots, pulled up stakes. The land didn't belong to anybody *per se*. The way those old guys figured, before you can own land, you have to know that it's there. You have to be able to find it on a map. And that's what your grandfather did: he put land on the map so people could own it and he picked this spot where you are now for himself and his family. But more importantly, he put land on the map so that people could prospect it, lay claim to it, mine it. Think about it. Who did your grandfather work for?"

"The Crown," Verna replied slowly.

"What part of the Crown?"

"The Bureau of Mining."

"And why did the Crown and the Bureau of Mining want the region mapped?" Carmen asked. "Any reason you can think of?"

"Gold and silver had been discovered," said Verna. "But that was a long time ago. The place was uninhabited, well," she glanced apologetically at Winonah and Granny, "except for a few Native tribes and some trappers. Now people live here. They own property. They have property rights."

"And they owned property back then, too," Carmen assured her. "They owned the *surface* rights to property. The Crown didn't necessarily cede them the mineral rights to that same property. As often as not, it held those rights in reserve. Remember that governments like natural resources; they like them more than they like property rights."

Verna tried to take this all in. "So you're saying that this man has the right to stake my property?"

"You can go to the Land Registry Office in North Bay and have a look at your title," said Carmen, "but, if I had to put money on it, I'd say you're pretty well screwed."

"Damn!" said Verna. "But what makes him think that there's anything worth digging for on my land?"

"You've heard of the Precambrian Shield?" asked Carmen. "That slab of rock we're both standing on right this minute? Well, actually, I'm sitting, but you take my point. That's where they find most of the minerals and metals mined in Ontario. Only one in a thousand drill tests results in a mine, but, if you're going to find something, you're going to find it in northern Ontario."

"But surely you just can't stake randomly," Verna objected. "Surely there are restrictions of some sort."

"There are," said Carmen. "Let me see if I can pull them up on my computer. Give me a minute."

At the kitchen table Winonah lit a cigarette. "'We own this land,'" she said. "That's what my people said. A lot of good it did us."

Verna put her hand over the phone's mouthpiece. "This is different," she said. "You were the oppressed; we were the oppressors. The oppressors shouldn't be oppressing the oppressors. That's not how it's supposed to work."

"Thanks for clearing that up," said Winonah. "I feel much better now."

"I'm not saying that it's right," Verna defended herself.

Carmen came back on the line. "Okay, I'm on the website of the Ministry of Northern Development and Mines," she said. "Here's your list of places you can't claim stake. Ready?"

"Ready."

"Subdivisions, railway lands, Crown town sites, Ministry of Natural Resources summer resort locations, lands certified by Ministry of Transportation for public purposes,

Indian reserves, and provincial parks. Does your property conform to any of the aforementioned types?"

"No." Verna's heart sunk.

"Is there a dwelling, cemetery, church, public building, dam, garden, vineyard, orchards, or crops that could be damaged on the part he staked?"

"Well, maybe. Sort of. A cemetery."

"A *pet* cemetery," Winonah clarified.

Verna scowled at her. "Winonah says it's supposed to be the site of an old Ojibway burial ground, but we don't have any proof of that. I don't suppose ashes count? Scattered ones, I mean."

"I wouldn't think so," said Carmen.

"Damn," said Verna. She racked her brain, trying to think of loopholes. "But he trespassed! Can't I charge him with trespassing?"

"The Mining Act gives anyone who holds a prospector's licence right of entry on land open for staking. Sorry, Verna, but the laws weren't written for you; they were written for prospectors."

"So there's absolutely nothing I can do to keep this guy from digging up my birch grove?"

"Nothing legal," replied Carmen. "Course he could be a lazy son of a bitch and not work the claim. If a year goes by and he hasn't spent at least four hundred dollars on it, the claim's forfeit."

"What are the chances of that?"

"Who knows?"

"So, you're telling me it's just watch and wait? That there's nothing I can do?"

"Pretty much," said Carmen. "If he's going to dig, you get twenty-four hours' notice. You'll see it coming."

Verna felt sick to her stomach. "I can't believe this. It isn't right. This shouldn't be happening. Not on my watch."

"Shit happens," said Carmen. "Shit doesn't know whose watch it is and shit doesn't care. That's shit for you. What'd you say this guy's name was?"

"J.R. Eubanks."

"Doesn't ring a bell. Probably some drifter."

"Drifter?" Verna asked. "That's not very reassuring."

"All it takes to get a prospector's licence is twenty-five bucks and one piece of photo ID," Carmen told her. "They don't do a background check or nothing."

"That's ridiculous." Verna fumed. "Absolutely ridiculous."

"So," said Carmen, "what do you plan on doing?"

"I don't know. Maybe I can reason with him."

"Your average prospector isn't exactly what you'd call an upstanding citizen. More like a coyote. Try and buy him. That's what I'd try if I were you. Or you could kill him."

The last suggestion so shocked Verna that she could think of no response.

"Just kidding." Carmen said smoothly. "And now, if you don't mind, I'm signing off. Time for my daily meditation to Tibetan Singing Bowls."

There was a sudden commotion on the porch: the sound of the screen door squeaking open and slamming shut, the creak of floorboards, laughter, footfalls and a scramble of claws.

"We're home," cried Romy.

So shocked were Paisley and Tai by the lack of whole or fresh foods in the cottage larder that they decided to go into Beverley that afternoon to stock up on healthier fare. Romy tagged along for the ride and to purchase the ingredients needed for her "special vegan diet." As for Winonah, she had spent the afternoon stolidly caulking the downstairs windows and doors, while Granny, curled up tight as the frond of a fiddlehead fern under the black-green-and-blue afghan, napped on the couch. Verna stewed confusedly on the porch, alternating between trying to stretch her hitherto fairly rigid idea of the past enough so that she could wrap it around Paisley's story and consider the light it shed on aspects of her sister's life that had, up to now, been unknown to her and trying to figure out just what the hell she was going to do about J.R. Eubanks.

When the dial-drop clock in the study hazarded a guess that it was five o'clock, Winonah shook Granny as gently from her nap as she might have a beloved child and told Verna, "We're out of here." She glanced over at the ladder that remained propped up against the back shed. "Don't take the ladder down. I still have to caulk the upstairs windows and cut back that larch."

Left on her own in the cottage in the middle of the bush, Verna became restless. Strange, because she was used to being alone; indeed, she had almost always preferred it, there being less scope in solitude for recrimination. And, besides, she was not alone. Not really. She had the dog, Jude, her very own happy-go-lucky idiot child. What better company? Uncritical, enthusiastic, alive in the moment ...

Still she felt at loose ends, rattled, even panicky. Well, that was where the word *panic* came from, wasn't it? The fear a person experienced upon finding him or herself alone in the woods, that inner flutter, that tripping heart. Except it was not the Greek demigod Pan who was the teasing author of her unease, but this Eubanks character. It wasn't that she was frightened of him. She had been, initially, when Romy had first spotted him, but now that she knew his intentions were directed toward her property, she was less concerned with their personal safety. Still there were questions. Where had he come from? They were miles from the highway, from the spur road. She had heard no truck, seen no ATV or car. No, he had simply materialized at the opposite end of the lake and disappeared as quickly. He couldn't just have been wandering around in the bush, randomly claim-staking, could he? That didn't seem logical.

She couldn't sit still. "Come on," she told Jude. "I've got ants in my pants."

She vaguely remembered a kind of rudimentary trail cut into the bush out back near the spring that fed the pump; it had, to the best of her recollection and with a few, brief digressions, followed the lake's eastern shore to the lily pad colony and possibly beyond — a twenty-minute walk, perhaps more. If it was still there. After all it had been thirty-eight years since she had last walked it. Still it was something to do. Something to pass the time. She set forth, with the dog now going up ahead, now dropping behind, according to the information provided by his nose. No sooner, however, had she entered their riparian realm, than a cloud of blackflies descended upon her, buzzing and crawling and browsing and biting. She put up with them for five minutes, then gave up. "The bastards! I can't believe I forgot to put vinegar on my face," she told Jude. "Damn! Next time."

When she arrived back at the porch door, frazzled and bothered, she saw that an official-looking brown envelope had been wedged in between the porch door and its sill. She yanked it free. The words PROPERTY OWNER were written on it in a childish scrawl.

"What …?"

With a sense of dark foreboding, she tore it open. Inside was a battered form of some sort, entitled, "Notice of Intention to Perform Assessment Work."

"Shit!" she said. "Shit!" She waved the form at the dog. "It's my notice. The one Carmen told me about. Wait a minute. Did you hear a car? I didn't hear a car. Why didn't we hear a car? We were only gone ten minutes."

Jude looked confused. Canting his head to one side, he wagged his tail tentatively.

She scanned the notice. "He intends to start work on Tuesday! *Tuesday!* That's two frigging days from now and tomorrow's Sunday and Monday's a holiday. How can I get hold of anybody in a government office on a holiday? It's impossible!" She sat down on the stoop and buried her head in her hands. "What the hell am I going to do?"

There was the low burr of an approaching automobile. *Wait a minute,* she thought. Was that Eubanks? Was he coming back? Adrenaline crackled down her spine. Maybe this was her chance — her chance to talk him out of trenching the glen! Her heart skipped a beat and she lifted her head from her hands.

But it was only Tai's Camry emerging from under the leafy arch of forest into the open parking area.

"I don't understand, Auntie Verna," Romy protested. They were in the kitchen making dinner. At least Tai and Paisley were making dinner — a pasta dish revolving around a rather wizened-looking chicken — purportedly free-range, which struck Verna as credible given the bird's obviously low BMI. By this time she was on her third vodka and tonic and seated — or, to be more precise, *planted* at the table, her stance wide to maintain an increasingly fragile equilibrium. "How long were you gone, anyway?"

"Ten minutes," replied Verna morosely. "If that."

"And you didn't hear anything?" Romy sat opposite Verna, vibrating. She reminded Verna of a hovercraft. "No car or truck or anything? No engine noise?"

"Nope."

Paisley, who was sautéing peppers and zucchini in olive oil, shook her head. "That's so strange. You'd have thought you'd hear something. It's so quiet here."

"Unless Eubanks is lurking around in the bush somewhere nearby," suggested Romy. "And just popped out to drop off the notice." She turned to Tai. "I hope you're not planning to be a surgeon. The way you're cutting that chicken."

"A urologist, actually," said Tai, "and I hardly think Mr. Eubanks is hiding in the bushes."

"Hardly?" Romy asked. *"Hardly!"*

"A urologist?" wondered Verna. *That could be useful,* she thought. *In my doubtless rapid decline, which is due to begin any moment now.*

"What about yesterday?" Romy defended her theory. "When I saw him on the far side of the lake? First he was there and then he wasn't. Isn't that so, Auntie Verna?"

"Yep," said Verna glumly. She wished Romy would stop vibrating; she was all blurred. "What's that you're doing anyway? That bouncing thing?"

"I'm micro-exercising. You can burn calories even while sitting."

"Well, stop it," Verna told her. "It's making me ... I don't know. Carsick."

"And that's the other thing," said Romy. "No car. We didn't hear one. No engine noise whatsoever. Just now you see him, now you don't."

Verna sighed. Clearly Romy did not intend to stop vibrating. She felt defeated and not a little wobbly. She turned her chair slightly so that she no longer had to look directly at her niece. "Right," she said. "It's all very mysterious." Then, "We're totally screwed."

"Don't talk like that, Auntie Verna," Paisley enjoined her. "We'll think of something. Won't we, Tai? Hot stuff coming through!" Picking up the pot of boiling pasta, she carried it to the sink and dumped its steaming contents into a colander. She took the colander by its handles and shook it to drain the water. "Fettuccini," she announced, sliding a heap of pasta onto Verna's plate. She was about to do the same with her sister's plate, but Romy snatched it away. "What? It's pasta, Romy. Vegans eat pasta."

"And how do we know that the machine that made this pasta wasn't used for making egg noodles and not cleaned properly?"

"Romy!" said Paisley.

"Don't be idiotic," Tai told her.

"What? There could be traces of egg. You don't know!"

"And that would kill you?" Tai asked, spooning bits of chicken and sautéed vegetables onto Verna's heap of pasta. "Traces of egg? At least have some vegetables."

"Vegetables tainted with chicken juice?" Romy was disdainful. "No thanks. I'll make my own supper later."

Everyone looked at her.

"What?" she asked. "I will! I like to dine fashionably late. Now is too early." Paisley and Tai had suggested eating by six-thirty so that they could catch the seven-thirty showing of Mel Gibson's *Passion of the Christ*. That afternoon they had discovered an unlikely thing — a shabby little second-run movie theatre in Beverley open only on Saturday nights. Romy had declined to join them; she had seen the movie on one of the Birches' entertainment outings. "Because if there's anything that cheers a depressed anorexic up, it's *Passion of the Christ*. Honestly, it's worse than a slasher flick. And the ending sucks."

While Paisley was checking in with Jill on the telephone in the study, Tai joined Verna on the front porch. Romy had shooed them from the kitchen. She was making her dinner. "Cooking is a very private thing for me," she had explained. "Personal. I don't like people watching. There are things that must be done in a certain order. Rules — hard and fast ones. Counting is involved. I can't be distracted or the whole thing goes up in smoke and I have to start all over again. It's complicated. Don't ask."

Surface Rights • 227

"So, Tai, you're the doctor," Verna began. She drew her heavy flannel shirt closer around her; it had grown chilly and the clouds that had begun to fill up the sky promised rain. "What was that — that stuff back there with Romy — what was that all about?"

Tai shook his head. He ran his fingers through his sooty hair, leaving it on end, his expression concentrated and concerned. Verna remembered that he had been a serious boy, one who took things hard. "Elaborate food rituals," he said. "It's typical of eating disorders. It's like she's dealing with an angry, vengeful, and capricious god — one whom she can only propitiate by performing some complicated ritual that she has dreamed up and perfected over the years. And she is both that god and herself."

"So what you're saying is, she's crazy."

"Basically."

"Yeah, well, I sort of knew that."

"No, really, she's not thinking straight," said Tai. "She's too depleted. Malnutrition takes its toll on the central nervous system, on the brain. This isn't Romy. This isn't my baby sister. This is Romy's body trying desperately to stay alive."

"So, what am I going to do with her?" *I* with *her*, Verna thought. *What will I do with her?* It seemed strange — having to do something with a person whom she had met only two days' prior. Yet it was absolutely clear to her that something was going to have to be done with Romy and that she was the one who must do it. She was, after all, for better or for worse, the adult. Nieces and nephews did not count as adults, regardless of how old they were. At least not until it came time for them to take away your car keys and put you in a nursing home.

"She needs to go back to that place — back to the Birches," Tai said. "And it needs to be soon. I don't know what she weighs, but I'd be willing to bet she's less than a hundred pounds. It's hard to tell with all those clothes."

"I've seen her naked," confessed Verna, "and, believe me, next to her, Biafrans look chunky."

"If she loses any more weight, I think she's at real risk."

"Real risk of what?"

"Dying," said Tai flatly. "A third of anorexics die of the disease." His face convulsed. "God!" he said, his voice strained. "How could this have happened?"

"It wasn't your fault."

"Well, it was somebody's fault. That it was allowed to get to this point. When I think of her as this little toddler ... so happy. So carefree."

Verna went dredging around in her memory and came up with a snotty-nosed urchin with dirty feet, plantar warts, squawking because she had just gotten gum stuck in her blond curls. "Yeah, well ..."

"It just breaks my heart," said Tai. "That's all."

They sat in silence for a moment. Then, "What about you, Tai?"

"What about me?"

"Paisley has issues. Romy has an eating disorder. What about you? How are you?"

Tai sighed. He rubbed his forehead. "Oh, let's see. I was taken away from the mother I dearly loved and my two sisters in the middle of the night by a gang of uncles and raised by a woman I continue to hate to this day. A vicious harridan who has always resented me because — needless to say — I am the son of a woman my father never stopped loving. I guess I have a few hang-ups. I don't sleep well, for starters. I have difficulty with relationships. Mostly I'm just sad. And angry. I feel like there's something broken inside."

"Me, too," said Verna.

"Well, there you have it," said Tai. "We're broken."

Paisley appeared in the door. "Ready?" she asked. "It's seven o'clock."

"Ready," said Tai. He stood. "Oh, yeah. Before I forget. My stepmother told me to 'get the tapestry that whore stole. Get the tapestry.' Does that mean anything to you?"

"Oh, yes," said Verna.

It turned out that not only did Romy dislike people watching her while she cooked, she also didn't like them watching her while she ate. "I got enough of that at the Birches," she told Verna. "Watching, watching. Always watching your every mouthful. Like goddamned border collies." She was standing in the door when she told Verna this, holding a large mixing bowl heaped with steaming vegetables.

"What's in there?" Verna asked. "Besides onions." She could smell the onions.

"Celery," said Romy. "Cucumber. Zucchini. Carrots. Cabbage. Broccoli. Cauliflower. Good stuff."

"But what about protein?" Verna objected. "You've got to have some protein, Romy. What about starch?"

"What about protein? What about starch? What about minding your own bee's wax, Auntie Verna? What I eat is my business. It's my body, not yours."

"Yes, but ..."

Romy huffed off, headed upstairs with her bowl of vegetables and brandishing chop sticks. *Where did she get chopsticks?* Verna wondered.

"I bet she travels with them." A familiar voice to her left. "So she can eat slow, eh?"

"Hi, Lionel," said Verna. "Yeah, you're probably right. She probably does travel with them." There he was, where he always was, sitting on the porch floor, looking out at the lake.

"That girl of yours," Lionel continued, "that Romy there, eh, she's pretty sick."

"She's not *my* girl," retorted Verna. "And what do you expect with Fern for a mother?"

"No," Lionel corrected her. "She had a mother and then she didn't. That's what happens when you have no mother. You get sick. You don't know how to live. Mothers teach you how to live."

"Hey!" Verna reached for the bottle of Russian Prince and slopped another finger of the vodka into her glass. "I didn't have a mother and you don't see me starving myself to death!"

"No," said Lionel. "Just drinking yourself to death."

Verna flushed. "Not to death," she protested. "I'm just knocking off a few of those crappy years toward the end when you'd rather be dead, anyway, not dependent on strangers, not all by yourself in some nursing home."

"You should put Romy in the lake," Lionel suggested. "Let the Nebaunaubaequaewuk heal her."

Verna laughed. "Look, I'll make a deal with you. Me feeling better is one thing, but Romy ... well, let's just say that, when the mermaids cure Romy, that's when I'll believe in them."

Lionel shook his head. "They don't ask you to believe in them," he told her. "They're not like that Jesus guy. They are not like Tinkerbelle."

"It's a moot point in any case," Verna told him. "She can't swim. Can you believe that? Nobody taught her how to swim."

"Then you teach her."

"Me?"

"You're a good swimmer," said Lionel. "You teach her to swim."

"No way," she objected. "That is so not my responsibility."

"Then whose responsibility is it?"

Suddenly there came a loud crash from outside and around back, followed by a piercing scream from upstairs. Verna leapt to her feet at the same time as Jude, who had been sleeping in the hall at the foot of the stairs, arose in a scramble of claws and four splaying feet and galloped upstairs. Barking frantically, he began to hurl himself over and over again at the door to Fern's bedroom.

Verna raced upstairs, and, reaching over Jude, pushed the door to Fern's bedroom open a crack. The Lab immediately wedged himself into the opening, and, together, they half-burst, half-toppled into the room. There was Romy, cowering in Fern's bed, with the mixing bowl of flaccid vegetables clutched to her sunken chest. Eyes wide with terror, she pointed toward the latched window.

Verna gulped. Craning her neck, she squinted hard at the window. Through its glass pane she could just make out a man's haggard face, patchily bearded. The sight jolted her. She gasped and staggered back a step. Jude bounded forward, positioning himself between the window and the women. He growled, hackles up, tail held low and motionless. "Who's there?" Verna managed. Barely.

"Jesus H. Christ! Is that dog vicious?" This from the man on the other side of the window.

Verna heard fear in his voice and fought for breath. "He'll rip your throat out if I tell him to," she lied.

"Well, don't tell him to. Please," the man pleaded — a broken tenor, scratchy and nodular. "Don't mean no harm!"

"Who are you?" Verna grew braver. "Why are you breaking into my house?"

"J.R. Eubanks! I'm J.R. Eubanks — the one left the notice. The prospector. Shit, lady. I just come to get my smokes! I saw the others leave and you on the porch and figured I'd just come up the ladder. Not disturb you. Didn't know there was anybody in Fern's room. Then," pointing to Romy, "that one there, she goes off like a goddamned car alarm. Don't think I haven't heard that before. Scares the bejesus out of me. Made me knock the ladder over. Now, you going to call your dog off? Cause I don't like dogs. I never did."

"He won't hurt you if you don't give him cause," replied Verna. "Otherwise I can't answer for what he'll do. He's got a real mean streak." Crossing over to Jude, she bent down and pulled back his flews; his array of teeth was impressive. "Show me some ID. Hold it up to the window so I can see it."

There was a pause while the man foraged around in his pockets. He surfaced a moment later with an Ontario driver's licence, which he held against the window. Verna leaned forward to inspect it. "You don't have a beard in this photo," she said suspiciously.

"Back then I had a razor."

"How do I know that this is not some fake ID?"

"Look, I just come to get my Camels. That's all. Please. It's getting cold out here and I'm pretty sick."

"Your Camels?" Romy decompressed and entered the fray. "Were those *your* Camels?"

Verna turned from the window. "I'm going to call the O.P.P."

"Hey, Verna, please!" He sounded panicked, stricken. "Don't do that. You can't do that. Please!"

Verna stopped in her tracks. She turned back to the window. "How did you know my name? Never mind that — how did you know my sister's name? And how did you know that this was her room?"

"I knew her, okay? She was ..." he hesitated for a moment, then, shyly, proudly, "she was my old lady."

"Your 'old lady'?" Verna repeated, incredulous. "Your 'old lady'? Good Lord! What were you? A singer in the band? Christ Almighty!" Closing her eyes and hitting herself in the forehead with the heel of her hand, she flopped down on the bed and lay back. "Fern, you slut!"

"Hey!" Romy objected. "That's my mother you're talking about!"

"Please, Verna, please let me in," J.R. whined. "These bugs are eating me alive and it's fixing to rain."

Verna sat up. She closed her eyes, sighed, and shook her head. "Yeah, well. What the hell! Join the party!" Rising, she unlatched the window and pushed up the sash.

J.R. eyed Jude apprehensively. "What about him? He's not going to bite me, now, is he?"

"Here, Fang." Verna took hold of Jude's collar and yanked him toward her. "Don't eat the boyfriend. Not unless I tell you to. Good dog."

J.R. thrust his head tentatively into the room, blinking at the light with rheumy, red-rimmed eyes the washed-out colour of old denim. His nose was red and bulbous, riven with spider veins, and a scruffy mange of rusty beard obscured the lower part of his leathery, sunken face. What of his sallow face the beard did not hide was dotted with rubbery-looking purple lesions.

"Ooh!" hissed Romy. "Dude! What's on your face?"

He bristled. "Acne," he said defensively. "Rosacea."

"Yeah, well. It looks like bugs."

Verna peered hard at the intruder, trying to gauge his age. Judging by appearance alone, she might equally have said forty or sixty or anywhere in between. That's how weathered, how eroded and windswept, how *distressed* he appeared. However, there was about him a certain awkward callowness that made her think he might be younger than he appeared.

"Didn't nobody ever tell you it's rude to make personal remarks?"

"Didn't nobody ever tell you it's against the law to break into other peoples' houses?"

"Didn't *any*body ever tell either of you not to use double negatives?" Verna was exasperated. "Are you coming in or not? Because, if you aren't, I'm closing the goddamned window and you can just hurl yourself off the roof and into the elderberry bushes for all I care!"

"All right! I'm coming!"

J.R. clambered in through the window, using one hand to keep a black baseball cap sporting the name and logo of the Toronto Blue Jays affixed to his head, and straightened up, tentatively, one vertebra at a time, as though the process pained him. In the end he fell several inches short of his full height of perhaps six feet, seemingly not having the wherewithal to stand much straighter than a stoop. His breathing was laboured — heavy, deep, and stertorous; his sunken chest rose and fell on its tide. Under filthy clothing well on its way to becoming rags — a tattered red flannel shirt, torn, smoke-stained blue jeans — he appeared to be little more than bone and loose skin.

"Okay. What's this about you and my sister?" Verna asked.

"Fern and me, we was going to get married," J.R. explained, his voice thick with expectoration. "Before. But she took sick and I … I, well …" He blinked at Verna and Romy. He coughed, trying unsuccessfully to clear a throat clogged with phlegm, then turned to Romy. "You her kid?"

Romy wrinkled up her nose. "Yeah and P.U.! You stink."
He did stink. Verna tried to identify the various strains of odour and settled on a combination of wood smoke, stale, sour sweat, and something else besides — some sweet sort of rot.

He swallowed, absorbing this information. Then, "Right," he said, wobbling. "Anyway, I just come for my smokes."

"Well, you're fresh out of luck," Romy told him.

"Excuse me?"

J.R. was shaking like a dog. Verna noticed that his splotchy forehead was beaded with perspiration. Was he running a fever?

"Because they're gone."

"Gone?" J.R. repeated, not computing. "But ... I ... where did they go?"

"I smoked them, asshole," said Romy. "And why are you shaking like that, anyway? Are you some sort of Powder Monkey? Are you ... like ... riding the White Pony?"

J.R. shook his head. "Nah. I'm clean. I'm sick. Pneumonia or the flu or something. Sleeping out in the bush these couple of nights ... goddamned bugs. Can I sit down? I feel dizzy." Without waiting for an answer, he careened over to the peacock chair and plopped himself down. He leaned his head back and carefully closed his eyes. "I can't believe you smoked my Camels!" He began to keen softly, rolling his head from side to side.

Verna turned to Romy. "Powder Monkey? White Pony?"

"Meth," Romy explained. "As in 'methadrine.' As in crystal meth."

"I find the fact that you know these things deeply disturbing," Verna told her.

"I was in a rehab centre," Romy pointed out.

"My last pack!" J.R. moaned. "What am I going to do now?"

"Well and how the hell was I supposed to know it was your last pack?" Romy demanded. "And what were they doing in my mother's bedroom in the first place? Huh? Answer me that!"

J.R. opened his eyes. "I was sort of hanging out here." Then, "Well! She give me a key, didn't she?" He glanced at Verna. "And then you came along and I didn't know what was up with that, so I took off. Left in a hurry. "

Verna held up a hand. "Wait a minute. Hold on. You were squatting here?"

"Yeah."

"In this house?"

"I told you."

"And you only left on Tuesday?"

"She give me a key!" J.R. defended himself. "It's not squatting when they give you the key." He pulled a key with a green tag from his shirt pocket and waggled it at her.

"It's squatting when a dead person gave you a key however long ago and years later you decide you're going to use it to break into a house and squat there!" Verna countered.

"Well," said J.R. stubbornly, "that's not how I see it." He returned the key to his pocket. "Fern was my fiancée, and, if her and me had gotten married like she wanted to ... like we planned, this'd be part of the matrimonial property — it'd belong to me. Part of it, anyway. I figured that'd give me the right to stay here, at least until I get myself sorted out. Wasn't hurting anything or anybody. Then you had to come along. And those others."

While this exchange was going on, Romy had been working things out. "You said you took off. How?"

"Waited until Verna here was inside, then I climbed out the window," said J.R. "Slid down the roof of the shed. Cut my leg on a rusty drainpipe going down." He glanced down at his right leg; a dirty rag was wrapped tightly around his lower calf. "Hasn't healed. I think it's festering."

Romy turned to Verna. "That explains it."

"Explains what?" Verna asked. "The smell?"

"No! Explains why the window was left open and the door was locked from inside. And the Camels. Mom would have never smoked Camels. Camels are foul. Worse than those butt-legged puffers of Winonah's."

J.R. took umbrage at this. "If they're so disgusting, why did you smoke them?"

"I was desperate," retorted Romy, "just like Mom must have been desperate to hook up with a loser like you. Ew!"

"I was different when your mother knew me," J.R. defended himself. "Good-looking. Strong. Not like now. I've had a hard life. Not my fault things turned out like they did."

"Well, whose fault is it?"

Verna interceded wearily. "Romy, please. What's done is done. Let's just move on."

"Yeah," said J.R. "We gotta move on. Look to the future."

"Which brings me to this." Verna retrieved the Notice of Intention to Perform Assessment Work from the pocket of her overalls and waved it at him. "How hell do you get off thinking you can stake a claim on my property?"

"*Our* property," Romy corrected her.

"Our property."

J.R. shrugged. "What about it? I got a licence. It's my right. It's anybody's right got a licence."

"But what do you hope to gain by it?"

He laughed. A ragged laugh that escalated into a dry racking cough; it sounded like there was a ball rolling around loose in his trachea. Then, in a ravaged voice, "Gold."

"Gold?"

"One way or another."

"What do you mean by that?"

J.R. looked at her through narrowed, blinking eyes. Through their glazed pupils she could just glimpse his reptilian brain firing. "Don't tell me I have to spell it out, Verna."

It took her a moment, then, "Oh," she said. "You mean extortion." Relief flooded her — relief that he had just beaten her to a plan she had already settled on. Hard on its heels, however, came anger. How dare he put her in such a bind?

"Call it whatever you like, but I got myself to look after. And I'm sick. Real sick. I need medicine — expensive medicine. I need a place to stay. I gotta eat. And, like I said, Fern was my lady. This ... what was hers ... I figure I got a right to some of part of that. That's what I figure. And I don't expect for a minute that you'd give it to me out of the kindness of your heart. Fern said you were cold. *Cold as ice.* Her words."

238 • Melissa Hardy

Verna flinched to hear Fern's estimation of her charity; it tore the sting right out of her anger. *Well and what did I expect?* she thought, freefalling. She had kicked Fern out of her house and contrived never to see her again and now.... Well, now it was too late. And it had been too late for a very long time. Years. "Okay," she said roughly. "Let's you and I talk dollars and cents. But downstairs. I need a drink."

"What about me?" Romy wailed.

"Finish your dinner."

"But I don't like people watching me while I eat!"

"Stay up here until you finish, then come downstairs."

"But it takes me forever! Hours!" Romy protested. "Can't I just skip it tonight? Just this once?"

"No," said Verna, "or I swear, Romy, I'll call 911. And I'm taking one of your cigarettes. For Romeo here."

"What?" Romy was outraged. "No!"

Verna reached for the pack of Virginia Slims on the bedside table. So did Romy. The brief tug of war ended in an easy triumph for Verna — Romy was as weak as a sick cat. "Ah-ha!" Verna crowed. "For that I'll take two! Come on, Romy! Paisley got you a whole carton."

Romy collapsed back into a stack of pillows and crossed her stick arms over her sunken chest. She pouted. "You better not do anything bad to my Auntie Verna," she told J.R. "Or Jude will rip you open and tear you limb from limb. He'll eat your balls, too. He specially likes balls."

J.R. blinked. "I thought his name was Fang."

"So, fill me in on my sister's life," Verna said to J.R. She was standing at the counter in the kitchen, building J.R. a rum and Diet Coke. He sat at the kitchen table, cracking his knuckles and his neck and picking his venous ruin of a nose. Every few moments he would cough — a dry, inconclusive rattle. Unproductive. That was how doctors described such coughs. "How did you meet her?" she asked. "You don't exactly seem like her type." And what had Fern's type been, anyway? Pretty, marginal, faintly artistic. Of these attributes only "marginal" would seem to apply to J.R.

"Well, uh ... in Toronto," he muttered, glancing sideways at Jude, whose body language — hackles high, tail low — continued to send a message of vigilance, as did the soft, low-pitched ruffle of a growl that emanated, every few minutes, from his throat. "In ninety-seven," he added.

Ninety-seven, thought Verna. *Eight years ago. This goes back awhile.* "So you're not from around here?"

"No."

"But you came here because of her? Because of Fern?"

"You could say that."

She handed him the drink, noting, as she did, the tremor in his hands when he took the glass from her. Like an old man's tremor. Like Donald's, toward the end. Returning to the counter she made herself yet another vodka and tonic — possibly her fifth, no, probably her fifth — but no matter. As it turned out, finding a strange man on the roof outside her dead sister's window had had a remarkably sobering effect upon her; in fact, she felt downright lucid. "Where have you been staying? After I showed up, that is."

"I told you." He was cranky, restless. "Outdoors. On the other side of the lake. Why do you think I'm so sick? Sleeping on the ground in my condition. I got an old pup tent, but it's mouldy and it leaks. Bought it in a yard sale. Somebody else's old junk. The bastard who sold me said it didn't leak. Swore to it. He lied."

Verna glanced around. After the dimly lit bedroom, the yellow kitchen seemed to blaze with light. In all this radiance J.R. appeared even pastier and sweatier than he had upstairs; he had collapsed back upon himself as though aware that the degree of scrutiny afforded by so bright a space worked to his disadvantage. He reminded her of a grub worm, slimy, unnaturally pale. She wrinkled up her nose. "It's way too bright in here," she said. "Why don't we go onto the porch?"

"Yeah. Good." J.R. seemed relieved at the prospect of darkness. He followed her out to the porch, taking the Heywood rocker farthest from the door. She sat in the other rocker and Jude positioned himself between them. She glanced to where Lionel had been earlier in the evening. She was relieved to find that he was still there, sitting cross-legged and gazing out towards the lake. *Thank you*, she thought.

"Don't mention it," Lionel said.

"I'll have that cigarette now," J.R. said.

Verna handed him both Virginia Slims. He looked confused and tried to give one back. Verna shook her head. "No," she said. "I don't smoke."

"That's right," said J.R. "Your type never does."

"What type is that?"

"Miss Prissy."

The phone rang, startling J.R. He jumped, splattering some of his drink on his mud-caked jeans, then shuddered back into his chair. Verna rose from the rocker. Miss Prissy! A version of Super Grammarian, she supposed. "Don't get your knickers in a knot," she told him. "It's probably just Carmen checking in on Romy." Then, when he continued to look uneasy, "A friend," she said. "Checking on a sick child."

"You going to take that dog with you?" J.R. tucked one of the cigarettes into his breast pocket and scrounged around in his pants pocket for a lighter.

"Why?" asked Verna, but Jude followed her into the house and down the hall to the kitchen, anyway. She picked up the phone.

It was Carmen. She sounded excited. "I found out something. Something about your mysterious J.R. Eubanks."

"He's here." Verna kept her voice low. "Eubanks, I mean. He's here."

"What do you mean?"

"'Here' as in on the porch," said Verna. "I caught him breaking into Fern's old bedroom."

"Breaking in?"

"It's a long story," said Verna. "Anyway, the bastard's pretty keen to be bought off. I'm just working out the details now."

"Okay, but first you'd better listen to this," Carmen told her. "Just so you know who you're dealing with. I have a membership in an online government public records database — for background checks. You know, criminal records, property records, bankruptcies and liens, sex offenders. That sort of thing. Very useful for checking out prospective clients."

"Yeah, and …?"

"So I did a search on your guy. Seems he's has been in and out of prison most of his life, from juvi onward. Botched B and Es for the most part, a couple of car thefts, small stuff, but — and this is the freaky part — in ninety-nine he was charged with aggravated assault — for the sexual transmission of HIV. Charged with infecting this woman with HIV."

Verna's heart turned over. "I'm sorry, Carmen. What did you say?"

"The sexual transmission of HIV," Carmen repeated. "You know. The AIDS virus. Some woman in Toronto — Fosbrink was her name. It seems he's known he was HIV-positive since the mid-nineties, but he didn't bother to tell her before sleeping with her. The case was thrown out of court. Some legal technicality. The trial judge had misdirected himself or something. It wasn't that Eubanks was innocent. He was guilty as hell and everybody knew it. Anyway, he ended up back in prison the following year, but on a different charge — a bar fight that spun out of control. He just got out of Beaver Creek in Gravenhurst last month. The Fosbrink woman died in 2002. Cause of death: some kind of pneumonia called PCP, common among AIDS patients."

Ninety-nine, Verna thought, and Fern had died in 2001. "Excuse me, when did he go back to prison? This last time, I mean."

"2000."

"2000," Verna repeated. "Thanks for this, Carmen. This is really helpful information. More helpful than you know. But I'd better go."

"Keep me posted."

"I will."

"Oh, and Verna?"

"What?"

"Whatever you do, don't sleep with him!" Carmen hung up.

Verna replaced the receiver and leaned back against the counter, trying to work the chronology out. So J.R. had been in and out of prison all his life. That meant long exposure to shared needles and unsafe sex. He had been diagnosed with HIV in the mid-nineties — mid-nineties, what would that be? Ninety-four through ninety-six? In ninety-seven he had met Fern and their thing — whatever that thing had been — was presumably over by ninety-nine when he was tried, but not convicted for aggravated assault with a deadly penis. Then in 2000 he went to jail because of some bar fight, and, while he was incarcerated, both the the Fosbrink woman and Fern had died from AIDS-related causes. Clearly the Fosbrink woman was not the only person he had infected. He had infected Fern, as well. It was just that no one had made the connection until now — because no one had known about J.R. and Fern; because only she had known that Fern had tested positive for HIV and had died of an AIDS-related cancer. She looked at Jude. "It's official," she told him. "That son of a bitch killed my sister!"

Jude glanced at his bowl and wagged his tail hopefully.

"No, you don't understand. That goddamned son of a bitch killed my sister!"

Jude barked.

"What? You've had your dinner!"

Jude's ears drooped; his head dangled.

"Oh, all right. But only because you've been such a *mensch* tonight. Honestly, Jude, I've never thought you capable of conveying menace or anything really beyond a kind of goofy bonhomie, but tonight you rocked it as Fang. You really did." Jude trotted over to his bowl and stood before it. She crossed the floor, dropped to her knees and wrapped her arms around his neck. "Jude!" She pressed her mouth against his cheek and earflap and whispered, "He killed our Fern, Jude! What are we going to do? We've got to do something. But what?" She released the dog, stood, and bent over to scoop kibble out of the bag of Iams. As she did, the orange bottle of OxyContin that she had removed from Romy's discarded clothing earlier in the evening popped out of the front pocket of her overalls and into the bag of dog food. She was reaching into the bag to fish it out when a thought occurred to her. Going to the front door, she leaned out. "How's your drink?" she asked the shadowy, hunched figure in the rocker.

"Gone."

"How about I freshen it up for you? After all, the night is young."

"Sure!"

She took the glass he offered her, and, returning to the kitchen, extracted a grey marble mortar and pestle from the cabinet. *Let's make this a double*, she thought. *No, on second thought, let's make it a triple*. Plucking three OxyContins from the bottle, she proceeded to crush them into a fine powder. The lucidity that had prevailed since she had seen

J.R. through the window of Fern's bedroom crumbled away. Verna was now officially drunk. And very pissed off.

Ten minutes into his doctored rum and Coke, Verna, who was watching carefully, like a spider, noticed a distinct difference in J.R.'s demeanour. All his tense urgency seemed to drain away and he began to slump in the rocker and slide slowly down until he lay sprawled in it, almost prone, the glass half full on his sunken belly.

"So, about Fern," Verna began. "How did you meet her?"

Up to that point getting any information out of J.R. had been like prying shrapnel from a wound. Under the influence of the painkillers, however, he became more forthcoming. "Underground parking garage," he said. "Queen Street West area. I was the attendant. An attendant. That's the only kind of job you can get when you got a record — a lousy one. Ex-cons and sand niggers, that's who they hire. All day long stuck underground in this little booth. You never see the sun. Well, you never see the sun in Toronto, anyway. But still. Underground. It's like you died and they buried you. You do know I got a record?"

"No," lied Verna. "Why would I?"

He didn't seem to register the coldness in her voice, the barely suppressed fury. He looked like he was enjoying himself. He probably thought they were having a pleasant conversation.

"Well, you do now." He sighed. "I guess I just assume people know. Like it's branded on my forehead or something. According to most people, it's the most important thing about me, the only thing worth knowing. But it's not the only thing worth knowing. Nossir. I got my good points and she saw 'em — Fern did. Lot of people won't have nothing to do with you if you got a record. Treat you like dirt. But not Fern."

"So she knew you had a record?"

"Sure she did. After a while. Once we'd … you know. You don't just say 'Hi, that'll be seven dollars. I got a record.'"

"So, paint me a picture," said Verna. "You met her … how? When she got her parking ticket?"

J.R. shook his head. "No, that was automatic. The machine did that. It was when she paid. You paid the attendant. You know. Me."

Damn you, Fern, Verna thought. *Always so goddamned friendly. Always giving people the benefit of the doubt.* She had never thought in terms of boundaries, limits; hers were open borders, in sharp contrast to Verna's heavily fortified and guarded ones.

"She parked there pretty regular," J.R. reminisced. "Liked to walk up and down Queen Street and look at the stores, then she'd stop in one of those cafés and have a fancy coffee. And she always had … you know … a good word to say. One day she asked my name, what the J.R. stands for. I had one of those tags, you know, with my name on it."

"What does it stand for?"

"Don't know. That was what was wrote on the birth certificate. Just the initials. My mother was long gone by the time I thought to ask."

"So your family …"

"Don't have one so far as I can tell. Foster homes growing up. Four of 'em. I didn't get along too good with any of my foster parents. They were just in it for the money. Didn't care about me or nothing."

"That must have been rough."

J.R. snorted. "Sucked is what it did. Big time. Those bastards. You'd better believe I gave as good as I got. Didn't let nobody get away with nothing. I was tough."

"I bet."

He struggled to a slightly more upright position to slurp at his drink. "So, after she asked about my name, we'd talk whenever she parked in the garage. Sometimes she'd even bring me a cup of joe from one of those fancy places. But you couldn't have a good conversation — not with cars waiting, so one day she asked me if I'd like to go for a cup of coffee with her when I got off and I said yes. And that was how it all started. The best year of my life."

"You were together a year?"

"Or thereabouts. A little less. Ten months, maybe."

"And you actually lived together?"

J.R. shook his head. "I didn't want my parole officer to know I had a girlfriend."

"Why?" Verna already knew the answer: the parole officer would have made sure Fern knew J.R. was HIV-positive.

But Eubanks was evasive. "They give you a rough time, that's all. But we were planning to. Live together, that is. She was moving up north. She didn't want to live in T.O. anymore. Too expensive and too much pollution. She told me about this place here — somewhere we could start over, together. We were just waiting for my parole to end, so I could come with her." He fell silent.

After a moment, Verna prompted him. "We all need to start over."

J.R. shrugged. "She didn't tell me about the bugs," he said despondently. "Fucking, cock-sucking bugs." He stared ahead for a moment, his expression blank. Then his eyelids began to waver.

Reaching over, Verna poked him hard. "Hey! Are you falling asleep on me?"

J.R. jerked to attention. "What? No."

"So what happened next?"

J.R. shook his head dolefully. "All I know is we had this fight and I went and got in trouble and, before I knew it, I was back in the slammer." His upper lip started to wobble. "Never saw her again. She died while I was in. Beautiful

Fern. The only woman who truly loved me." He began to cry. It was a harsh, ugly sound.

Verna waited for a moment, listening to him wetly blubber, then, "How's your drink?"

"Verna!" Lionel warned her. "Careful!"

"*Sssshhh!*" Verna hissed. "The bastard killed my sister!"

J.R. stopped crying. "Who are you talking to?" He glanced from side to side. Verna noticed that his speech was beginning to slur; he sounded punch drunk. "Are you talking to somebody? Is somebody else here?"

"Nah!" Verna joshed. "Nobody here but you and me and Fang." Then, with icy solicitude, "How's your drink doing there, J.R., old buddy, old pal?"

"It's gone!" he sobbed.

"How about I get you another?"

Once again Verna careened to the kitchen where she ground up three more OxyContins and poured fresh rum and Diet Coke into J.R.'s glass. This time she did not pour herself another drink; she could tell that she was perilously close to that spinny, throwing-up state and her brain could not afford to go AWOL, not now. Returning to the porch, she found J.R. practically prone in the rocker, snoring.

"J.R.! Wake up!" Taking him by his bony shoulder, she rattled him.

"What? Oh, yeah. Must have dozed off," he mumbled, struggling to sit up.

"Here you go," Verna said, handing him the doctored rum and Coke. She pulled her rocker around so that she was facing him head on.

He eyed her apprehensively. "What are you doing that for?"

"Just want to look at you," replied Verna. "My dead sister's last lover. The last of her many, many lovers. I'm wondering what she saw in you. To tell you the truth, I'm having kind of a hard time seeing it."

J.R. looked abashed. "I know I'm not much to look at now. But I was."

Verna looked skeptical.

"I was!" he insisted. "You should have seen me then. Then you'd know. Do you know what Fern used to call me?"

"I can't begin to imagine."

"Her beautiful boy. That's what."

"Of course she did."

"I was younger than her. A lot younger."

"You were her boy toy."

"That's right."

"Not so beautiful now, though. Are you?"

"Well, you're nothin' to write home about neither," J.R. mumbled, shifting miserably in his chair. "Why do you have to be so mean?"

Verna sighed. She stood and dragged her rocker back to its former position. Sitting, she stared glumly out at the lake. After a moment she said, "Did you know we were twins, J.R.? Me and Fern. Not just sisters, but twins."

"I knew that."

"But did you know that twins have a special bond?"

J.R. turned nasty. "I know you hated her. That's what she said. She loved you, but you hated her. Is that the special bond you're talking about?"

"Drink your rum and Coke," Verna told him. "And I didn't hate her. I resented her. I was envious of her. There's a difference."

"She used to cry about you," he said. "You made her cry."

"Shut up!" Verna snapped. "Just shut up." Her throat constricted; it was as though a hand were compressing her heart. Why had she let Bob come between her and Fern — Bob whom she had come (let's be real about this) to loathe, Bob who ultimately turned out to be the dispos- able one and not Fern. She had a lot to answer for, but not to J.R. "We need to talk about this claim you've staked," she said shortly.

"We do? What?" J.R. looked confused now, all turned around, as though he had lost his bearings. He gaped at her, slack-mouthed.

"The claim," Verna repeated.

"Oh, yeah," said J.R. vaguely. "That. Gotta get what's coming to me. I give up everything for her. Need some compensation for my trouble. If I don't stand up for myself, who's gonna stand up for me? Eh? Tell me that."

"And what did she get for her trouble, J.R.?" Verna asked. "What did Fern get?"

"She got love," J.R. replied. "That's all Fern ever wanted. She said so. 'All I want is love.' Her words."

"I'll tell you what you gave her. You gave her AIDS. Didn't you? You gave my sister AIDS."

J.R. blinked at her, muddled by the OxyContin. "But, what about me?" he blurted out at last. "Look at these fucking spots?" He lifted up his flannel shirt to reveal more purplish lesions on his stomach and chest. "I didn't sign on for this. How is that fair? How did I deserve this? Why me? When I've had such a rotten life! And now I'm going to die!" He burst into ragged sobs.

"Oh, stop it, you big sissy," Verna told him. "I'm getting you another drink." She wrangled the glass out of his clammy hand and stood up.

"Slippery slope, Verna," warned Lionel. "The Thunderbirds are coming from the south. Do you hear that?"

A distant boom sounded like a faraway bass drum.

"That there is *bodreudang*," Lionel said. "What our people call 'Approaching Thunderer.'"

Verna glanced out towards the lake. Grey clouds had swallowed up the Milky Way and the wind had picked up; it rattled the new leaves and troubled the water.

"Oh, hush," she told Lionel.

Verna returned to find J.R. curled up in a fetal position on the floor of the porch beside the rocker.

"J.R.?"

She prodded him with her toe.

"Oh, J.R.!"

No response.

"J.R., stop fooling around. You're scaring me." She knelt down next to him, and, with some difficulty, managed to roll him over onto his back. He was breathing, but very shallowly. His skin felt cold, clammy to the touch. She pried open one eyelid — a pinpoint of a pupil stared unseeingly back at her. Verna's heart bumped in her chest. "Oh, shit, Lionel! Don't tell me I've killed him!"

"Okay," Lionel said.

"What?" she demanded. "Do you think I have? Do you think I've … like … given him an overdose and now he's in a coma?"

"How should I know?" Lionel asked. "Maybe he's sleeping."

"Are you kidding? I fed him six OxyContins!"

"Could be taking a nap."

Verna stood. "Shit! What am I going to do? What?" She paced up and down the length of the porch. She wrung her hands. "What about an antidote? Is there an antidote? Milk, maybe? Oh, I know! Ipecac! But I don't have any ipecac. Maybe I should feed him lots of bread …"

"That's for when a dog, eh, eats a chicken bone," Lionel pointed out.

"Oh, shit, you're right," said Verna. "I'll have to call 911."

"You could try and let him sleep it off," Lionel called after her as she headed inside.

She was halfway across the living room on her way to the study, when a voice came from the depths of the sofa, "I wouldn't do that if I were you. Call 911, I mean." Verna whirled around to see Romy, curled up on the couch under Grandmother Frieda's afghan.

Verna clutched her chest. She had been so focused on J.R. that she had completely forgotten her niece's existence, much less her presence in the house. "Romy! For Christ's sake! You scared the daylights out of me!"

"Think about it, Auntie Verna. What you did looks a whole heck of a lot like attempted murder. What? Did you honestly think I was going to stay upstairs while you talked to that white trash trailer park mulletino?"

Verna sighed. She put her hand to her forehead. Closed her eyes. "I suppose not. How long have you been here?"

"If you're asking how much did I *hear*, I'd say pretty much *everything?*" the girl replied. "When the two of you went out on the porch, that's when I snuck down the stairs and hid in the corner by the window." She drew the throw closer around her. Shivered. "Is it true about Mom? That she had AIDS? You told me she died of cancer. No, come to think of it, you told me she died of *putrefaction*."

"Yeah, well, technically, she did," Verna replied. "Putrefy, that is. The sepsis was the result of the cancer and the cancer was the result of a weakened immune system. Look, nobody knew about this but me, Romy. I asked the doctor to keep it quiet. I didn't tell my husband. Not even your grandfather knew. I wanted to spare him. I didn't want people to know what she died of. It was ... well, it was embarrassing." She sank into a lumpy armchair and stared into the cold, sooty mouth of the riverstone fireplace.

"Yeah, well," conceded Romy. "I guess I can see that. Still, it's pretty shitty."

"Yeah," agreed Verna. "It is."

"So you gave six Oxys to AIDS Boy?"

"Uh-huh," said Verna mournfully.

"You did know they were eighties, didn't you?"

Verna nodded. "Yup."

"And you ... what? Crushed them?"

"Ground them into a powder. With a mortar and pestle."

"Whoa!" Romy was impressed. "Auntie Verna!"

"I'm glad you approve," said Verna. "But that doesn't solve the problem of what to do about an ex-con on the front porch whom I may have just killed."

"Hey, Verna!" This from Lionel on the porch. "The cavalry has arrived. I can see headlights through the trees."

"Tai and Paisley! They're back from the movie. Oh, thank God. Tai's a doctor. Surely he'll know what to do!"

"Oops!" said Lionel. "Now there's another car!"

"What the ...?" Verna stood.

"What? Where are you going?" asked Romy, but Verna was already out the front door. Harrumphing, the girl stood, arranged the afghan so it draped her bony frame like a fusty toga, and followed her aunt outside, giving J.R.'s prone body a wide berth as she went.

It was not the Camry, but the bulky Carmen-mobile that was pulling up alongside the Volvo.

"Moby Rapper?" hissed Romy. "What's she doing here?"

"She called me earlier to tell me that J.R. had a criminal record," Verna told her. "She probably got worried and decided to check on us."

"Or she's a ginormous nosy-parker!"

"Give it a break, why don't you? Carmen's a friend." She was a friend, Verna realized. How had that happened?

In the meantime, the realtor had decanted herself from the Buick and was flowing toward them like slow-moving lava in her purple jalaba and high-top shoes. "Are you all right?" she asked. "Is Eubanks still here?"

"Not really and yes," said Verna.

"It's very fraught," Romy added breathlessly. Then, "Auntie Verna, look!" Winonah's Impala, glimmering a ghostly white, appeared in the laneway. "Oh, please! Isn't it bad enough that we have to spend all day with her?"

"Did you call Winonah?" Verna asked Carmen.

Carmen shook her head. "Not me."

The Impala, wheezing, lurched itself into position next to the aubergine Buick. As its engine died in a series of hollow clanks, Winonah emerged from the driver's side, and, exhibiting a high degree of dudgeon, crossed around to the passenger's door, where she took Granny under the armpits, hauled her out of the car and onto her feet.

"Hey!" Verna greeted the women. "What are you guys doing here?"

Winonah was bitter. "Granny made me come."

"I had a dream," said Granny.

"What kind of dream?" asked Romy.

"An important one," Granny replied.

By this time the wind had picked up, causing trees to twist and thrash and stippling the surface of the lake. Lightning lit up the clouds from within. The heavens crackled. In fact, there was so much ambient noise that no one heard the sound of the Camry smoothly negotiating the gravel laneway until it suddenly hove into view from between the trees.

Between the time that Verna had gone inside the cottage with the intention of calling 911 and the others had arrived at the cottage, J.R. Eubanks, aged thirty-six and lying all by himself on the porch floor, stopped breathing and quietly expired — his precise time of death was 9:58 p.m. Eastern Standard Time on May 20, 2005. What neither he nor Verna could have known was that the yeasty fungus causing that peculiar form of pneumonia to which people with surrepressed autoimmune function are particularly susceptible — pneumocystis pneumonia, the same type of pneumonia that carried off the Fosbrink woman in Toronto — had been preying upon the interstitial, fibrous tissue of his lungs for some time now, thickening his alveoli, making it more difficult for oxygen to diffuse into his blood. The low-grade fever that had swaddled his cognitive processes in a miasmal fog over the past week or so, the night sweats that had jacked him awake in the middle of interminable nights spent huddled in his makeshift camp, the stabbing shortness of breath whenever he exerted himself at all (claim-staking the glen had exhausted him; he had had to crawl back to his pup tent and rest for the remainder of that day), not to mention his chronic cough — all symptoms of pneumocystis pneumonia. The six tablets of eighty milligrams of OxyContin that Verna had fed him would not have killed a healthy man; a healthy man could have slept the overdose off. Eubanks, however, was not a healthy man. Conseqently the overdose became for him a kind of tipping point — that point at which life turns into death. Its effect had been simply this: to suppress an already suppressed respiratory system. That was all. It was, however, enough. J.R. — so-called because his mother had been a big fan of the hit TV series *Dallas* (although this, as all else about her, would have been news to him) — was dead. His last word, thickly spoken in a hoarse whisper, was, "Fern!" But there was only Lionel to hear.

Tai knelt beside J.R.'s body, rooting around for a pulse. Then he glanced up at the women anxiously gathered round and shook his head. "I think he's dead." He sounded amazed.

"What'd you mean, *think?*" demanded Romy. "You're a

doctor, for Pete's sake. Can't you tell when somebody is dead?"

"Hey!" Tai defended himself. "I'm a medical student, not a doctor. And cut me some slack here! I wasn't exactly expecting to come back from a movie with my long-lost sister to find that my aunt, whom I haven't seen since I was a kid, has murdered somebody at the family cottage."

At the word *murdered*, Verna staggered backwards a step, then turned and crumpled into a chair. "How can that be? He was alive twenty minutes ago! Less! Wasn't he, Romy? Wasn't he alive?"

"In a dying sort of way," she replied.

"See? He was alive," said Verna. "How can somebody be dead when he was just alive?"

"News flash, Verna," Winonah said. "It only takes a moment to die."

"It took me five minutes," said Lionel. He shook his head. "Those were some bad-ass five minutes."

"And he wasn't just anybody," Romy told her brother and sister. "Oh, you are *so* not going to believe this!"

"What?" Paisley demanded.

"He was her last lover! Mom's."

Paisley moaned. "Oh, man!"

"You've got to be kidding!" said Tai.

"I know," said Romy. "Isn't it embarrassing?"

Carmen peered at J.R., then shook her head. "There's just no accounting for taste, is there? I guess I didn't know Fern all that well. I thought I did."

"What do you mean?" asked Verna. "She had terrible taste in men. She always did."

"I don't know," said Granny. "Looks broken. All rusted out."

"But that's not all," said Romy. "This is the real kicker: he gave her AIDS."

"*What?*"

"You heard me!"

"Tabernak!" Carmen said. "I never knew that!"

"Nobody did," said Verna. "I didn't until tonight. I mean, I knew that Fern was HIV-positive, but I didn't know that he was the one responsible."

"Those spots on his face and his chest," Tai realized. "They look to me like Kaposi's sarcoma. That's one of the hallmarks of late-stage AIDS."

Romy prodded J.R.'s back with her toe. "I've never seen a dead person before. Oh, wait! There was Angela at the Birches. Just down the hall. An electrolyte imbalance gone terribly wrong. She was bluer somehow."

"Dear God," Verna croaked. "So I really did kill him! I killed a man." She buried her face in her hands. Was this actually happening? It didn't seem real somehow.

"Oh, it's real, all right," Lionel assured her.

"Do you believe in God?" Romy asked. "I don't." She plunked herself down on one of the Bar Harbour chairs. "Besides, you didn't mean to kill him."

"You don't know that! *I* don't know that. I think maybe I did. I think maybe I wanted him dead." Suddenly she felt lightheaded; the porch floor seemed to have taken it upon itself to tilt towards the east. "Dizzy," she managed. *"Glup!"*

"Up we go!" Carmen hauled Verna to her feet and steered her through the screen door and out in front of the house. It had begun to rain by this time — plump, loose drops with a slick, thick surface, like Concord grapes. Verna sunk to her knees and vomited a sour stew of vodka and pasta into the elderberry bushes.

"I'm sorry!" she sobbed after a moment. She wiped her mouth with the back of her hand. "I'm so sorry!"

"Come on," Carmen reassured her. "You're going to be all right."

"I am? How? How am I going to be all right?"

"We're going to take care of it," Carmen told her. "You'll see."

"You're a good friend, Carmen," Verna said drunkenly. "Why are you such a good friend?"

"I have no idea," said Carmen. Helping Verna to her feet, she led her back to the porch. "Come on," she said to the others. "Let's go inside. We're not doing this guy any good standing around here."

"I'll start a fire!" Filled with sudden purpose, Paisley headed inside, followed by Winonah and Granny.

Tai took Verna over from Carmen. "Calm down. Stop worrying."

"Stop worrying? I just killed somebody!"

Tai put his arm around her shoulder and led her into the house. "We'll fix it."

"Fix it? How are we going to fix it?"

Once again the porch lit up — a greenish tint, like the light exuded by a lightning bug. It began to rain in earnest now, not in drops so much as wavering sheets of water that broke against the house like waves.

Romy, in the meantime, had spotted the second of the two cigarettes Verna had taken from her pack of Ultra Slims and given J.R.; its filter protruded from the breast pocket of the dead man's flannel shirt. "Bonus!" She swooped down to retrieve it. As she pulled it free, she dislodged the pocket's other contents: a penknife, a house key tagged "Fern's cottage," and a legal-sized envelope that had been folded in two. She pocketed the penknife and the key and peered at the envelope. "What's this?"

Carmen took Romy by her stick arm and steered her towards the door. "Lord Thunderin' Jesus, girl! You're like a rag bag of bones!"

"And you're bus-like in your enormity!"

As Carmen closed the door behind them, the darkened porch lit up for a moment, illuminating J.R.'s corpse before letting it slip back into darkness.

Romy plopped herself down in one of the armchairs and studied the envelope she had plucked from J.R.'s shirt pocket. "Provincial Mining Recorder," she read the address portion, "Ministry of ..."

"Let me see that!" Carmen snatched the envelope from her and tore it open. "Application to Record Staked Mining Claims'" She looked up. "It's the claim! Don't you see? This is good news!"

Verna stared at her blankly, then closed her eyes and swayed. Somehow she had let it all get away from her, lost control. Things had gone off the rails, run amok, gone asunder. The centre had not held. She had come undone. What was more and possibly even worse was the fact that, now that she had inadvertently murdered J.R., the job of disposing of his mortal remains appeared to have passed to these guiltless others. At least that's what they seemed to think. How had that happened? Was that fair? What had she gotten them into? Was this fresh sin to be heaped on top of her already overburdened conscience? She didn't know whether she could handle that or anything else, for that matter. She sagged momentarily against the diminutive Tai, who staggered under her weight before sidestepping over to the sofa and lowering her down onto it. He went to sit cross-legged on the floor in front of the fireplace next to Jude, whom the imminent thunderstorm had reduced to a cowering mound of jelly.

"This is the claim. Eubanks didn't mail it," Carmen explained. "That's means there's nothing to link him to this place, to you. No paper trail. Well, at least, not now there isn't." She tore the form in two and handed the pieces to

Paisley, who tossed the them onto the pile of newspapers and kindling she had been constructing in the fireplace's grate and lit them with her Zippo.

"Gonzo," said Paisley.

"Now, where can I park this hunk of junk?" Carmen asked. "The blood's pooling in my ankles." After surveying the available furniture, she settled for a place on the sofa, squeezing Verna into its furthest corner. Verna did not mind; somehow it was comforting, being pressed by all that flesh.

Winonah settled Granny in the other armchair and drew up one of the chairs from the card table under the window for herself. "Where'd you get that guy there?" Granny asked. She pointed to the moth-eaten moose head over the door to the study.

"That's Bullwinkle," said Verna.

"Looks sad." Granny shook her head. "Why do white people do that?"

Carmen took charge. "Okay. Let's take stock. What do we know about this Eubanks guy? I know that he was in and out of jail his whole life. Mostly small stuff — burglary, car theft, getting into fights, but he was also charged with aggravated assault for the sexual transmission of HIV. That was in 1999."

"What?" asked Paisley. "This creep sexually assaulted Mom?"

Carmen shook her head. "It was another woman who charged him — a Toronto woman. She died later of an AIDS-related illness." She turned to Verna. "Okay, Verna. What did you find out about him? Don't fall apart now. That's not going to help."

Verna tried to rally herself. "Uh … hmm …"

"Never mind her. I heard it all," Romy interceded. "He said that he didn't have a family that he knew of. He bounced from foster home to foster home — four of them. Didn't work out. You could tell he'd been a real juvi bastard."

"But that's good," said Carmen. "Don't you see, Verna? That's good. No family to miss him. No family to go looking for him."

"He met Mom in ninety-seven," Romy continued. "At a parking garage in Toronto. He was the parking-lot attendant. They had split by the time he was charged with the assault."

"He was diagnosed in the mid-nineties," Carmen put it together for them. "He met Fern in ninety-seven. Presumably he knew he was HIV-positive at the time."

"Ew," said Romy. "A parking-lot attendant!" She wrinkled her nose.

Verna found her tongue. "It was her nature," she said, remembering Fern's easy empathy, the dwelling in the moment that precluded any consideration of consequences; finally it had been this that had proven to be her great undoing. "She didn't know that she was not supposed to be friendly with parking-lot attendants. Social markers didn't register with her."

Tai shook his head. "Still! I can't believe she slept with him."

"I know," said Paisley, poking distractedly at the resulting flames with the poker. "He looks like a homeless person."

"Well, apparently he used to be a real hottie," said Romy. "According to him, at any rate."

"It happens," Carmen pointed out. "You should have seen me."

"Carmen was Miss Greater Gammage," Granny told them. "And Miss Moose Milk and Miss Congeniality at the Miss Dominion of Canada pageant in ... what year was that, Carmen?"

"1974," replied Carmen, blushing a little, expanding.

"I thought Fern died of cancer," said Winonah. "Now you're saying she died of AIDS. Which was it?"

"To be perfectly accurate, she died of putrefaction," said Romy.

"*What?*" demanded Tai.

"Sepsis," Verna said hastily. "She died of sepsis caused by a cancer that was AIDS-related." Then, looking up and then around the circle of faces, "I didn't tell anyone. There didn't seem to be much point and, besides, if I hadn't kept it under wraps, there would have been all these questions, questions I didn't know how to answer. That I didn't want answered, to tell you the truth. How did she get it? Who gave to her? Did she give it to anyone else? Would I have to hunt them down and tell them? Because I had to assume that she had contracted the virus from sex. I mean, that was what Fern did. She'd had no blood transfusions that I knew of, and, for all her faults, she didn't do hard drugs. No," she continued, the dam breaking, the words tumbling out, "she slept herself into that particular corner, the way she slept herself into all those other corners over the course of her brief, chaotic life and to tell you the absolute godawful truth, I didn't want to have to reconstruct the last several years of her bloody mess of a life one man at a time. What happened to her was her fault. Why should I have to clean up after her again? I was always cleaning up after her!"

"Are you finished?" Romy asked. "Because if you are, I have something I want to say."

"One more thing," insisted Verna tearfully. "Knowing that Fern died of AIDS would have broken my poor father's heart. Although, God knows, it should have come as no surprise to him, given her propensities." She paused for a breath. "Oh, but Fern! Poor, silly, romantic Fern! It wasn't her fault. Not all of it. I wasn't good to her. I only saw the bad things. I was so goddamned jealous." For the first time since her death, Verna experienced her sister's loss as something real, something visceral; it was as though she had been slit open with a sharp, clean knife from stem to stern. The searing pain took her breath away for a moment. She gasped and closed her eyes, waiting for it to pass, then, "Sorry," she mumbled. "I lost it there." But she hadn't lost it. She'd found it. Finally she had untangled it from the other. Pulled it loose and free. The love. Because she had loved Fern. She had. She looked around and gulped. "Now I'm finished."

Romy cleared her throat. "Well, I would like to say that, as far as I'm concerned, J.R. Eubanks killed my mother. Murdered her as sure as if he'd taken an axe to her. And not just her. Who knows how many women other than the one who charged him he might have infected? If you ask me, he got what was coming to him. An eye for an eye. Maybe an eye for a whole lot of other eyes. I don't think you should worry yourself one bit that you killed him, Auntie Verna."

"But …"

"And he did have AIDS, Verna," Carmen said. "From the looks of him, pretty full-blown. The way I see it, he had one foot out the door. You just gave him a teensy, tiny shove."

"Still …"

"Euthanasia," decided Paisley, wiping sooty hands on the thighs of her jeans and standing up. "That's what it was. It's how they do it in the hospital — just up the morphine drip. That's what they did with Dad, at any rate."

"Only you used OxyContin," said Tai. "Otherwise, same thing."

"Guys …"

"And lest we forget: that hoser died higher than a kite," said Romy. "The way I see it, you did him a super huge favour. What a way to go! We should all have it so good!"

"I don't know what to say," mumbled Verna and burst into tears. Carmen flung an arm around her and squashed her into her armpit; she smelled like tobacco and patchouli. They sat there for a moment as Verna sobbed and the rain pelted the roof. Then Romy bestirred herself. "So," she said. "How are we going to get rid of the body?"

Granny tugged at Winonah's sleeve and whispered something in her ear.

Winonah nodded. "It's time for Granny to tell you her dream," she announced.

Lightning struck the Hydro pole outside, triggering a flashover arc that painted the sky a pulsating turquoise for a few moments before consigning it once again to darkness. Jude yelped once, exploded from the room, and took cover under the big oak desk in the study. Then the power went out.

There was a resounding clap of thunder, then another, ending with an emphatic crack. From the sanctuary afforded by the oak desk in the study, Jude whimpered.

"Storm candles!" Verna announced abruptly, galvanized by the sudden, overwhelming descent of darkness. Wriggling out from under Carmen's vast arm, she stood and stumbled toward the kitchen, groping her way with her hands. She felt beside herself — besonders, as her father would say — literally. It was as though she were tagging along with some grizzly somnambulant whom she was charged with keeping out of mischief. *Too late,* she thought. That horse, as her father used to say, yes, that horse had already left the barn. She wondered vaguely how long the outage would last. Hours? Days? Power had always been inconstant at this remote edge of the grid. In any blackouts that took place, the Macouns were always the first to lose power and the last to regain it. That was what you got for living on the grid's periphery, for teetering on its trembling edge. While this had been the source of considerable distress to Verna and Fern growing up, Donald had embraced whatever random opportunities wind and weather afforded him to haul out bags of marshmallows and his stock of storm candles and his Coleman stove and lantern. Indeed, blackouts were his idea of a good time.

And, really, when she came to think of it, what better time for a blackout than this dark and bloody night? "Well, maybe not bloody, but you know what I mean," she muttered to herself as she rooted in a kitchen drawer for storm candles.

"I do," replied Lionel.

She looked up and over her right shoulder. Sure enough, there he was — or what could be said to be him — a presence composed of a different, more concentrated kind of gloom than mere darkness, opaque where darkness is sheer, with mass and shape and pull — and he was not on the porch for a change, but here, in the hall.

"What are you doing in here?"

"That guy out there, the one you killed?" Lionel sounded aggrieved. "You know what he just called me?"

"J.R.? But he's … oh, Lord, you don't mean he's …?" *But of course*, she thought. *Why not?* Fern was rattling around here somewhere, if Romy and Lionel were to be believed —and Donald, too. If they were here, why not J.R. Eubanks?

"A bush nigger," said Lionel. "He called me a bush nigger."

"He didn't! He referred to a 'sand nigger' earlier. I think he meant someone of Arabic extraction. You have to ignore him, Lionel. He's kind of a scum bag."

"Kind of? He's a racist is what he is. The sooner we get rid of that spotted moon-cricket the better."

"Moon-cricket?"

"You heard me!"

"Auntie Verna!" Paisley called from the living room. "Are you all right? Who are you talking to?"

"Coming!" called Verna. "Nobody! I'm looking for candles. Hang on," she hissed to Lionel. "We're working on it."

"I'm not going back out there, eh? Not 'til he's gone. By the way, the candles are in the drawer by the sink, but there's a Coleman lantern in the pantry. On the top shelf, eh? It was stored with some fuel in the tank, but there's a propane tank in the tool shed if it runs out. And one of them big utility flashlights from Canadian Tire. Next to the Coleman."

Verna crammed the various pockets of her overalls with stubby storm candles and a box of safety matches and lit her way back to the living room with the flashlight, the handle of the Coleman lantern dangling from her left hand. "Does anybody know how to light this thing?"

"Me," said Paisley. "Do we have propane?"

"Apparently there's still some in it,"

"That's not cool," said Paisley. "Eventually that causes a buildup on the fuel tube, which restricts fuel flow to the generator and burner."

"You are *so* butch!" Romy declared.

"Don't knock it," said Tai. "Do you know how to light one of those things? I don't. One of the things you'll never see a middle-class Indian family do is camp. It's like horrible déjà vu."

"Best to light it outdoors," Paisley said with an air of solemn, but gratified authority. *Fire Maiden*, Verna christened her mentally, admiringly. How competent she was! Just like Donald. "In case there's a leak. These things blow up sometimes." Taking the flashlight, the box of matches, and the Coleman lantern, Paisley headed briskly for the front door before remembering that J.R.'s body lay just outside on the porch. She did a one-eighty and made for the back porch instead, returning a moment later with the lit Coleman. She placed this in the centre of the coffee table, knelt down to adjust the fuel valve for maximum brightness, and sat on the floor beside Tai. Everyone turned expectantly to Granny.

"Tell us about your dream," Carmen said.

"First we better offer these Thunderers our respects," the old woman said, casting her eyes toward the noisy heavens. Her voice scratched like an old record; it crackled like a fire. "We want them to help us, eh? Not strike us down with their arrows. Not burn this house down. They are our grandfathers, some of them — First Thunder, the Searching Thunder, and Thunder that is Going to Hit. These are their names."

"They've got *names?*" Romy asked.

Granny removed a soapstone pipe from her pocket along with a pouch of loose tobacco. Pinching some tobacco from the pouch, she packed it into the bowl of the pipe. Paisley handed her a Zippo. Granny lit the pipe, took a puff, then tilted her head back and blew the smoke upwards. It smelled vaguely of cherries. "Thunderbirds, how you doing, eh?" she began in a conversational tone. "How was your trip down south? Did you have a good winter? That's good. Glad to hear it. One thing we ask for down here — it's your help — help getting rid of this body, eh? We don't want Verna here to get nailed for killing this no-good white man."

"She's talking to *thunder?*" Romy hissed.

Winonah made a low, growling noise, shook her head the way a bull does before it charges, and reached for her cigarettes. This had all the other smokers reaching for their cigarettes. Carmen took a pack of Du Mauriers from her Le Bag knockoff and Romy and Paisley dug around in their pockets for their Ultra Slims.

"I can't even begin to tell you how bad smoking is for all of you," Tai said reproachfully. (*Thank God,* thought Verna, *another non-smoker!)* Then, "I only started because it drove my stepmother crazy and now damned if I can stop. Can I bum one, Pais?"

Granny waited until everyone but Verna had a lit ciga-rette. "Okay," she said. "Now I'm going to tell you my dream and you must listen carefully, because it was sent to me for Verna." She cleared her throat. "Not so long ago, *pawaganak* came to me. Dream visitors. It was just after supper. Was that tonight? Seems so long ago! Anyway, these pawaganak, they took me to see Geezhigo-Quae, Sky Woman, the mother of our people. I got to ride on the back of a Thunderbird, eh? Pretty exciting. Remember that convertible that your Uncle had, Winonah? That was what it was like, riding in that con-vertible. I was afraid my hair would blow off, but it must be stuck on good, 'cause I still got it." She grinned. "Now Sky Woman, when I see her, oh! She was so beautiful and like a sunset — all different colours. And she says, 'Old woman, I know why the spirit of your grandson — that guy that choked there — has not gone to the Sky World. I looked down where you are and saw a bear walker sneaking around.'"

"What's a bear walker?" Tai asked.

"A bad shaman," Winonah explained. "One who takes the shape of a bear. Or some other animal. Maybe a dog. Sometimes he appears as light."

"Thanks for clearing that up!" Romy snorted.

"Romy!" Carmen warned the girl. "Go on, Granny."

"So I say, 'What can I do, Sky Woman? If there's a bear walker going around the place, I'm going to stay inside and not come out until he is gone far, far off.' And she says, 'No, no, Old Woman. You got to do something. You got to feed the bear walker to the mishepishu. The mishepishu is hungry and that bear walker's no good. Your grandson is not going to be able to find his way to me with that bear walker around.'"

At the word *mishepishu*, Verna felt a fluttering sensation in her heart, like the beating of a bird's wings. "Dad told us about the mishepishu. Fern and I figured that it must live in the water under the floor of the boathouse. It drowns people. Drags them under."

"Like the Ball Grabber," said Paisley.

Verna shook her head. "The Ball Grabber lives in outhouse holes."

"They are both manitou," explained Winonah. "The Ball Grabber is an underground manitou, while mishepishu is an underwater manitou."

"Where exactly is this manatee supposed to be?" Romy asked. "In the boathouse? Because you didn't tell me there was a manatee in the boathouse."

Winonah winced. "*Manitou!*" she repeated. "Is there something wrong with your ears? Or is it your big head?" They glared at one another.

"Mishepishu is not in the boathouse," Granny said. "Mishepishu is in the lake."

"Which lake?" Romy asked.

Granny pointed. "That lake." As she did, a bolt of white lightning poked at the lake, illuminating its roiling surface.

"You did not just do that," said Paisley.

Granny smiled, revealing a scattering of worn teeth.

"And then what happened?" Carmen asked Granny. "In your dream, I mean?"

Granny blinked. "I woke up."

"And that's it?" Paisley asked. "That's your dream?"

Granny nodded.

There was a moment of silence. "And this means ... what?" Tai ventured.

"Isn't it clear?" Winonah asked.

"Not exactly," said Tai.

Winonah sighed. "We should throw J.R. into the lake," she explained. "That's what the dream is telling us."

"What?" Verna asked in disbelief. "Begging Granny's pardon and all, but . . . you know … it's just a dream!"

"What do you mean *just* a dream?" said Winonah. "The manitou sent it to Granny for a reason — so that you would know what Sky Woman wants us to do. Why else would she have sent Granny such a dream?"

"But that's crazy," said Verna. "We can't throw J.R. in the lake just because Granny had a dream. I mean, just imagine what would happen if everybody did that."

"Well, it makes perfect sense to me," Carmen chimed in. "I mean, there it is — a deep lake, probably at least sixty feet if it's like the other lakes around here — as deep as a six-storey building — and you own it and all the land around it. Where else are you going to dump him?"

"We have to get rid of the body somehow," Paisley pointed out.

"Think about it, Verna!" Carmen urged her. "This is a guy nobody's looking for. *Nobody.* No family. No friends. He's not on anyone's radar and, honey, this is northern Ontario — it's a big old place to go looking for somebody nobody knows is lost, somebody nobody wants to find. People disappear up here. They go into the bush and never come out. Or somebody comes across their bones later on and everybody says, 'Gee, I wonder who the hell that poor bastard was? Bear must have got him.'"

"But won't he just … I don't know — swell up and rise to the surface and bob around." Verna asked. "Accusingly? Isn't that what corpses do?"

"Don't look at me!" Carmen begged off. "I don't know what corpses do."

Verna turned to her nephew. "Tai?"

"He's nothing but skin and bones," Tai said. "No fat to

float him. And the lake's deep and cold. Chances are he'd stay down pretty good."

"We could put stones in his pockets!" Romy suggested. "Just to make sure."

"You and your stones in the pocket!" Verna said. "And what if he doesn't stay down? What then?"

"You're forgetting something," said Winonah. "The mishepishu will eat him. There won't be anything left to bob around."

"Come on, Winonah," Verna protested. "You don't honestly believe there's some sort of monster in the lake. If there was, I would know it."

"How?" asked Winonah.

"Because I was in the lake," replied Verna. "Today. This morning."

"Were you in the *whole* Lake?" Winonah asked.

"Girls! Girls!" Granny interceded. "The mishepishu doesn't *live* in the lake. The mishepishu moves around. Sometimes he's in Whitefish Lake, sometimes Georgian Bay, sometimes Lake Manitou. All the lakes are connected. By underground passages. He would eat this bad guy here and then go off somewhere else. To eat some other bad guy thrown into some other lake."

"You know, this just might work," Tai said. "And what if he does surface? Heart failure, drug overdose, hitting your head…. They all look like drowning if you don't look too close. Sometimes even if you do."

"And it wasn't like he had anything to live for," Paisley pointed out. "He was dying, after all. Who knows? Maybe he took those painkillers himself …"

"That's it, Paisley!" Tai cried. "Bingo!"

"Bingo?" repeated Granny.

"Suicide," explained Tai. "He committed suicide. Where's that bottle of OxyContin?"

"In the kitchen. On the counter. But …"

"I'll get it!" Romy volunteered. Leaping to her feet, she grabbed the utility lantern and headed for the kitchen.

"We'll put the empty bottle in one of his pockets," said Tai. "That would explain why the drug was in his system if he turned up and they ran a toxicology screen on him."

Romy returned with the orange pharmacy bottle and handed it to Tai.

"What about fingerprints?" asked Paisley. "On the bottle, that is."

"I don't think they'd survive under water," said Tai. "We'll wipe it clean, in any case. I have Latex gloves in my bag and wipes."

"Wipes?" asked Romy.

"My stepmother is very clean. I inhabit a wiped universe."

"Don't forget his glass — the glass he drank out of," said Paisley. "And the mortar and pestle."

"We'll clean them with bleach."

In the meantime Romy had been working up a scenario. "How about this?" she asked excitedly. "J.R. gets out of prison and where does he go? To this cottage, where the love of his life — a woman whose death is on his conscience — died. To this cottage where they were going to build a life together. To this cottage to which he has a key." She produced the cottage key she had taken from J.R.'s pocket." "He feels a terrible despair, deep remorse. He knows that his own days are numbered and that he will probably die in pain and all alone. So he has a few drinks and decides to end it all. And what better way than by overdosing on his dead lover's medication … so that they can be reunited again in death!"

"Hey!" said Carmen. "You know, I have to say I'm impressed."

"Let's make sure he has the key on him," said Paisley. "In the same pocket as the bottle."

Romy tossed her the key, which she caught deftly.

272 • Melissa Hardy

"And when does this happen?" Tai asked.

"Just before Auntie Verna comes to the cottage," replied Romy. "Last Tuesday. He was squatting here, after all. Right up until she arrived."

"That could work," said Tai. "Time of death is very hard to pin down when somebody's been in the water for more than forty-eight hours. There are ways to tell if someone has died by drowning — the position of the body, the appearance of the eyes — but we're not suggesting that he drowned, so that won't be a problem."

"This is ... like ... reverse CSI!" said Romy.

"And, if he turns up, who's more surprised than us?" said Paisley. "We never heard of the guy. We didn't even know that Mom had AIDS."

"So how does he end up in the lake?" Carmen asked. "Does he walk into it?"

Tai shook his head. "He's got to be in deeper water if we've to have any chance of keeping him down."

"Guys ..." Verna protested. They were acting like this was a game. Didn't they realize that being accessories to murder was a serious matter? "Maybe I should just turn myself in. Throw myself on the mercy of the court. I don't want you all putting yourselves in jeopardy for a crime I committed. Surely to God they would take extenuating circumstances into account."

"Don't be crazy, Auntie Verna," said Tai. "They'll throw the book at you. Manslaughter, for sure. And that carries a four-year minimum sentence."

"You would *so* not look good in an orange jumpsuit," Romy told her.

"You're not to say another word about it, Auntie Verna," said Paisley. "You were avenging our mother. And you're all we have left. Everyone else is gone. We won't hear of it." She turned to the others. "Will we?"

Romy and Tai shook their heads.

"We're just doing what Sky Woman told us," Granny pointed out.

Paisley turned to the realtor. "And you're okay with this?"

"A-ok," Carmen replied. "The bastard killed Fern and that other gal besides. And, trust me, this probably won't be the lake's first secret. Or its last, I warrant. This is northern Ontario, after all."

"We're agreed, then,'" said Paisley. "Now, where were we? Oh, yes. What if he jumps off the dock?"

Tai turned to Verna. "How deep is it at the end of the dock?" he asked.

"Five feet. Maybe six. But ..."

"Too shallow," Tai said. "If we could only get him to the middle of the lake, that would be perfect."

Romy and Winonah looked at each other. Their eyes lit up. Twinkled. For once they were in agreement.

"Now where did Lionel put that duct tape?" asked Winonah.

That was when Verna officially gave up and withdrew into herself, curling into a ball that occupied only the small corner of the sofa into which Carmen had not spread. Eventually she unfurled herself, stood, and wandered off to the study. From its accustomed place on the credenza, Donald's Macallan Highland single malt winked its golden eye at her from within its Bohemian lead crystal decanter — like a cat's eye, it glowed in the dark. She located the decanter with trembling fingers on the credenza, poured herself a glass, and sat down at her father's desk to drink it. Jude, who continued to be tormented by the Thunderbirds, whimpered and flinched in the knee hole below, while the others talked deep into the night, planning how they would get the body to the boathouse (there was a wheelbarrow in the tool shed), how they might get the skiff to the centre of the lake (they would repatch the hole with duct tape, tether the skiff to the canoe, tow it there, and then cut it loose), when they would do it (when the storm broke), and how they would remove all traces of the crime from the house — the glass from which J.R. had drunk, the mortar and pestle (bleach, antiseptic wipes). They talked of other things, too. Of the cult from which Paisley had been rescued by her father. This had been news to Romy, who was too young to remember her own rescue from the same cult. Of Paul Doucette's numerous wives, each younger than the last and Romy's own downward spiral into anorexia. Of Tai's stepmother and the bitter vendetta she continued to wage against his father's memory of Fern. Of residential schools and beatings and humiliation. Of the brother who had choked to death at a pow-wow. Some of this Verna heard snippets of, but most of their conversation she registered as a low, muffled drone under the thunderstorm's ongoing racket. Later she curled up on the floor next to the shivering dog and slept brokenly until grey dawn leaked over the horizon and poked her awake with sly and chilly jabs.

Saturday, May 21, 2005

"Huh?" Verna hoisted herself up on one elbow and looked blearily around. Floor to ceiling shelves crammed with moldering books and old magazines, the English drop-dial wall clock that thought it might be six o'clock ... six o'clock? In the morning? What was she doing on the floor of the study?

"Jude?" she whispered urgently.

But the dog was not there.

"Damn!" Verna crawled up onto her knees, then used the chair to pull herself upright. It felt like someone had whacked her a few good ones with a baseball bat. Her head throbbed and her mouth tasted like kitty litter. "Jesus!" she muttered. "What the ...?" She eyed the empty decanter and winced. Then she remembered. "Shit! J.R!"

She limped into the living room to find Granny asleep on the sofa. Someone had covered her with the afghan. In the cold light of dawn the old woman looked incredibly

278 • Melissa Hardy

fragile, skin like ancient parchment, bird-boned; the orbs of her eyes roiled beneath papery lids — the dreamer was in.

Verna tiptoed to the window and peered out towards the lake. It was still as glass under a cloudless sky, its eastern edge a blaze of reflected light. There on the dock stood Romy and Carmen — Jack Spratt who could eat no fat, his wife who could eat no lean — and beside them, Jude, dancing with impatience. Winonah stood at dock end, her two hands raised to shade her eyes against the newly risen sun's glare as she peered out towards the lake's centre.

Verna stole to the front door, closed her eyes, and steeled herself. She had never seen a dead person before. Well, not sober or, at least, relatively sober, and not in the light of day. Things happened to corpses. Lividity. Rigor Mortis. *He's bound to look just awful,* she told herself. *Prepare yourself.* Then she opened the door, and, a moment later, managed to convince herself to crank her eyes open just enough to discern that there was no body on the porch.

She blinked. Rubbed her eyes. Looked again.

Still no body.

"What the …?" Verna stepped out onto the porch and, crossing to the screen door, opened it. Wheelbarrow tracks cut deep into the soggy lawn heading towards the boathouse. Oh, man! Did they actually go through with it? If that was the case, where were Tai and Paisley? Verna stepped outside and, cupping her mouth with her hands, cawed crowlike, "Romy! Carmen!"

Romy turned. "Auntie Verna!" she called. She waved broadly, standing on tiptoes and rocking from side to side like an eager child.

Verna lurched across the sopping lawn (at some point during the previous evening she seemed to have lost a shoe) and climbed the steps to the dock, which creaked like an old tire swing in the dawn breeze that blew off the lake. "Where is he?"

Romy pointed excitedly towards the centre of the lake. Her lips were blue. She was white as whey. "Yay!" She threw her arms around Verna and gave her a hug — it was like being hugged by a Halloween skeleton, jangling, hapless and cheerful. "You're just in time! Look."

Verna untangled herself from Romy's embrace, shaded her eyes with her hand, and peered in the direction of her niece's finger — there at the approximate centre of the lake were Paisley and Tai in the cottonwood canoe. Tethered to the canoe was the skiff, which she could see was riding very low in the water. Tai, who was seated in the back of the canoe, turned around, leaned over the stern deck, and untied the tether. Then he and Paisley appeared to confer for a moment before reverse paddling a few strokes. Once portside the other craft, they began poking at the skiff with their paddles, causing it to take on more water, to sink faster.

"Oh, man!" Verna moaned. "I can't believe this is actually happening."

"What? You can't believe you actually murdered your sister's lover and now her children are disposing of the body?" asked Carmen.

"We are so a team," said Romy.

They watched as the skiff sank lower and lower in the water before keeling a little to the leeside and disappearing from view with a slurp that could be heard all the way to the dock. Tai and Paisley sat for a moment, looking intently down at the water, before starting back to the boathouse.

Winonah abandoned the end of the dock and came towards them, smoking a butt-legged cigarette and slapping at blackflies. "These bastards are really biting. I'm getting out of here before they eat me alive."

"I'll come with you," said Carmen. "I could use some coffee. We all could use some coffee."

"I think there's a Coleman stove in the pantry," said Winonah. "And some propane in the shed." The two women lumbered towards the house.

The canoe pulled up beside the dock and for a moment the four of them — Verna, Romy, Paisley and Tai — sat there in silence. Paisley was ashen under her tan; Tai looked exhausted — for him, it had been a second night without sleep.

It was Paisley who broke the silence. "What should we do with this?" She was referring to the canoe. "Is it all right to leave here or should we put it in the boathouse?"

Verna roused herself. "Just tie it up here." Paisley and Tai climbed out of the canoe and Paisley tethered it to the dock. "Thank you," Verna managed, in a voice that crumbled into chunks half way through. It seemed so inadequate — "Thank you" — too little and much, much too late. And yet somehow here they were — Fern's dirty, badly behaved, inconvenient children — their arms thrown around each other and her, too, gathering her close for a moment and holding on for dear life. Fern's children, but her blood, too, and all there was left of her family. She whispered fiercely, "Paisley, you are so like your grandfather. And, you, Tai ... in ways you are like Fern. And you, Romy ... oh, God, Romy, you remind me of myself sometimes. It's true."

But Jude had spotted something in the water. He barked excitedly, then flung himself off the dock and started swimming toward the centre of the lake. Twenty-five feet in, he veered leeward, plucked an object from the water and headed back to shore.

"Here, Jude!" Tai called him. "Come here, boy!" He walked to the end of the dock and onto the beach. Jude emerged from the water, shook, and came toward him. Tai hunkered down. "Give," he told the dog, holding his hand out.

Obediently Jude relinquished J.R.'s soggy black Blue Jays baseball cap. Tai turned it over in his hands, then, spotting something on its inner band, peered more closely. He closed his eyes. His hand went to his forehead.

"What?" asked Verna. She followed him onto the beach, trailed by Romy and Paisley.

He handed the ball cap to her, pointing to an inscription written in Fern's unmistakable childish scrawl on the inner band. TO J.R., ALL MY LOVE, ALWAYS, FERN.

J.R. sank. Slowly at first, then, as the greater density of the water (eight times that of air) began to compress his fungi-pocked lungs, more quickly. Thanks to the rocks in his pockets, the only piece of Fern's last lover to escape a watery grave was the baseball cap Jude retrieved; it disengaged itself from his head when the skiff keeled over and floated away.

This realm of the cold-blooded was much darker than above the surface and more sombre in hue — with every ten feet of depth, a colour drops off the spectrum, so that, at ten feet, red appears black or dark gray; at twenty, orange ceases to exist; and at thirty, yellow disappears. This world through which J.R. descended — through schools of whitefish cruising for darters and insect larvae and solitary large northern pikes on the prowl for ciscoes and slimy eelponts — was coloured blue and green with an occasional, startling jolt of violet; it resonated with the purr, knock, and drum of gliding, darting fish and the clicking of invertebrates, and, for a time at least, the thick drag of a canoe paddle far above.

Finally, after a descent of some sixty feet, J.R. came to rest on the lake's silty bottom. There he would remain among the benthos — the midge and mayfly larvae and the common suckers — until the mishepishu swooped down and gobbled him up.

Or not.

This is how it came to pass that J.R. Eubanks became a secret kept fast by the lake. Another secret. One among many.

Like tall, slender dancers clad in frilly white bark, the birches gathered around the mossy pocket of open forest floor that was the glen. Of those who had come to Verna's aid the previous evening — Winonah and Granny, Carmen, her nieces and nephew — only Carmen had declined Verna's invitation to join them for a joint scattering of Fern, Donald, and Lionel's cremains in the glen. "There's not a canoe big enough."

"I can't begin to thank you," Verna had told her.

But Carmen had just squeezed her arm. "You can thank me by not selling the cottage. I need another commission like I need a hole in the head, and, besides, it wouldn't be right. I'm thinking that you belong here. That here is where you need to be for all kinds of reasons."

Winonah, Granny, Jude, and Verna, along with the LCBO bag containing the three cartons of cremains, journeyed to the lake's farther end by canoe. (Since Romy refused to venture out onto the water, Fern's three children were compelled to retrace their previous buggy slough through the bush to the alvar.) Midway across the lake, Granny asked Winonah to stop for a moment while she crumbled tobacco between her fingers and sprinkled it onto the surface of the water, muttering in Algonquin. When Verna asked what she was doing, she told her, "Mishepishu might want a smoke, eh? After his big breakfast."

After they had pulled up the various wooden posts that J.R. had driven into the ground in and around the glen, the old woman took charge of the formalities, announcing, "*N'gah auttissookae!* I'm calling the Grandfathers. The Grandmothers, too. Gonna ask them to help our loved ones on their journey to the Sky World." Reaching into the LCBO bag, she retrieved the three cartons of cremains. To Winonah she gave Lionel's cremains; to Verna, Donald's; and to Paisley, Fern's. "You're the oldest," she explained. Then she turned towards the east and held up her hands. Winonah, taking her cue from her, also turned in that direction.

"This way!" hissed Winonah over her shoulder — uncertain as to what the proper protocol might be under such circumstances, the others found themselves at a loss as to how to proceed. "Face this way!"

It was as though she had poked them with a cattle prod. Everyone quickly shuffled into place.

"Grandmother East," Granny chanted in a kind of sing-song, "from you comes the sun, which brings life to us all; please make the sun shine on our friends here and bring a new life to them — but one without all the pain and sadness of the world, eh? Could you do that for them?"

She turned towards the south; again she held up her hands. Everyone followed suit. "Grandfather South, you bring the Thunderbirds from down below and the rains that make things grow and live. Be gentle when you fall on our friends. Let the rain wash away their pain and their sadness. How about it?"

To the west, "Grandmother West, it's you who takes the sun from us and cradles it in your arms. You bring darkness so that every creature can get some rest. We only ask this, that when you bring the darkness to our friends here, do you think you could leave the nightmares outside the door? Could you let your stars and moon shine on our friends nice and gentle?"

She turned to face north. "Grandfather North, you are the warrior, ride alongside our friends and help them to be at peace with everything that was and is. You are the doorway to wisdom, the place of elders."

Casting her eyes upwards, she intoned, "Grandfather Sky: May your songs of the winds and clouds sweep the pain and sadness out of our friends' hearts; as they hear those songs, let them know the spirits who are with those songs are at peace."

Finally, with Winonah's assistance, the old woman knelt and directed her words down toward the earth, "Grandmother Earth, all spirits come from your womb," she said. "I have asked all those other Grandfathers and Grandmothers to help our friends rid themselves of the troubles that weigh so heavy on their hearts. This way, the weight they carry will be less; and they will walk more softly on you." She gestured to Winonah, who helped her to her feet.

"And now we have come full circle," she said. "To the eastern doorway, I say *meegwetch*. To the southern doorway, I say *meegwetch*. To the western doorway, *meegwetch*, and to the northern doorway, *meegwetch*. May the Great Spirit watch over you and may you be at peace."

Romy tugged on Winonah's sleeve. "Meg who?" she hissed. "What's she talking about."

Winonah glared at her. "*Meegwetch*. It means 'thank you.'"

Granny was satisfied with the proceedings. "Okay. It's time."

"Let's do this!" agreed Romy.

"Wait a minute," said Paisley. "Tai? Romy?" Opening the carton, she untwisted the tie from the plastic bag that held Fern's cremains and held the box out to her brother and sister. "We should all do this. Not just me. Here. Take some." Tai gulped, then reaching into the carton, he wiggled his hand through the bag's opening and grabbed a handful of cremains — they looked like grey sand.

"That doesn't look like ashes," Romy objected.

"It's not," said Tai. "It's dried bone fragments that have been pulverized in a cremulator."

"What? You're kidding!"

"A *cremulator?*" asked Verna.

Tai nodded grimly. "I had a friend who had a summer job at a crematorium."

Romy winced, closed her eyes and thrust her hand into the bag. "Ooh!" She sounded surprised. "Gritty."

Verna and Winonah opened their cartons, hauled out the bags, untwisted the ties.

"One, two, three!" said Granny and for a moment unfurling ribbons of sand-like powder glittered in the hazy cylinder of pale golden sunlight that bored through the canopy before settling. Out of the corner of Verna's eye she thought she glimpsed the spirit of Lionel slipping away between the birches, another wavering verticality, then gone.

"Lionel?"

She must have spoken aloud, for Granny shushed her urgently, seizing her by the wrist and pressing her bony index finger to her lips. "Don't say his name, Verna! When you say his name, you call him back. You got to let him go. You got to let them all go."

Victoria Day
Monday, May 23, 2005

Paisley and Tai left early on the holiday Monday. Paisley needed to get back to her business and Tai was on call at the hospital. Before they left, Paisley asked if her and Jill's wedding could take place at the cottage the following spring. She was certain that Jill would accept her proposal of marriage now that she had dealt with her baggage.

"That's one way to describe what happened here this weekend," said Tai.

"You've got to promise me that nobody tells anybody about this," Verna insisted. "Not Jill. Not your dad, Tai. Not yours, Romy. Nobody."

"Of course not," Paisley assured her. "It's our very own skeleton in the closet. We get it, Auntie Verna." She turned to Tai. "I'm hoping you'll agree to be my best man?"

"I would be honored," said Tai.

"What about me?" Romy cried. "Can I be a bridesmaid?"

"Only if you go back to the Birches," Paisley told her sternly. "Jill's not going to want a bridesmaid who looks like Jack Skellington."

Verna, Paisley, and Tai had decided between them that Romy must go back into rehab. Verna was to call Paul Doucette that night and the Birches the following day — there could be no hope of raising anybody at the centre on the first long weekend of the summer.

"Unfortunately, by signing herself out the way she did, she's almost certainly forfeited her bed," said Tai. "There are waiting lists for these places. She'll probably have to queue up again and wait her turn. It could be months. I just hope she can make it until then."

"Auntie Verna," Romy began. Tai and Paisley had just driven off and they were having coffee on the porch. "About those OxyContins …"

"About those. I didn't think that bottle was empty."

Romy smiled at her. The cat who ate the canary.

Verna held out her hand. "Let me have them."

Romy shook her head. "No way, José! Uh-uh!"

"Let me have those pills!" Verna insisted. "I mean it, young lady!"

"Hey! Like you can be trusted with them?" retorted Romy. "The murder weapon!"

Verna realized Romy had a point. "Oh," she said. "Right. Sorry."

"There were two left," Romy told her. "We could each take one right now and that would be the end of them."

Verna thought for a moment. "Oh, sure. Why not? It's not like I can set you any worse an example."

"You're not so bad." Delving about in her voluminous folds, she surfaced with the two pills and handed one to Verna. "Remember to chew."

"Oh, I remember!" Verna assured her. She stared out at the lake as she ground the OxyContin between her teeth, reflecting that, on any given day, it could appear to be midnight blue, azure, cerulean, or ultramarine, but always, always blue. Most of the lakes in this region were the colour of tea. That was because the forest was largely coniferous and needles are slow to degrade. Not Lake Marguerite. Its colour was a reflection of the sky above. It was the sky's mirror. From the bulrushes and cattails on the lake's western shore, a loon wailed, a long note followed by a second higher note and then a third. Plaintive. Haunting.

She said, "I can't do this anymore."

"Do what?"

"Live like this."

"Like what?"

"Drink like this."

Romy considered this. "Well, you could, but it wouldn't be so hot."

"I'm an alcoholic."

"Well, yeah, but you don't get falling-down drunk," Romy pointed out. "Not like my dad."

"Was Paul a drunk?" Verna asked. "Of course, I scarcely knew him. I scarcely knew any of them — Fern's men. I scarcely knew her."

"That makes two of us. What?" Romy turned to look at her. "Are you going to cry again?"

"I'm sorry. I can't help it." Verna swiped at her eyes and dripping nose with a piece of soggy Kleenex.

"Come on!" Romy protested. "You're supposed to be the strong one!"

"Who said I was the strong one? I'm a basket case. I'm not strong!"

"You're stronger than me! At least you'd better be. Now, snap out of it!" Taking Verna by her shoulders, she shook her.

"Okay! Okay!" Verna conceded. "I've got a hangover! Ouch!"

Romy released her and went back to staring fixedly at the lake.

Some time later it dawned on Verna that the OxyContin was kicking in. Suddenly she felt vague, warm, comfortable. That was an unusual feeling — comfort. "Why are you staring that way?" she asked Romy. "It looks like your eyes might pop out of their sockets."

"I'm watching," replied Romy.

"For what?"

"That manatee."

"The mishepishu."

"Whatever."

"What? Do you think it might suddenly appear? Like the Loch Ness monster?"

"I don't know," said Romy. "But if it does, I'll see it."

Time slipped away. At some point in the course of this slippage, Verna realized that her memory of Fern was not of how she was, but how she was *when* she was. In other words, Fern had ceased at long, long last to be a presence and become, instead, an absence. This struck her as an important insight. "Hey, Romy." She tugged on the girl's sleeve. Romy tore her gaze away from the lake. "My sister no longer exists in time. I mean Fern, your mother. She exists somewhere other than time. Time is reality. It is the definition of reality. Transcendence, on the other hand, is outside time!"

Romy stared at her for a moment. Then she said, "I'm glad you cleared that up."

They returned to looking at the lake.

"So, Auntie Verna, what are you going to do now?"

"What do you mean?"

"Are you going to sell the place?"

Verna thought about it. Then she slowly shook her head. "I don't think I can."

"Why?"

"Because everyone is here."

"Everyone?"

"My grandfather is here and my mother ... and now my father and my sister. Everyone. I ... I can't leave."

"I like it here," Romy said. "It's nice. It's really nice. Auntie Verna, can I stay with you? Until a bed comes free at the Birches? I don't want to go live with my father and his new wife."

"Here?" Verna was as surprised as one can be on prescription drugs. "With me?"

"You're as close to being my mother as anyone else could ever be. And we've already been through a lot together."

"But I'm not good with children."

"I'm not a child."

Verna thought about this. "Okay," she said cautiously. "All right. But there are conditions."

Romy clapped her hands. "Goody! What?"

"You have to eat enough to stay alive. I can't have you dying on me."

"I promise!"

"And that's not all. You have to learn to swim."

Romy's face fell? "What?"

"You have to learn to swim," Verna repeated.

"Why?"

"Because you can't live on a lake and not swim," Verna replied. "Because swimming is intrinsically a very good thing to be able to do." *Because there are mermaids in the lake who might help you*, she thought, *who might even make you well.* That's what Lionel had said and it was worth a shot. "I'll teach you," she promised. "I'm a good swimmer. I'm not good at very much else, but I am a good swimmer."

294 • Melissa Hardy

"And that's the only way I can stay? If I learn to swim?"

Verna nodded. "The only way."

Romy sighed. "Okay," she said reluctantly. "If that's the only way … it's a deal. I'll learn to swim."

"Good," said Verna. "That's good."

"Will you call me 'my little Roo'?"

"No," said Verna. "Well, maybe sometimes." Then, "It's not going to be easy, Romy. You know that, don't you?"

Romy nodded. "I know. It never is. Easy, that is. If there's one thing I know, that's it."

"Okay," said Verna. "As long as you know."

Romy stood. "Can we go inside, Auntie Verna? All of a sudden I'm feeling kind of hungry."

"Yes, my little Roo," replied Verna, rousing herself.

Of Related Interest

Family Album
Kerry Kelly
978-1459701595
$19.99

A former literary notable, Cynthia Wilkes is looking down the barrel of an empty nest, an empty desk, and an endless supply of empty pages when an unlikely *protégé* comes calling, setting in motion a chain of events that will force Cynthia, and those closest to her, to redefine the idea of family and of self. This novel is a humorous look at the creation and reconstruction of family and the lingering hold of the people we keep close and those we try to let go ... the siblings and step-siblings, parents and step-parents, spouses and exes, the friends, the colleagues, and the others we call family.

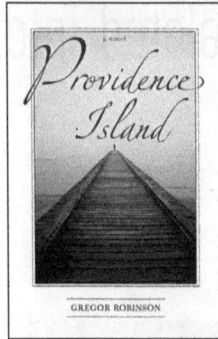

Providence Island
Gregor Robinson
978-1554887712
$21.99

Returning to Ontario's northern lakes as an adult to bury his father, Ray Carrier is taken back not only to a tangled romance in that green paradise, but also to the forests and lonesome swamps that have haunted his dreams. As a teenager, Ray was enchanted by the grace and privilege of the Miller family on Providence Island, part of the wealthy resort community up the road from the farm where Ray and his widowed father spent their summers. Ray's father had always said that he was too impressed by money. But it was more than that. There was Quentin Miller, a beautiful girl, older than Ray, who thought nothing of strolling to the end of a dock, stripping naked, and diving into the lake. But something happened near the abandoned railway tracks long ago something that shattered Ray's illusions of love and money. And now something must be settled before Ray can achieve peace and let go of Providence Island and the Millers once and for all.

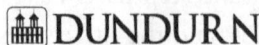

🏛 **DUNDURN**

Visit us at
Dundurn.com | @dundurnpress
Facebook.com/dundurnpress | Pinterest.com/Dundurnpress